PRAISE FOR CRAIG WOLF

"Craig Wolf's *Queen of All the Nightbirds* is a powerful, compulsive examination on the tenuous nature of friendship, the dark agony of lust, and the tantalizing shine of acceptance, rocketing along page after page. I literally, at times, could not put this book down, possessed by the need to Find Out What Happens Next, the best drug a writer possesses. You must read this book."

—Paul Michael Anderson, author of *Bones Are Made to be Broken* and *I Can Give You Life*

"What happens when the girl of your dreams drags you into the most depraved nightmare? Craig Wolf's *Queen of All the Nightbirds* is a sharp, reality-bending ride through a teen fantasy that twists into raw terror. I couldn't put it down."

—Sheri Sebastian-Gabriel, author of *Spirits*

QUEEN OF ALL THE NIGHTBIRDS

ChiZine Publications

Distributed in Canada by
Fitzhenry & Whiteside Limited
195 Allstate Parkway
Markham, Ontario L3R 4T8
Phone: (905) 477-9700
e-mail: bookinfo@fitzhenry.ca

Distributed in the U.S. by
Consortium Book Sales & Distribution
34 Thirteenth Avenue, NE, Suite 101
Minneapolis, MN 55413
Phone: (612) 746-2600
e-mail: sales.orders@cbsd.com

Library and Archives Canada Cataloguing in Publication

Title: Queen of all the nightbirds / Craig Wolf.
Names: Wolf, Craig, 1969- author.
Identifiers: Canadiana (print) 20190103396 | Canadiana (ebook) 2019010340X | ISBN 9781771484947
 (softcover) | ISBN 9781771485258 (hardcover) | ISBN 9781771484954 (PDF)
Classification: LCC PS3623.O4349 Q44 2019 | DDC 813/.6—dc23

CHIZINE PUBLICATIONS
Peterborough, Canada
www.chizinepub.com
info@chizinepub.com

Edited by Sandra Kasturi
Copyedited and proofread by Leigh Teetzel

Canada Council   Conseil des arts
for the Arts   du Canada

We acknowledge the support of the Canada Council for the Arts which last year invested $20.1 million in writing and publishing throughout Canada.

ONTARIO ARTS COUNCIL
CONSEIL DES ARTS DE L'ONTARIO
an Ontario government agency
un organisme du gouvernement de l'Ontario

Published with the generous assistance of the Ontario Arts Council.

Printed in Canada

CRAIG
WOLF

QUEEN
OF ALL THE
NIGHTBIRDS

THIS IS A WORK of fiction. Seriously. Check the spine if you don't believe me. And though this novel is set in a very specific time and place, both locale and era serve only as the canvas on which I painted my story. Which is to say that I occasionally took liberties, and if those liberties trouble you, you most likely wanted a map, not a painting.

This one's for Charles:
May the good old days just keep on piling up for us,
but not too fast, right?

PROLOGUE

WHAT YOU NEED TO know up front is this: my name is Eric Lynch, my youth is a receding memory, and I will never walk again, never dance again, never be free again.

And if mercy exists, I won't fall in love again.

My many doctors over the last twenty-eight years have concluded that I suffer from schizophrenia, or from anosognosia—that I am utterly incapable of discerning that my delusions are delusions. So these numerous kind men and women have fired countless meds at my allegedly dysfunctional brain, these very smart men and women have resorted to one therapy after another as fads have waxed and waned—and still the problem child won't change his story, his wild fanciful tale of other layers of realities and the dark things that swim up from the depths of them. As far as they're concerned, my mind remains as twisted as my face and body. They don't say it, but they think it. I'm crippled, not blind.

Have there been more than a couple of these witch doctors who suspect me of malingering? Of sticking to a preposterous story because Oklahoma is a "treat until competent" state, and should I ever become competent . . .

Well, that would be interesting. Even after nearly three decades, plenty of people would be happy to see me get the needle. They'd line up to do the job.

The problem is my doctors are full of shit.

They are full of shit because I was there and I know good and goddamned well that it all happened. All the grief, the loss, the blood—it *all* happened. I've had three decades plus to relive it over and over, even in my dreams. Hell, always in my dreams.

Three decades? Shit, *yesterday* as far as I'm concerned.

1987.

Reagan's Iran-Contra fuck up. Gorbachev talking *glastnost* and *perestroika, da*, with Soviet troops bogged to their necks in Afghanistan. Iraq blasting the USS Stark. Oliver North. Jim Bakker. Nuclear fear. Nuclear hype.

None of that mattered a shit if you were seventeen.

What mattered was Eddie Murphy and da Ahnold, *Beverly Hills Cop 2* and *Predator*, Whitesnake and Genesis and U2, and a new band called Guns N' Roses. *Moonlighting* and *L.A. Law*. Midnight movies. The Bangles walking like Egyptians. Pink Floyd mostly back together. Spuds MacKenzie. Guess jeans and Swatch. God help us, Whitney Houston and Tiffany. And, hey, getting laid. Getting wasted. Getting away.

All of that was in style, and when you're seventeen, *everything* relates to style, pro or con.

Except love. That always trumps style.

And death. That beats style, too.

Even in 1987.

Yeah, even then.

PART ONE: STRANGE BIRDS

1

"I DUNNO," SAID STAN Russell, "she's probably a real woofer, you know?"

So here we were, the end of our first week of senior year at Woodrow Wilson High, a week out from Labor Day, sweating out the last efforts of another flamethrower Oklahoma summer. Stan and I were waiting for the rest of our pals to show up at the Pizza Inn about a mile from campus. Our manners were as good as ever. My mouth was too stuffed with deep-dish supreme pizza to answer Stan, and anyway he rarely asked anything but generally rhetorical questions, which was a good thing, seeing how we so seldom listened to them anyway.

"I mean," he gravely continued, "let's face it. When's the last time one of us had a real babe?"

Such sensitivity.

I shrugged and inhaled my own pizza. I was the fastest guy alive when it came to eating in that fabled year of 1987. It had been timed, it was official. Eric Lynch, Champion Garbage Gut of Oklahoma City. Of course, I looked like it. What the hell. One could be thin or one could enjoy life, I believed, but not both.

We were waiting on our pals Doug Driscoll and Mick Cornwell, and of course the Mystery Girl. They were supposed to meet us here at the Pizza Inn, a few longish blocks from Woodrow Wilson High School. Doug had mentioned he might bring a new "friend" with him, someone named Rebecca. Well. Since girls were not a usual presence in our circle, you can just *imagine* the waves of interest and anxiety this caused. Interest because we were curious who had chosen him (guys like us didn't do the choosing, you understand) and anxious because it meant we were chosen as well. Did Mystery Girl have some pretty fucking low standards, or what?

Take me and Stan. I was a fat, curly-haired schlub. I looked like an acne-ridden, mustache-free version of the guy in the Doritos commercials. Not because of glands, or a psychological issue, or because my mommy and daddy didn't love me. Fuck, I just liked to eat. And while Stan was not as mega-porky as me, you could at least see in me that if I laid off the damn burritos, there might be a skinny person inside. Stan was one of those people who will always seem somehow thick and put together in slabs, with thick short limbs and a blocky head. His long hair didn't hide that as much as he liked to hope. He always wore a sort of puffy, stupefied expression that made him look dumber than he was. He was a good guy, usually, and he put up with us so we put up with him. But what I'm working at here is that neither of us were a hit with the girls, you know?

Stan, afflicted with the attention span of a mayfly, started raving about his latest musical wet dream.

"Was in Driver's yesterday," he said between chews, "and they had this blue Yamaha that was just fuckin' primo."

Driver's was our musical Mecca. Stan was a guitar player of mediocre abilities and I was a bassist who had aspirations to become at least average. We had vague but intensely hopeful delusions of forming a band. Some time ago we'd decided on the name Shogun and had several logos drawn up. Couldn't write a note of original music and could only barely play "Smoke on the Water" but we had that logo, yes sir.

"How much?"

"Oh," said Stan, "a little."

"Yeah, a little more than you got."

"Not so much."

"Oh Jesus, Livingston." It was a nickname Doug had given him for some obtuse reason, and he hated it. Naturally, we wore it out.

He shrugged. "Don't—"

"—call you Livingston, yeah yeah. Listen, you didn't put it on layaway like you did that Gibson, did you?" That had been one of his less wise financial decisions. Never got the damned thing, and lost the money he put down on it.

"No, *Eric*, I didn't."

He might have bitched more but Mick slapped a hand on his shoulder. "Hey, Livingston, save some for the rest of us!"

"Shit," said Stan, wiping a smear of grease away from his mouth and shaking his not-so-golden tresses. "That's Eric you got me mixed up with."

Mick looked a lot like he'd just run a marathon, which he was built for. If there was an ounce of fat on his body, I couldn't have told you where. Sweat stained the front of his western shirt, plastered his fine blond hair down onto his forehead.

"Sorry we're late," he said. "Doug forgot where he parked, and I hung around in case he needed a ride."

Stan said, "Where *is* Driscoll? And whatsername?"

Mick nodded. My guess was that was supposed to answer both questions. He launched for the buffet.

As if on cue, here came Doug, heading for our table.

And hell came after. But oh, what a hell.

A slender, crazy-beautiful girl with black, black hair and startlingly white skin, as though she'd emerged from some lightless world, walked beside Doug. She was taller than Doug, and Doug was no dwarf. She should have seemed delicate—like one of those emaciated models on some catwalk—but that wasn't the impression I got. Instead, she gave off a sense of coiled grace, steel-spring strength. She wore black jeans that tightly revealed the slightest curves and a plain black T-shirt. She smiled at us as they approached, and my breath caught on her beauty like a fish on a gleaming hook. I'd been in the presence of beautiful girls before—hell, Doug's sister Samantha was no slouch in the looks department, even if she was sort of a pain in the ass—but this was something on an altogether different level. I could not have imagined a more beautiful girl if I'd spent my life trying. And I had.

You know what? Maybe even then I thought there was gonna be trouble.

And if I didn't think it, I should have *known* it.

Doug was the perfect gentleman. He pulled a chair out for her, stood behind her while she sat. Only after he sat and nudged his glasses back up his thin nose did he speak.

"Guys, this is Rebecca Connors. Becca, that's Stan, and that's Eric." Becca already? *That* was fast.

"I'm the village idiot," I said.

"How nearly pleasant."

"Why, thank you. Hardly anyone appreciates just how much work it takes to be thoroughly stupid. I mean, you'd be surprised how many—"

"I am hungry," she said. Her eyes, a disquieting gray, were smiling, which made her cool in my book. But the first thought that popped into my head was: *Hungry for* what?

I say it again: I should have *known*. We *all* should have known.

She rose, and Doug got up with her, and they were off to the buffet. Stan and I, a pair of pigs, watched her go.

"Wow," said Stan.

Yeah, wow. She was slim, *slim*, with narrow but straight shoulders. She had a very nice ass, which is crude, middle-aged me knows, but '80s teen me of course didn't. Her legs went on for-fucking-ever, thin and long. She made you want to cover your eyes; looking at her was too much like staring at the sun.

"Shit," I offered. Prayer or despair, who could say?

Mick came back, saw which way we were staring, and said nothing. There was no need for color commentary.

"New here, huh?" said Stan.

"Doug said she transferred from Kansas," Mick replied. "Hutchinson or somewhere like that."

"No shit," said Stan, wonderingly.

I gobbled the rest of my now cold pizza, belched, and announced that I was going back for more. I passed Rebecca on my way there, as she headed back to the table. We were close, for a quick second, and I was caught by her scent. The scent made me embarrassingly hard in a hurry—not that surprising for a teen dude, but I'd never had that reaction just from a smell before. It affected my walk, like Stan was fond of saying. Part of it was a perfume, a sweet and high fragrance, like roses, but it was more than that. It was her. Some ancient part of my brain that remembered swinging through the trees responded with sudden, energetic glee. Not that I hadn't felt it before, you know, but I hadn't felt it like *this*.

But on the heels of that, scattershot images, a bona fide vision: a still rope hanging over a clay stained pool of water covered by a cathedral of trees, a dark tunnel gaping like a hungry mouth, blood red roses in exploding blooming profusion, a boy's bloodied hand grasping for something, something . . .

"Goddamn," I muttered. My feet moved forward again. One thing you could say for my body: no matter how bumfuzzled my brain was, it could find food on complete autopilot.

But I glanced back at Rebecca and she was looking at me, dark creases of worry defacing that alabaster forehead. Then the look flashed away and she smiled. The smile didn't seem to fit, like it was a mask someone was trying on for the first time.

I looked away, shaking my head, and got to the buffet.

Plate loaded, I sat back down and dove in. Rebecca was saying, "You must be the Floyd freaks Doug's told me about."

Stan leaned toward at her, almost leering. "You like Floyd?"

She shrugged. God, her face was so exotic; high cheekbones and full wide lips and those gray eyes—all softness over gentle planes and angles. "I like them enough well. Yes. Yes . . . I do like them."

She sounded less from Kansas and more from Lower Slobbovia or somewhere. But then, I can't lie: none of us gave a damn what she sounded like.

Stan grinned. "Me too, but I'm more of a Boston man."

"More of an idiot," I mumbled around a mouthful.

"No, Eric," Doug said, "Livingston's just a dork. You do idiots a disservice."

Stan aimed the bird in our general vicinity.

"They've got a new one out, don't they?" asked Rebecca.

Doug said, "Yes, but it's terrible. Waters *was* Floyd."

"Ah, Christ, not this again!" I groaned and stood. "It's been nice and I'm pleased as hell to meet ya, Rebecca, but I got fourth-hour English and I'd rather face Shakespeare than more of Dougie's 'Waters is God' bullcrap."

She smiled. Yeah, so did Helen of Troy.

Mick stood, patted his stomach in a contented manner, fighting or feigning a belch. "Yeah, I've got class, too."

"Debatable," I said.

"Blow me, Lynch."

"Only in your wildest dreams, Cornwell."

Mick rolled his eyes.

Such was our dignified exit.

"What do you think?" I asked him when we were outside.

He shook a Marlboro Light out of a hardpack and thought about it for a second. "I bet you she's smarter than the rest of us put together."

"Yeah, well, throw me in and that ain't too hard. I sort of drag the average down, you know?"

"I don't help the curve none either," he said, blowing out a jet of smoke. "She's all right. I guess. Wonder if Doug can handle her."

"Hah. Like you could."

He squinted at me through a shroud of smoke. "Probably not."

It was hot as Satan's scrotum out. It was almost technically fall, but in Oklahoma things sometimes broil far into October. Sweat pooled in the small of my back, rolled down my gut.

"Well," I said, happy to change the subject. "First full week down. Eternity to go." Senioritis already.

"Yeah. Hey, I'm gonna be late. Catch you at work."

I watched him stroll off to his car, a Camaro cobbled together from the corpses of Camaros past. It was a car of many colors. The unifying shade was primer. Mick wasn't a car guy; most of the money he pulled in from work went into his wardrobe. Unlike the rest of us, the dude knew threads and how to wear them.

I found my own wheels, got in, cranked the window down to let the hot air out, and started the engine. In the rearview, I saw Doug and Rebecca leave, holding hands. My groin stirred and my heart wrenched at once. Pretty shitty way to react when your best friend hooks up with a beautiful girl. Fucking graceless.

That was bad enough. But why were my hands shaking?

I strangled the steering wheel, and somehow pulled out without screeching the tires, and instead of heading back to school, I drove aimlessly, listening to Iron Maiden, driving and driving without thought until I had no choice but to go home and get ready for work.

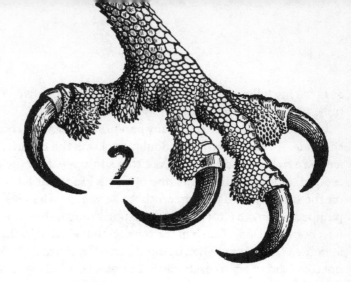

2

I WAS THANKFUL MY mom's battered tan station wagon was not in the driveway. I let myself in, glancing up as a long growl of thunder tore through the air. Storm clouds were nearly overhead, and the gray reminded me of Rebecca's eyes. Just what I needed. Rebecca was Doug's girl, wasn't she? Which made them a couple, which put her off-limits, as opposed to merely out of reach. I didn't like getting hot over my best friend's girl. It felt far too much like stealing, somehow. Or conspiracy. Or a shitty pop song by The Cars. Or something.

What a fucking great start this school year was off to.

I made a raid on the fridge. A note was taped to the door, the one place I'd be sure to see it:

> Eric,
>   I am at Lottie's for a while. Have a tv
> diner. Come strait home from work. You
> have to help you're father tomorrow.
> Mom

Wonderful. Helping my father no doubt meant cleaning up the garage. My old man was a mechanic, had his own shop, barely brought in enough business to keep food on the table. He was good at what he did, but he didn't do enough of it to be able to afford to hire help. Which meant that I was often pressed into service. I worked at Tate's at four. So much for a fun-filled Saturday on Planet Eric.

I flipped the note over and jotted that I was spending the night at Doug's, which I could get away with because my man Driscoll was some kind of saint as far as my folks were concerned, put it back on the fridge, poured a glass of milk, and went to my room.

Understand that when I say my parents were devout I mean they were just this side of Jonestowning it. Soul purity was the order of the day, because we were to be—and I don't make this shit up—"faith believers." Seemed a redundancy. My father was one of those kind that left a Jack Chick tract on the table instead of a tip on those occasions when we ate out. My mom pumped money to Oral Roberts on a fairly routine basis, something I told no one, not even Doug. Much of the tension that existed in the Lynch household stemmed from their belief, or more correctly, from my failure to share it. It's not like I didn't try to pretend that I was a true believer, but I guess I wasn't wholly convincing. And no effort was spared to correct my waywardness.

Thus my room did not really have my decorating touch.

I would have preferred a couple of Maiden posters, maybe Dio, and that knockout Budweiser poster with the three babes on the blanket. Maybe you know the one. A Paulina poster, maybe.

What I got was white walls with a set of shelves on one side, lined with oddball consolation trophies I'd accumulated through years of earnest failure, as well as those stupid ribbons they gave you for showing up and acting like you were participating in the school track meet. I had one green honorable mention ribbon for every grade, one through six. Happily they give that shit up by junior high. I had my dresser, my bed, and a banged-up Army surplus desk my dad got in trade for fixing a carburetor on some guy's Ford Grenada. One small bookcase, filled mostly with Hardy Boys books I hadn't read in years. Harmless framed pen-and-ink landscapes. The obligatory portrait of Jesus, which I respectfully refrained from drawing a mustache on. A boring room. Very vanilla.

The only real touch that was mine rested in the corner.

I still had a little time to kill, so I downed the rest of my glass of milk and dug my bass out of its scuffed case.

I owned a beautiful red Peavey T-120 that I'd bought secondhand (or third, who the hell knew?) from a friend of a friend. I'd only been allowed to have it on the condition that I learn some hymn-type stuff so that I could play at church. I obliged, but played so terribly that this obligation was forgotten by all. There *are* mercies.

Stan and I still practiced together a lot. He kept wanting to do Boston and I wanted to do something more like Maiden or Priest. Stan claimed to only know Boston parts, and as God or Whoever is my witness, to this day I almost puke if I even think about a Boston song.

I fucked around on the bass too long and ran late. Worse, it started pouring as I pulled into the parking lot of Tate's Discount Grocery. That "discount" part was a bald lie, by the way. I ran in from the rain, soaked, and dashed to the time clock. My tacky blue tie was plastered to my gut, and my sneakers made punky squishing noises as I sprinted into the office. Roger Craw, assistant manager and bane of my very existence, sat at the one battered desk that all the assistants used, marking out forms. He glanced up at me as I flicked my finger down the time cards in the rack.

"Late," he said.

"Car trouble," I replied, thinking, *Fuck off, man.*

He grunted and returned to his paperwork, but I knew he was filing away my tardiness in some mental folder. Craw liked to develop his arsenal against the hourlies. It made him feel significant in a large, uncaring universe.

Zeke Thomas was the floor manager that night, and he told me which check stand to take. It was my crummy luck that he placed me next to Monica Arden.

Monica was hotter than hot, okay? She was small, almost pixie-ish, and part Hispanic. I liked Monica just fine, and love would have been okay too, but I must speak the truth here and tell you that I had a typical overweight teen boy's wholly unrealizable but constant longing to explore her body. That notwithstanding, one of her finer points was that she was at least quick to smile, to laugh, and was moderately civil even to under-attractive walking zeros such as myself.

It was a sort of sweet hell to have to work when Monica did. My checking mistakes multiplied like zits the night before a dance whenever I was stationed next to her. Even if my self-discipline was such that I could restrain myself from looking over at her, there was always the occasional faint whiff of her perfume or the happy bubble of her voice bobbing to the surface of the din.

If Monica's presence wasn't enough, any hopes I had for a little comic relief that night were dashed when neither Livingston nor Mick showed up for work. All I had were snotty customers with food stamps, tyrannical assistant managers with attitudes, and that luscious scent from the next check stand over. You tell me, does that sound like a hot Friday night to you?

About nine-thirty, that changed.

Our payday rush had trickled out about an hour before, and the persistent rain outside was keeping business down. Every time it seemed like the rain was going to let up, another storm cell would move in with a drumroll of thunder and strobes of lightning. Half the checkers got sent home early, and I was aggravated that I was not among them. Neither was Monica. It was circumstances like these that sometimes convinced me that there was indeed a god, or God if you must, and that He, She or It was a sick, perverse fuck.

As I rang up an order for a fat grouchy old lady who smelled like wet cats, I saw Doug Driscoll's thin shape drift into my field of vision. A second later came Rebecca, all elegant grace, dressed in black jeans and a tight black T-shirt that made her soft bright skin glow. My fingers jumbled on the register, and the old lady scowled.

"I know that goddamned coffee ain't no seven thirty-two," she hissed, although without her dentures, I had to actively stop and allow my brain to translate her mush. The horrible rancid stench of her breath, like maybe hot dirty diapers or something, made this chore even more difficult.

"Yes, ma'am," I said, voiding the transaction. It was only through great force of effort that I did not curse. This old biddy always, and I mean *always*, got me. I did not look at Doug and Rebecca. I was suddenly tired. "I'm voiding it off."

"Goddamned place, al'ays tryin t' rip me off."

I sighed. "I'm voiding it off."

Her yellowed old eyes glared at me from wrinkled fatty caves. If I'd been the type of person susceptible to a faith in the supernatural, I'd have thought her some sort of persistent payback visited upon me by some vengeful old gypsy I'd wronged. A curse with no cure.

And it didn't help, it really didn't, that Doug was standing back there in line holding his stomach and acting like he was going to laugh his internals out. Rebecca merely smiled in a way that I could not read.

"I'm terribly sorry for the inconvenience, ma'am," I told her, and I'm sure I was as convincing as a funeral home director on laughing gas. The ancient doughbag snorted at me and glared at the hapless sacker who came to carry her groceries out.

Soon enough, Doug and Rebecca drew up. Doug had a bottle of orange juice and a bag of pretzels, and a couple of big tall candles. The orange juice I could figure, the pretzels were just munchie fodder, but on the candles I drew a blank. I rang 'em up anyway, as three packs of gum. It was the unofficial Tate's employee discount, which extended to friends and family, unless management or other customers were present.

"Hey guys," I said, mostly at Doug. I still was not sure I trusted myself enough to squarely look at Rebecca.

"Having fun tonight?" asked Doug.

"Oh, loads. I get done with this, I might go home and pull out all my toenails, you know, add to the mood."

Doug handed me a dollar to cover the purchases. "What are you doing after you get off?"

If he'd been alone, I would have said "Using Kleenex, numbnuts." But Rebecca was there. So instead I blinked in mock astonishment. "Are you trying to pick me up, young man?"

Rebecca smiled. "I might so do," she said.

Doug's smiled got knocked a little crooked and my own heart stuttered. Her tone said she was kidding . . . probably.

"Well," Doug said. "Seriously."

I shrugged and bagged the stuff. "Nothing. Why?"

"I—we thought it might be fun to go Walling."

One of the cineplexes still ran midnight movies on three screens every weekend. *The Rocky Horror Picture Show* ran on one, *The Wall* on another, and the third varied from weekend to weekend. Once a month or so we caught *The Wall*. I hadn't planned on going to see it, but what the fuck.

"Sure," I said. "I gotta see if my folks're sacked out."

Which was kind of a dumb thing to say since they crashed out about eight o'clock on any given night. Still, safety first—that was likely to be my motto if I ever settled on one.

"Sure," said Doug, who knew the drill. "You're off at ten?"

"Yeah. Crash at your place?"

"No problem. Hungry?"

"Fuck yes, I'm hungry."

Rebecca said, "We'll wait for you then."

Yeah, I thought, *you do that.*

"Where, out there?" The rain still poured. I expected to see pairs of animals trooping by at any time.

"Yeah, why not?" said Doug.

They walked out together and I watched them dash out to the Doug's little Datsun 310, a car that I think was Japan's half-assed answer to the Gremlin.

"Your friend Dan finally got a girlfriend, huh?"

It was Monica. I looked at her, incredulous that she had spoken to me. Most of the time we were on the same planet but different worlds, hers much more elevated than mine. Felt like the natural order. And here she was violating it. She was looking out at the departing couple.

"Yeah," I managed, not correcting her name-wise. It wasn't as though we never talked, but it was damned rare. And usually she avoided me when I was feeling particularly lusty, like she had a hormone radar. Or maybe—probably—she'd wised up to dumbasses in lust a long time ago.

Monica shook her head a little wistfully. "I always thought he was kind of cute, in a geeky little way."

I had no idea what to say.

I PUNCHED OUT FIVE minutes early and ran to my car, as though that would prevent me from getting absolutely drenched. I shot into, my car, which I had affectionately, if ironically, dubbed the Cherry Bomb (it was neither a cherry nor a bomb) shivering and sopping, like some poor half-drowned cur. The drumming of the rain on the roof of the car was loud and lonely. I scanned the parking lot through the rain-battered windshield, and after a minute I saw Doug's Datsun. I started the Bomb, stuck some Dio in the deck, and eased up the slight incline of the lot and up next to Doug's car. I rolled my window down, got a face full of rain for my trouble.

Doug's face appeared in his window. I could see Rebecca beyond him, face softly lit by the dashboard lights. God, it was like that damned Meatloaf song.

"Gotta go by my place," I yelled, to remind them.

Doug nodded and rolled his window up. I cranked mine up gingerly, since the handle was loose and figured to come off just any time now.

Before I pulled away, I could just see the white ghost of Rebecca's face moving near, connecting with Doug's.

I felt that I showed great self-control by not peeling out.

The thing is this: at seventeen I felt at least some degree of attraction to about eighty percent of the female populace at any given time. Fuck it, blame hormones. Still, it wasn't just that. Some crushes came and went like strange tides. Some endured for years. There are one or two that survive to this day. Just crushes, that's all, but in most cases I'd have given anything outside of my sexual equipment to nurture them into more.

Monica Arden was one of those. A girl I'd known since fourth grade, a stunning smiling sprite named Jocelyn Foster, was another.

But all were so out of reach.

And let's not forget Samantha Driscoll.

But I'd never had what you could call a steady girlfriend, and the only time I'd ever been laid was almost by accident. I only barely knew the girl, and we were both so drunk that when we snuck out behind the toolshed at the party we were at, we could barely remember our own names, much less each other's. I really wish it had never happened. Most of the time, if I was dumb lucky, I went out with a girl a time or two, and then she decided that she liked me so much that she could not possibly destroy our friendship by becoming romantically involved. What a fucking line. You hear it all the time. And mostly what it meant for me was that a girl had better options than the fat guy.

My response to all of this frustration was to get mad and mope a lot. My response to getting mad and moping a lot was to get drunk as often as possible. All I can say is it always seemed like a good idea back then.

So much does when you're seventeen.

There was a break in the rain as I pulled up in front of my house. I got out and took a deep breath of the moist, fresh air.

I used to love the clean smell just after a rain. I haven't smelled it in over three decades.

There was still a good deal of thunder and lightning about, and I was pretty sure that this calm wouldn't last.

I waited for Doug to show, and about two minutes later his car pulled around the corner and eased behind the Bomb. I walked over to his window, waited for him to roll it down.

"It looks like they're asleep," I said, "but I need to make sure. I also need to change."

"Yeah," Doug said, "that tie sucks, Lynch."

I flipped him off.

Rebecca smiled warmly at me, and I could think of nothing to say, so I slapped the Datsun and headed for the house.

"We'll wait here," I heard Doug say for Rebecca's benefit.

No way in heaven, hell, or earth would my parents ever let me go to a midnight movie, even if it had been *The Ten Commandments* personally hosted by Jesus Christ. To even stay out past ten was some kind of mortal sin to them. So I usually told them I was staying over at somebody's house (Doug was the usual alibi) or I went home long enough for them to crash. Once they were out, they were *out*.

And tonight, they slept the slumbers of the snoring dead.

I navigated the dark house like a cat burglar and changed without a light in my room, throwing on jeans and some concert shirt, it didn't matter which one. Let it be a nice surprise. Tour shirt roulette. Finished, I reached up under my bed, into the box spring, for the bottle of Everclear I had stashed there. It was a small bottle, mostly full. I'd gotten one of the older guys at Tate's to get it for me. I tucked it into my jeans and dashed back outside to Doug's car. Doug got out and let me in, folding his seat forward. Doug was always the driver.

I had never seen *The Wall* sober. Doug, the opposite.

Rebecca twisted around in the front passenger seat, watching me pull the Everclear out. God, her sweet smell . . .

"What thing that is?"

I could not hear her voice without getting mild pleasant shivers, but sometimes her syntax seemed just a little off, and I paused before answering.

"Liquid fixation."

She gave me a puzzled look over the top of the seat. I could hear Doug chuckling from his seat. His eyes, as best I could make them out in the rearview, were filled with amusement.

"Everclear," I said. "Useful as an antifreeze." I belatedly hoped Rebecca wasn't a teetotaler.

"Ah."

Doug said, "You lush. Should be a cup back there. OJ's on the back seat."

I guessed that meant Rebecca wasn't on the Temperance Board.

"Thanks," I said, and rummaged. It didn't take long. The Datsun was a small car, made by short people for short people.

Success! A little OJ, a lot of Everclear, bottoms up.

Doug's cheap Targa radio was on—the KATT, 100.5 FM, coming through, occasionally punctuated by a burst of lightning-spiked static. It was their block party weekend, and they were playing Rush, starting with the new one, "Force Ten." I lay back against the seat and closed my eyes, tired from standing in front of a check stand all night, just sort of catching my second wind and letting the groove of the Rush tune wash over me. I pictured Rebecca in my mind even as she said something to Doug, and before I knew it, I was hard. I flashed on a strong mental image: me, Rebecca, naked, fucking, her straddling me and riding up and down. Her smooth skin soft against mine, my black pubic hair indistinguishable from hers when we thrust together. Her round, strong breasts moving with our rhythm, nipples stiff and tight. Her moans, my own matching them, my hands sliding, finding, gripping as she moved with urgency. Those gray eyes, those unreal gray eyes . . .

An angular, bony form swimming up from a great depth . . .

Blood in dirty water, blood . . .

And screaming that would not end.

I gasped, not realizing that I had drifted to sleep. It took me several moments to blink away my dream. When I did, I saw Rebecca looking at me with a trace of concern pulling at her features, but it quickly vanished, and for a long time, I thought I'd dreamed that, too.

Fuck it. Bottoms up.

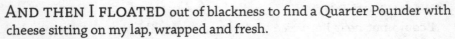

AND THEN I FLOATED out of blackness to find a Quarter Pounder with cheese sitting on my lap, wrapped and fresh.

"Wuzza?" I asked.

Doug regarded me in the rearview. "You ordered it."

I had?

I started to unwrap it, looked down at my belly, looked at Rebecca looking at me, and something like a whisper, like a feather, touched my brain.

"Oh," I said, and passed back out.

DOUG HAD ONE ARM. Rebecca had the other. They helped me out of the car. I woke up in the middle of it.

"Huh," I said.

"We're here, and please don't breathe on me," said Doug. "You could melt my glasses."

I blinked, shook my rubber head, smiled at Rebecca (and oh, miracle, she smiled back) and tried to focus. It was hard to concentrate when I was in physical contact with Rebecca. Never mind the booze. My nervous system wanted to fry out, my hormones wanted to geyser out of my chest.

"Here" apparently was the parking lot of the AMC Memorial 8. The lot was mostly full, other misfits and drunks gathering to worship at the midnight altar. The lovebirds tentatively let go of me when I convinced them that I could indeed walk.

Trickster me. They should make pavement softer.

3

I DON'T KNOW WHAT a midnight showing of *The Wall* was like in other places, but in our admittedly backward neck of the woods, it was a catalog, a dim-lit museum display of misery. *The Wall* is not the most uplifting or inspiring piece of filmmaking to ever shine on the screen, but then those of us who flocked to it repeatedly were not terribly interested in inspiration. You could get all of that shit on the Sunday morning idiot box. Damn near everybody went to it drunk or stoned out of their gourds, which might have been a problem if you were going to see, say, *Children of a Lesser God*. But *The Wall* (and also *Evil Dead* and *Highlander*, other midnight flickage in our times) was enriched for the chemical activity. Some have argued that *The Wall* makes no sense if one is sober. I have never put this theory to the test.

So the idea was to get so smashed you couldn't stand up, get someone to drive you to the movie, and then buy so much popcorn and candy that you made yourself sick. Also, when you woke up the next morning, your wallet was sucked dry and for all you could remember, and judging by the state of your pounding skull, you might well have been robbed. You got points for not puking during the film. Points also were awarded for staying awake for the whole thing, no mean feat. Bob Geldof in this film is not magnetism personified, if ever he was. So, you're in a theater full of drunks and potheads who are ralphing, snoring, or yelling dementedly at the screen; watching one of the most incoherent, confusing, and disjointed films ever created, in Armageddon Dolby so that "In the Flesh" blasts yours off the bone; and when you leave you're nauseated, bleary-eyed, wobbly, and deaf.

Heaven, I tell you.

We went Walling. By the time we got to the AMC up on Memorial, the Everclear and OJ had wrapped me in a nice fuzzy numbness.

A pleasant surprise awaited us in the lobby: Stan and Mick had decided to go Walling as well. Stan was skunk smashed.

"Hey, Mick, it's Tweedledum and, uh, Tweedledummer."

I grinned, weaved over to Mick and gave him a high-five. Only barely missed. Rebecca seemed amused by this, which made me grin even more foolishly.

"Tsup?" I asked Mick.

"Nada," Mick replied. He wore black jeans and a crisp, snappy white shirt, his best snakeskin boots. His thick blond hair was immaculate, nothing out of place. You took a look at him, and it was easy to wonder why he didn't get more dates than he did.

"Hey, Doug," he said, over my shoulder.

"Hey," Doug said in that peculiarly parsimonious way of his.

I shuffled over to Stan. "Hey."

"You're shitfaced, man," Stan said to me.

"Duh."

He was wearing his jean jacket, even though it wasn't at all cold out, and he held one side open to let me see the top of a bottle of what looked like schnapps.

"Peach," he confided solemnly.

"Jesus Christ!" I looked wildly around the cavernous lobby for the two cops who always picked up some mad money by providing security at the midnight movies. I saw lots of drunks and plenty of geeks up for *Rocky Horror* in all that shamelessly bright DayGlo paint and pointless neon, but no cops. "Put that shit away! They'll kick us out!"

We went and got popcorn and Cokes, found the rest of the gang and went in to be pummeled.

Mayhem erupted on the screen, Pink Floyd cacophony. I glanced once at the popcorn but it made me queasy, which was weird, because normally I'd be cramming the greasy puffs in as fast as I could. Stan was less restrained, if also less efficient; it took every ounce of his concentration to get a handful from bucket to mouth, and he dropped more than he ate.

I could not feel my face. Good thing I didn't need to.

Every time I looked over at Doug, he was looking at Rebecca as if she were the lost city of Cibola, all golden and shining, and he was Coronado at the end of his quest. I could, even drunk, feel Doug's reaction, frustrated, hot, and frightened because she was, after all, beautiful. I felt it because it was my reaction as well.

I nudged Stan and motioned for him to hand over that bottle of schnapps.

I didn't remember much for a while, then I phased in to see Bob Geldof shaving himself in areas that would have the Schick folks shrieking. I looked down at the popcorn bucket, which was empty, then at Stan, who was, too. His eyes seemed to have been sprayed with a liberal coat of polyurethane. He muttered something that I could not hear, but which looked like "shit."

My hand held the schnapps bottle, and it was mostly empty. Shit was right. I felt very much not there. Untethered. With a great amount of effort, I made my head turn around and I saw Rebecca leaning over Doug, their faces fusing together at the lips. One of Doug's hands caressed one of Rebecca's breasts, but it was dark and I was far beyond drunk and I couldn't tell you which hand or which breast.

I tried to get interested in the movie again, but I felt too much heat from that side of me. Also, a great pressure grew in my bladder, seeming to achieve, truly, a malign sentience. I thought of *Alien*. I thought of the restroom.

"Gotta go," I pronounced, and tried to get up.

On the fourth or fifth try, I made it. I stumbled over Stan, nearly fell, got past Mick, made the aisle, and was nearly undone by the fact that it sloped upward. Things swayed for a minute, lazy and liquid. The soundtrack ate at me. I was seriously loose. This was largely okay with me.

"The Swing," I said, a babbling idiot.

Like Frankenstein's monster with a whopping attack of vertigo, I lurched up out of the theater. I turned down towards where I thought a bathroom might be. Navigation was not one of my strong suits at the moment, but amazingly, I found one.

I shambled in. It was empty, stark white, and silent. My bladder was a giant water balloon. I swerved toward the nearest urinal, passing the sinks with their attendant mirrors. It took a long time to wring my bladder dry. I almost passed out pissing, it took so long. Finished, I weaved back toward the door, passing the sinks once more.

Their attendant mirrors.

The first three I passed, I was okay. Out of the corner of my eye I saw only my drunken self. In the fourth, I saw something else. I saw water, a small slow creek. Trees. Red clay banks dappled with shadows. A thick rope dangled from a massive branch, directly over the muddy pool. On one bank, a bush of wild roses, their color a startling red. On the other, a much battered boombox. I knew without hearing anything that it was playing "Year of the Cat."

I couldn't catch my breath. Something wriggled in my thoughts, something that didn't want to be caught. Something about that seemingly innocent tableau scared the living shit out of me.

And that fear spiked right off the goddamn charts when someone spoke to me, because I was sure the bathroom was empty.

"Eric."

The voice, though I did not recognize it, was familiar.

A figure filled the mirror, swelling out of the previous scene, gaining clarity and substance.

"Eric."

I backed away from the sink, shaking my head, until I bumped into the hand dryer. My elbow pushed the button and the dryer whirred to life. It's a miracle I didn't shit myself. It didn't drown out the voice. It was a young boy's voice, the voice of a boy heading toward manhood, cracking and breaking, caught in vocal cord no-man's land.

"I don't know you," I whispered.

"You do. You just gotta try to remember. You have to fight it, you can't let it stay. This ain't about us, it never was, it wants the door open again, and there's no telling what'll follow. You gotta close the door, you gotta cut the line."

As I was hearing this, the shape in the mirror grew became a clear figure.

It was a thin young man, in jeans and an Adidas T-shirt. He wore wire-rim glasses and had bright golden hair.

And there was blood all over him. A ton of it, too much of it.

"We hung out once, remember? It's real important that you *remember*."

"No." But I wasn't really answering him.

"You and me and Doug and—"

"No."

And then he reached out of the mirror, one small, thin hand with long delicate fingers and ragged, bitten fingernails, blood smeared and streaked across tanned skin.

"She's no good, Eric, no good for any of you, no good for your whole damn world. Believe me. You have to try to remember it. Remember the Swing."

Reaching for me.

I shook my head violently

"She's empty. And she'll drink you up. She'll drink this world dry, her and everything that'll follow her."

I doubled over and vomited. I sucked in a breath and heaved again, and maybe I screamed after I did it. I emptied myself two, three times over until nothing but thick clear juices came out in dripping strings. Tears forced themselves out from between my clenched eyelids.

Sometime later, forever, I don't know, I looked up, and saw only my wasted self, slick with tears and cold sweat. I was alone again.

I took the only comfort I could from that: I passed out.

One of the others, Mick probably, came after me, and dragged me out of my own vomit and cleaned me up, but I don't remember that. I was lucky no one else had come in, although maybe they had. The crowd that went to *The Wall* was not lousy with good Samaritans. The next thing I really knew was Mick and Stan propping me up against Doug's car, Doug unlocking the door, everybody giving me hell. Except Rebecca. She stared at me with what I could only see as raw concern. But it didn't really feel like it was specifically directed at me.

Then I was dumped in the back seat, and I surrendered to the black again.

Doug and Rebecca parked out north of Oklahoma City, some place distant and hidden. I swam back up from unconsciousness, from the black, to hear the unmistakable sounds of two people making love. How this could be done in such a tiny car was vexing, and I thought of looking, but this seemed like a very bad idea in my state. Blinking seemed like a very bad idea in my state. Doug gasped and Rebecca let out a rising moan. I kept my eyes closed and did not move, and wondered at the jealousy and anger rising in me. After one or both of them came, when they lay against each other and whispered, I opened my eyes and saw flickering dancing light, picked up the smell of melting wax. At least I knew what the candles were for now. I faced the back window, and saw that the storm had moved on. The stars were bright and clear and cold and distant.

In the front seat, the lovers sighed.

I shut my eyes.

And that was the day the thing that called itself Rebecca Connors came back.

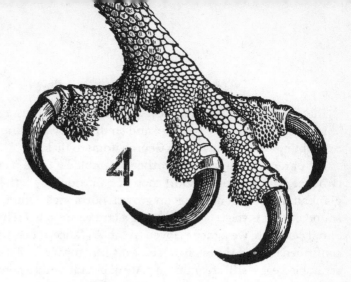

4

THE NEXT MORNING, I had ten pounds of brain stuffed inside a one-pound skull.

And that was the least of my concerns, at the moment. Daylight wasn't doing me any favors, and the greasy waft of food smells from the kitchen had my innards rising in armed revolt. Worse than the physical effects of this, though, was the sure knowledge that I was home, and that meant having to face my parents with a hangover the size of Mexico City.

I lay in my bed and tried not to move, tried not to think. Much of the previous night was fuzzy or gone altogether, but I remembered parts of it well enough. I thought it was pretty cruel that usually the stuff you don't want to remember when you're drunk is the garbage you can't flush from your head.

And what was that shit with the mirror in the bathroom? Wasn't I entirely too young to get the DTs? I didn't drink that often. Did I?

I resolved then to never get that drunk again.

I made this resolution about every three months. Something always happened.

The door to my bedroom opened, I could hear the bottom of it scrape across the plush carpet like a tidal roar. Probably my father, so though I really didn't want to, I decided I'd best open my eyes.

When I could focus, I smiled weakly at my father. He was not a man of great humor.

"Mornin'," I said to him. I think I almost sounded human.

He grunted. "Breakfast's ready. What time do you work?"

Work. Jesus. "Um . . . four, I think."

"Come eat, then. You can help me for a few hours."

He left, shutting the door behind him. I groaned and looked at my alarm clock.

7:15.

That was just not possible. Seven? Fifteen? As in the a.m.?

I groaned again. But I got up, and shuffled down to the kitchen, I'm sure resembling something from a George Romero flick.

My parents were fat. My mother resembled a large pale bowling ball on two tree stumps, with a short mop of hair atop. My father was more like a giant albino pear gone amok on growth hormones. I know how unkind that sounds, but it is the truth, and being a lardass myself, I felt qualified to judge. Simply enough, we Lynches loved to eat. A glance at breakfast that morning confirmed this: on the kitchen table sat a heaping plate of bacon, a large bowl of scrambled eggs, still steaming, a plate of biscuits, and a bowl of fried potatoes, also still steaming. An army could have fed on it. There were only three of us.

It was obvious that they were waiting grace on me, so I slid down into my chair and dutifully if insincerely bowed my swollen and heavy head. The smell of the food wrapped itself around me and made my stomach twist. Food really was the last thing on my mind. Which was odd, because even in my worst hangovers, I could still pack the chow away.

"Dear Father," my mother began, in her low mannish voice. I never thought of it as husky, really, because that implied too much sexuality. You don't like to think of your parents like that. But her voice must have sounded much like Lauren Bacall's when she was young, before the wrapping of body fat thickened it and squeezed it. I've always thought that must have been what hooked my father, but who can say? Something must have, back in those dark days before they got born again.

". . . we thank you for this food and ask that you bless it to our bodies . . ."

Yeah, I thought, *no salmonella please.*

The thought of actually eating any of that stuff spread out before me sent my stomach cramping again.

". . . in your precious name we pray. Amen."

I moved my lips in case they glanced my way. When you're in the presence of the terminally Saved, it's easier to fake it and go along to get along than it is to stand up for your own beliefs. Doug always argued otherwise, but he lived in a highly rational household. The Driscolls were moderate, mostly fallen away Lutherans. Different planets, man.

The prayer done, I raised my head up and filled my plate.

My mother asked, "How was work, Eric?"

I shrugged. "Okay, I guess. Kinda slow. The rain." My voice sent vibrations through my head that were not kind. My head wouldn't really be okay for a couple of days, after a stupid drunk like that.

"I thought you were going to spend the night at Doug's house," she continued.

"It didn't really work out. You guys were asleep when I got home after work."

My father spooned a heap of eggs onto his plate. This was followed by a half a hog's worth of bacon, and a trio of biscuits. I watched the food accumulate with a growing and unfamiliar sense of disgust. Was he really going to *eat* all that?

Between mouthfuls of egg, he said, "Need you to sweep up the garage today. Got some parts to soak, too."

"Okay," I said, carefully hiding my displeasure. Over the years I had gradually worked less at my father's garage, as other commitments took hold of me. I had no desire and no talent to be a mechanic, as my botched attempts at body work on the Bomb should have amply demonstrated. But dad had ideas about me taking over the business. It was concrete, and he was a man who, religious beliefs aside, held great faith in the concrete. Cars and engines were real, solid, steel and rubber and glass. Music was ephemeral, insubstantial in all respects, and I think that was the main reason that he crapped on my musical aspirations, my lack of talent notwithstanding.

Well, and rock 'n' roll was the devil's lure. There *was* that.

In another eight months, after graduation, I would leave, head to some place where even insubstantial dreams could be chased, and he would be alone with his shop. In the meantime, I was occasionally pressed into service, and most of the time I really did try to go about it with good grace.

"You're not eating," my mother pointed out, and indeed I wasn't. I looked down at my plate, and tried to temper my grimace. I felt as inclined to ingest this grub as I would have a dog turd. My stomach made a tight fist. I ate a bit anyway, as much out of habit and obligation as anything. But a weird feeling came over me: even the first bite made me hate myself for having taken it.

"Good," I said.

Maybe fifteen seconds later, I was bent over the toilet making the technicolor yawn. I thought maybe all of my vitals were being pulled out of my alimentary canal.

My mother filled the doorway. "Maybe," she said, "you shouldn't go into the shop today."

As it turned out, I didn't go into Tate's either. Stomach virus, I told them, but I could tell from the tone in the Roger Craw's voice that he thought hangover. Well, fuck him. I had worked through any number of hangovers, and *I* thought it was a virus. I spent the day in bed, didn't go anywhere that night, and even managed to get out of church Sunday.

I slept a lot, and dreamed of muddy water and dark places, black hair and soft white thighs, with no clue as to what any of it meant.

And didn't eat a bite.

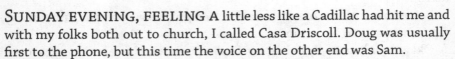

SUNDAY EVENING, FEELING A little less like a Cadillac had hit me and with my folks both out to church, I called Casa Driscoll. Doug was usually first to the phone, but this time the voice on the other end was Sam.

"Oh, God, no, not *you*, Sam-I-Am. Did they kick you out of school? Hitting on the Dean of Engineering in a desperate attempt to save your grades again? Trying to ensnare unwary exchange students into indentured servitude? Performing vile acts with the mascot? What was it this time, Sam? What terrible thing have they got you on this time?"

Not a "Hi, is Doug home?" Not, "Oh, hi, Sam." Nope. Always best to land the first blow where the vaunted Samantha Driscoll was concerned.

"I'm sorry," she countered, "I think we have a bad connection. What charity did you say you were with again? United Appeal for Sufferers of Tertiary Syphilis? I'm sorry, you might want to try the Lynch household. I hear there's a dork there whom you might be able to assist."

"Now, Sam, you know I don't know half of those words."

"Plus you have to have experienced physical relations to contract syphilis. My mistake, Lynch. I have a wicked head cold coming on. It's clouded my thoughts."

Unlikely as hell. The condition that could cloud Sam's thoughts hadn't come around. "Sorry to hear that. Your little brother around?"

"I'm completely whelmed by your sympathy, Eric. No, actually, he's having lunch with his girlfriend. Speaking of said girlfriend, that Rebecca person . . ."

Oh, yeah, speaking of.

"Well," I said, "she's got a hell of an S&M fetish."

"Uh-huh."

"What do you want me to say? I only met her Friday. She seems nice enough."

Eric Lynch, Master of Understatement.

"Were you wearing beer goggles or no?"

What the hell kind of a question was *that*? "What the *hell* kind of a question is that, Sammo?"

She said nothing. Silence scorched the phone line.

"At lunch, definitely no beer goggles," I said. "Later, maybe. Anyway, she's cute and she seems smart enough to keep up with Doug. What, you don't like her?"

She sighed with indecision. That was a sound you rarely heard out of a Driscoll.

"I dunno, Eric. I haven't met her. It's just that Doug won't shut up about her, and I'm worried baby brother's taking things too seriously."

"Not such a baby anymore. I don't know if you've noticed or not, he shaves and drives a car and looks at girls and stuff."

"Keep an eye on him, will you, Eric?" Twice within a minute she'd used my first name. Be calm, my heart.

"Sam, Doug can take care of himself. Probably better than I can."

No probably about it, actually.

Then a thought occurred to me. "Has he said anything about her to your folks yet?"

"I'm not sure he's girded his loins enough. I don't know why. I'm sure they'll just be relieved to death that he isn't gay. He isn't, is he? Wait, are *you* gay, Lynch? Are you planning on stealing my brother over to the dark side, the two of you listening to ABBA and watching John Waters movies?"

"I hate ABBA and have no idea who the hell John Waters is, so stop it." I fell into my best Gabby Hayes voice. "'Sides, he took one look at lil' ol' Miss Becca and got hisself a right proper little trouser tent."

Sam laughed. She had the best laugh I ever heard, and I miss it more than anything.

"Whatever, Lynch. Well, anyway, he isn't here, which is a relief, because it gives you no reason to come by and scare the children. They still have nightmares from your last visit."

"Yeah," I agreed. "Bogeyman-in-training, that's me. By the way, bite me, Driscoll."

"You'd just *love* that, wouldn't you?" Sam replied, and hung up. I don't know how I could tell she'd hung up with a grin, but I could.

I *never* got the last word in with her.

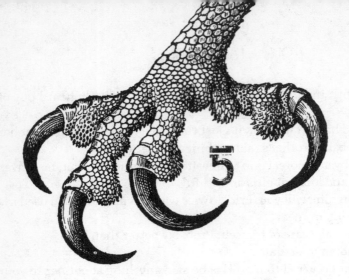

5

THE NEXT TIME I saw Doug was the end of the week. This would have been September 4th, the Friday before Labor Day.

School, to that point, had been Dull City. We were settling into our class routines now, and the homework was beginning to flow in earnest. I wound up getting transferred to second lunch, which meant that I now had to eat mostly by myself, to the degree that I actually ate. The giddy euphoria of eating out had given way to the bleakness of economic exile in the Wood Wilson cafeteria. I mostly spent my lunch hour in the Cherry Bomb reading a Stephen King paperback and nibbling halfheartedly on a granola bar or some such shit. I passed the others in the hallways only occasionally, mostly Stan and Mick. Once I thought I saw Rebecca, and I tried to catch up to her, but lost her in the rush between classes. She vanished into the bumping, shuffling mass of students. I stared after her, tried to find her, but it was useless. I cursed and wondered what it was that I'd thought I would say to her anyway.

The thing that pissed me off was Doug being AWOL. It shouldn't have, maybe, but it did.

ONE AFTERNOON AFTER SCHOOL I drove over to Stan's house to jam a little before going to work. I'd stuck my bass and amp in the car before heading out. Stan's parents rented a little place in Bethany, a small town that was surrounded on all sides by Oklahoma City, enveloped the way a bacterium is by an antibody. The Russell homestead was an older one, and in need of a few small repairs, like a new roof, a new driveway, a coat of paint, some grass that lived. When I got there and let myself in, Stan's dad was crashed on the couch, watching some dreadful horror flick on HBO. Stan's mom worked nights at Baptist hospital. I had only the vaguest notion of what she did there, only knew that it was stressful and depressing. Stan had told me recently that he figured that his folks would split once he moved out, that his dad was already pressuring him to go to Vermont for some fucking reason. Stan accepted this with a sort of casual resignation that was totally beyond me.

"Hey, Mr. Russell," I said to the scarecrow that lay on the couch, staring at the bloody mayhem on the television. The man was skin and bones, mostly, except for a shock of thinning white hair atop his head. He was in his mid-forties, I think, but looked closer to his mid-sixties. At the moment, judging from the odor in the living room, he was stoned out of his mind. He barely raised a hand at my greeting. Peace, man. An ex-flower child, except that he had a whole room full of guns and bladed weapons. I'd seen his collection once. It gave me the creeps. Pistols, ceremonial war swords, high-powered rifles, the whole nine yards. You wonder what orbits inside a guy like that, what kind of mad dark star spins without rest, without pause.

I went to Stan's room and let myself in.

"Okay, put your weenie away, schmuck. Royalty's here."

He was sprawled on his bed reading a copy of Circus, and without looking up from it he flipped me off. I found a chair, an ancient brown recliner one of his uncles had tossed out, shoved the pile of clothes on it to the floor, and plopped down. Stan had on his white shirt and blue tie on that he'd wear to work that evening.

"You gonna wear that to bed?"

"Not if you're joinin' me, man."

"Join this," I said, coupled with the age-old ball-cupping gesture. I wonder if Neanderthals did that to each other.

Stan's habitat was completely the opposite of mine. It was a mess. I doubt he had a stitch of clothing on a hanger or in a drawer. It was all on the floor or draped over his amp or in some other un-clothes-like place. It wasn't really dirty, no food growing under the bed (I think) or nasty unspeakable things procreating in his closet, but my god he knew nothing of tidiness. How can people live like that? Christ, I was fat, but I wasn't a slob. It drove me nuts sometimes. I shoved aside a stack of songbooks to set my amp down, and I just lowered my case down on some old clothes.

"'Peace of Mind'?" he asked me.

I tried not to groan. In addition to the fact that it is a fucking bland song, Stan was not so hot at playing it. But we only knew about four or five tunes, and you go with what you've got. Even when it's goddamn Boston.

We fucked around with that for a while, our noise banging off the walls, hardly muffled by his Whitesnake and Poison and Boston posters. Stan made ridiculous scrunched faces while he pulled notes, kicking and screaming, from his cheap red guitar. I was less enthusiastic, but it was fun nonetheless. I was frustrated by my own limited talent, by the lack of a real band kind of atmosphere; the two of us just jacking around didn't count. We needed other people to make our sound real, to push us to get better. And we didn't need to be playing fucking Boston.

After about an hour of trading riffs and the few new cool things we had learned (I had gotten down part of the bass line from "Tom Sawyer," and was pretty damn proud about it) Stan went out into the kitchen and came back with a pair of Coronas. His dad was probably passed out, or out in his gun room marveling over an instrument of death, seeking solace in all that steel. Stan handed a beer to me and sucked greedily at his.

I wasn't all that thirsty, and took mine more slowly. I'd have to eat a ton of mints before I went home to get ready for work.

"Man," said Stan, after a hearty belch, "we suck."

"*You* suck."

He flipped me off and reached over to his stereo, punched the power button, and grimaced when KATT came on, playing "Year of the Cat."

"I hate that fuckin' song," he said, switching to the tape deck. I recognized "Seven Wishes" from Night Ranger.

"I know this guy," Stan said, "goes to school at West, his brother's in my brother's frat, anyway, he's got a kit."

"Geez, Livingston, having one and being able to use it are two different things."

"What I hear from all your dates, man."

"Kiss my ass."

"So one of these days, maybe we all oughtta jam together."

I shrugged. Okay. Whatever. That sort of thing you believe when you see it. We sipped our beers. I found myself studying Stan's one nonmusical poster, an anonymous bimbo in a wet swimsuit on a Budweiser blanket. Stan followed my gaze.

"So, um, Doug got himself a real babe, huh?"

I frowned. Nearly the same damn thought had been going through my head. What I'd been thinking, actually, was how much better Rebecca looked than this minx of marketing. "Yeah."

Stan scooted back on his bed, set his Corona on top of his amp and folded his hands. "She's fuckin' hot, man."

I nodded abstractedly. I didn't really like where our thoughts were dwelling.

There's just-kidding-around dirty, you know, and then there's hurtful dirty.

"You think she's gonna hang with us next weekend?"

What he was asking on the surface was whether or not I thought Doug would bring Rebecca into our usual dork club hanging out. I thought about that, and about what he was really asking, which was "Do you think she'll get tired of him and go for one of us, hopefully me?" It was a shitty question, but we were both thinking it. I vaguely recalled my dreams since the night of the midnight movie.

"Yeah," I lied. But I wasn't sure which question I was lying about.

Stan nodded but looked doubtful.

"They're good for each other." Oh boy, was I convincing or what?

Stan said, "But good enough?"

I didn't know how to answer that.

He said, "You get a girl like that, you know, you'd have to kill to keep her, right? You think Doug would do that? Do anything to keep her?"

My throat was dry.

"Sure," I croaked.

Then Def Leppard came on the radio and we got into an argument over whether Hysteria sucked donkey dongs or not, and the subject of Rebecca Connors was passed over.

But it wasn't a topic that went away. Thursday night at Tate's, Mick was in, and we happened to go on break together.

I was sitting at the break table, which was really just an old cable drum with a disc of plywood dropped on top. The wood was held in place by some sort of glue that was losing the war with time. Once, the top had been painted lime green for some obscure reason, but now it was almost completely black from magic markers. Price stickers littered the surface like weird square lichen.

I was drinking a Diet Coke (even though I'd always hated diet drinks, the last few days, I'd been sucking them down) and reading a *Kerrang!* I'd swiped from the magazine rack when Mick sauntered in. His shirt was soaking wet, which meant he'd been back in produce all evening, spraying down the goods, and probably the other produce worker. Fights with the spray hoses were a fulfilling way to pass the time.

"Tsup?" he asked as he desultorily dropped into a chair that was turned backwards. He fished a cigarette out and lit up, inhaling with urgent gratefulness.

"Not much," I sighed. I would have given the same response were my hair on fire and badgers biting at my tenders.

"You were kinda fucked up at *The Wall* the other night." He grinned around his smoke as he said this.

I shrugged. Well, of course I'd been fucked up at the movie, I was always fucked up at that movie.

Mick took another long, greedy pull, and after a few moments let the smoke out in a smooth steady stream that broke apart into chaotic swirls. He stared at the smoke almost dreamily.

"She's really something, you know?"

"Who?" I asked, like I didn't already know.

Mick cocked his head at me, his grin slanted now. "Duh, fuck, 'Who'?"

I drained my Diet Coke. It tasted awful.

"Doug's real gone on her, ain't he?"

"Yeah," I said.

Mick said nothing, stared at his smoke, swirling, swirling.

"C'mon," I said. "She's a megafox."

He laughed, which turned into a couple of barking coughs. The slick eddies of smoke flew apart, reformed into stranger meanings.

"She's fuckin' trouble, is what she is," Mick said, when he'd regained his breath.

Sour grapes. "Right."

"I'm just saying, is all."

"I'm kind of thinking it really ain't none our business."

"He's your friend, don't that sort of make it your business?"

"Man, what the hell is *into* you?"

Mick said, "You seen Stan makin' eyes at her?"

Yes. "No."

"Well, he is. That bother you?"

"Might if it was the case, which it ain't."

"Eric, you got two eyes. I'm gonna suggest you start using 'em. I know it's something new, but you might be all right at it."

I crumpled my Diet Coke can. I might have thrown it at him if he hadn't looked so goddamned sad.

"Yeah," I said. "You know, even if what you're saying is true, it's not my problem. Stan's gonna have to get over it. Doug and Rebecca are a couple, and that's that."

Mick stared at me without saying a thing for a minute, then he only shrugged, and then Craw stuck his head in to inform me that my fifteen minutes were up. It was just about all Craw was really good for. Management, my hairy butt.

SO, AS I SAID, it was almost a full week before I saw Doug Driscoll again, the Friday night before Labor Day. This would have been the 4th of September. We'd been in class two full weeks at this point, but I hadn't seen him in the halls much. Of course, I knew who'd been monopolizing his time. I tried not to let it eat me too much, but you know how it is. Ordinarily I'd have expected him to at least swing by Tate's some night, or call, or something. We'd always hung out constantly, even in the summer. Of all the changes I had been preparing for, for my upcoming senior year, his absence in my day-to-day routine hadn't been one of them.

Friday when I got out of class I shot over to Tate's and picked up my paycheck, headed to the bank to cash it before I somehow managed to lose the damn thing, and then, cash in hand, sought my own brand of therapy.

The Rainbow Records on May Avenue is gone now, replaced, I am told, by a tire store, but in its glory days it was the best record store in Oklahoma City. In many ways, it was the only thing besides my friends that made life in Oklahoma bearable. I hated the wide spaces of the Oklahoma plains and the ugly red clay garishness of everything about it. The people, in my experience, were no great shakes either.

Ah, but Rainbow Records, where most of my money wound up. In no time at all, I was lost in the bins, panning for vinyl gold. So lost, that when someone tapped me on the shoulder I jumped a foot and almost shrieked.

Of course, it was Doug, grinning like a dork. Who else?

"Scared you."

"Bullshit"

"I did. You jumped a foot. Two feet."

I couldn't deny that so I didn't.

"I thought I'd find you here. What do you have there?"

I showed him. Doug wasn't the record hound I was, but usually displayed some interest in my purchases. It went both ways. I blew many afternoons in bookstores with him. I always acted like I thought Isaac Asimov paperbacks were hip as shit.

He frowned at a Maiden record, and actually sneered a little at an Al Stewart album. Doug's musical interest was prog rock, all that spacey shit, long epic songs about journeys to distant centers of parallel universes or some crap like that. Stuff like Genesis, Yes, Marillion. And Pink Floyd. Most especially, Pink Floyd. Even if he wasn't on speaking terms with David Gilmour right now. If he thought I was veering from my steadfast love for hair-metal bands, there was no telling what sort of nonsense he might proselytize me with.

"Not getting the Stewart record," I said quickly, shoving it back in the rack.

"Well, are you about done here?" He looked even more sober than normal.

I wasn't, but what the hell. "Yeah, why?"

"Denny's?"

"Sure."

Denny's ranked slightly below having a sinus drain when it came to my list of least favorite things. The food was not quite as tasty as freeze-dried cardboard, the waitresses looked and acted like ex-cons, and the prices bordered on illegal. The coffee, however, was tolerable. Also, they were open 24 hours and hardly ever kicked us out. We went there a lot after concerts and midnight movies, and it had come to serve as our jittery, fully-caffeinated home away from home.

It was dead when we got there, suffering the post-lunch-hour malaise. I sat across from Doug, sipping on my coffee and feeling it drip uneasily into my empty stomach. Doug clearly needed a heart-to-heart, and I was going to do my best not to be a smartass about it. This would not be easy. Especially since I kinda knew the topic was gonna revolve around his new girl, and it's hardwired into male genes to dish out good-natured shit over the sexual victories of our comrades. Particularly when we're jealous of them.

He nudged his glasses and leaned forward over the table and looked at me with such earnestness that I thought my cast iron stomach might empty what little it held all over my lap.

"So, what do you think of Rebecca?"

"I dunno, Doug, you might want to take a bag with you, you two go out. That is, if you can stand the public humiliation of being seen with her. I mean—"

His eyes narrowed. "I mean it, Eric. What do you think?"

"What, you need my seal of approval?"

He glared at me. Behind his glasses a tic twitched the corner of his left eye. Now I knew he was more than halfway to pissed off.

"Look, she's a babe and she seems like she's got half a brain at least, okay? I think you should marry her and settle down and have ten kids just like you were a good Catholic. Honest. That's my professional assessment having spent all of three hours in her company."

Well, and a few minutes one afternoon. I didn't want to talk about that.

My coffee was gone, so I poured more.

"Only half a brain?" Doug said.

"Well," I said, "she is goin' out with *you*."

"Yeah." Dreamy and contented.

"So what happened? You slip her some new kind of love potion you cooked up in Chemistry?"

"Chemistry—don't talk to me about that class, it's going to kill me," Doug smiled at me. "What was I wearing the first day of school?"

"Jesus, I don't know. A wedding dress, maybe? Parachute pants? A FRANKIE SAYS FUCK T-shirt? Women's underwear?"

Doug poured out the last of the coffee and set the empty thermal plastic carafe near the edge of the table. "Come on, Eric."

"My memory fails me in my old age."

"I happened to be wearing my Floyd shirt."

"Oh, duh. Which one, slick?" Hell, he only had a million Pink Floyd shirts. One for every occasion, all oversized and usually swimming around his beanpole body like a sail seeking wind.

"Wall Live."

Ah, the tattered nasty one with more holes than a PGA course. A more unattractive garment one would be hard-pressed to imagine. That shirt always reminded me of a textile version of the slush that gathers at curbs as a heavy snow melts.

"She asked me about it, asked if I like Floyd."

"Oh, poor Rebecca."

"Hey, she has a copy of *Ummagamma*."

"No accounting for taste."

"We kinda chatted about Floyd for a minute, and then I asked her out."

"Oh, like it was just that easy."

Doug looked a little uncomfortable. He pushed his glasses back up the bridge of his nose. "Well, it was."

I could think of nothing profound to say.

Doug flashed me his patented sardonic smile.

"Well," I said, "she seemed okay to me."

The smile did not waver.

"Okay, she's gorgeous as hell, and I'm jealous of you, you big hairy prick, and you could at least kindly not rub it in. Or let me know if she's got an older sister or something. Younger, too. Younger could work."

And we both laughed at that. I'm sure we did.

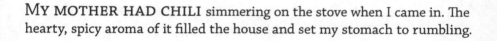

MY MOTHER HAD CHILI simmering on the stove when I came in. The hearty, spicy aroma of it filled the house and set my stomach to rumbling.

After zippo for lunch and bad Denny's coffee slopping around my stomach, I should have been starving. I lifted the lid off the pot. The simmering chili sent a flavored burst of steam up, and I inhaled deeply. Onions, cumin, tomato, chili powder. Good god, I could usually eat chili until I burst, but the thought of it now left me queasy.

"Stay out of that," my mother admonished as she came back into the kitchen. "How was your day at school?"

I shrugged. Like it was third grade and I was going to tell her all about my book report or something. It wasn't as if she was that interested anyway; this was merely small talk to fill unsightly spaces. My parents had gotten used to having birthed a dummy a long while back, so they didn't really hound me much about school. Besides, they were much more worried about my soul than my brain.

"When's Dad comin' in?" I asked her.

"He called and said he'd be late. He's got three cars to finish. Can you grate some cheese?"

I got a bowl down and took the grater from its hook. The cheddar had a nice sharp smell. My stomach flipped over.

"It's still okay if I hang out with Doug tonight?"

She gave me a sideways frown as she stirred the chili. "Your father could probably use a hand."

Great. "I've been working *every* night, I have to work *tomorrow* night, I just want this one night off." Jesus, I sounded like a pitiful whiner even to myself, and I have a high threshold.

My mom stirred longer than she had to, and regarded the chili far more than necessary. "Ask your father."

Which was a victory of sorts. "Okay."

I dialed the number of the shop after I finished with the cheese. The phone rang seven, eight times before my father picked it up, short of breath.

"Hey, Dad, it's me. You have any problem with me hanging out with Doug tonight?" I said this in the manner of one wishing to spend time with a loved one about to go off to war. Which wasn't totally off, you know; Doug had long talked of going to OU, but his tone had changed when he'd started getting brochures from Duke and Cornell earlier that summer. I think I got a mailer from ITT Technical College. Maybe. It was slowly dawning on me that my best friend might moving away, and it kind of stuck in my throat.

I crossed my fingers.

After a pause of maybe half a minute, he said, "No. No, that's fine."

"Cool," I said. "Thank you." And I meant it.

"You gonna eat then?" my mother asked.

My mom was looking at me with an odd slight frown on her face. Maybe I wasn't the only one worried about farewells rising on the horizon.

"Well, sure, yeah."

She nodded. "Set the table."

After I ate a little chili just for the sake of appearances, I showered. There was one bathroom in our house, and after I stepped out of the tub, I looked at my parents' scale, largely disused, shoved back up behind the toilet like a contrite and errant pet. I pulled it out and stepped on it, just curious. 215. I blinked and stepped off. That couldn't be right. I mean, yeah, my clothes had been a lot looser lately, but for cryin' out loud, that would mean I'd lost almost fifteen friggin' pounds over the last week. So I stepped on again. Oh, yeah, 215. How 'bout *that*, sports fans?

6

THAT EVENING, BEFORE I could call Doug, he called me.

"Do you have plans for tonight?"

I shrugged. "I guess you and Rebecca have something hot cooked up, like Indian bingo or something."

"Uh, well," Doug said, and hesitated. "Actually, she's out of town. Family trip."

"Ah." So, I was now permanently Plan B. I can't say I was thrilled. And I can't honestly say I might not have acted just as Doug had.

"Well," said Doug, "I thought we could maybe catch a flick."

"Sure."

"Seven okay?"

I hesitated. Then agreed. "Yeah."

And it was. It was as okay as anything was going to be for a while.

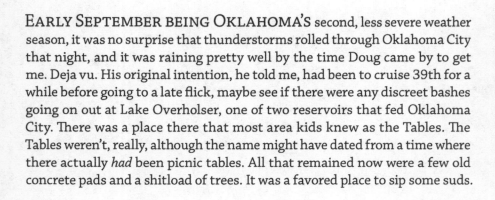

EARLY SEPTEMBER BEING OKLAHOMA'S second, less severe weather season, it was no surprise that thunderstorms rolled through Oklahoma City that night, and it was raining pretty well by the time Doug came by to get me. Deja vu. His original intention, he told me, had been to cruise 39th for a while before going to a late flick, maybe see if there were any discreet bashes going on out at Lake Overholser, one of two reservoirs that fed Oklahoma City. There was a place there that most area kids knew as the Tables. The Tables weren't, really, although the name might have dated from a time where there actually *had* been picnic tables. All that remained now were a few old concrete pads and a shitload of trees. It was a favored place to sip some suds.

Most Friday or Saturday nights it was a prime party spot, but those were no doubt washed out tonight.

We still drove around for a while, but jack shit was happening, so we took in *The Lost Boys*. If a stupider movie could be made, I have no idea what it might be. *Howard the Duck*, I guess. It would not be fair to say that we were not warned. Pete Carney, a guy we knew, was working the ticket window that night, and he did his best to talk us out of seeing it, but we (and by "we" I mean mostly me) were determined to see it, and so by god we did. By the time that murder of a perfectly good two hours was over, we found ourselves driving aimlessly again, having promised Carney that we'd listen next time.

This whole time, I heard not a word one about the singular Miss Connors. Suited me just fine. Let's give jealousy its due right now, but part of it was that I still had not shaken my base lust for her, and I really wanted to. I figured that maybe I could forget her. Maybe I could forget how to breathe, too. Maybe.

Doug had heard that there might be a party at Jason Grenick's house, which was up northwest, so we cruised over there. Beats me what channel Doug got his info from, but it was clearly jammed, because there were no signs of life at the Grenick homestead. Since we were up that far anyway, Doug suggested we go by Sam's apartment. I put forth no argument against this. But I didn't think she'd be home. On a Friday night? You shitting me? It was not unusual for us to come knocking when we were hard-pressed for something to do. She did not always shower us with gratitude for gracing her with our presence, but that never stopped knuckleheads like us. And hey, once in a while, she'd actually have something halfway fun in mind. A memorable, profanity-laced (much of it hers) game of mini golf remains one of the best memories of my life. Sam had a little of the devil in her, and when it came out, there was no one better to be around.

She lived in these mondo nice apartments in Edmond, about half a mile from Central State. Had to have cost a mint, but then her folks no doubt picked up the tab. She held no job that I knew of, except that of straight A student. We had to talk the guy at the security gate into letting us in, and the only reason the he finally did was because some dim part of his suspicious little brain finally recognized Doug from his numerous trips there. Doug nosed the Datsun through the maze of buildings in the complex, a jumble that I always got lost in.

"I always forget my ball of string," I said.

"No minotaurs here anyway."

"You *say* that, but . . ."

A small lake was the centerpiece of the property, and Sam's building sat just off it. Doug found it and picked the parking spot closest her door.

I looked out over the parking lot for Sam's car, a red '84 Fiero. Spotting it through the rain, I said, "Well, at least she's home." Brilliant deduction, Holmes, unless her date drove. Fuck off, Watson.

Doug nodded as he went up the walk, grocery sack in hand. I hurriedly caught up with him. My blood was running a little quick; for about the last five years or so, it had done that any time I was going to be around Sam Driscoll, even though I knew it was a lost cause.

"What's she doin' home on a Friday night?" I asked.

Doug shook his head. He rapped briskly on the door. A minute passed and he did it again. We waited. Finally, the door swung open, and there stood Sam.

Under the best of circumstances, Samantha Driscoll was a very, very pretty girl. She was tall and lithe, just short of athletic. Her blonde hair tended to be unruly, and usually fell over her bright blue eyes like strands of spun Sahara gold. She sported a tan most of the year, which sort of hid the small spray of freckles on her nose and cheeks. Her wide, expressive mouth was usually kinked into a slanted smile, unless she was in the grip of some fury.

Clearly, tonight was not the best of circumstances.

The bottom of my stomach fell away, because Sam was wearing her bathrobe, tight, but her hair was wet and undone, and the skin under her red eyes was puffy. She'd been crying recently. You don't have be head of Scotland Yard to know you've walked in on something bad.

Doug sighed. "What happened?"

Sam gave a weak sigh. "Nothing. What do you dweebs want?"

"Money," I said, "Barring that, drugs. Barring *that*, guns so we can blast our way out of the country, like Butch and Sundance."

She frowned at me and snuffled. "Um . . . I don't think so."

"What happened?" Doug asked again.

Sam let out a put upon sigh. "Look, nothing major, okay?"

"Adam?"

I looked at Doug, frowning. Adam? I had heard of no Adam.

Now she smiled, about the way a weak flashlight shines when the batteries are nearly dead.

"Can we come in?" I said. "It's raining and I gotta pee."

Sam stepped aside to let us enter. "Only if you promise to use the toilet this time, Lynch. I'm still trying to get rid of those stains."

"It's the smell that lingers," I said, heading straight for the bathroom, noting the scent of hot wax in the air.

Taste was a defining characteristic of the Driscolls, a genetic feature, some trait passed down by natural selection. Their Cro-Magnon forbearers had possessed the tidiest, homiest caves. Sam's apartment was spotless, clean, everything in its place. She had an Ansel Adams calendar hanging in the hall with a swarm of notes scrawled across the squares. The bathroom was a respectable green and white, towels neatly hung, air freshener suffusing the air. Above the toilet Sam had pasted an Escher print. Just the thing I needed to see while pissing, something that fucked with my perception. And why would a woman put a poster over the toilet? I didn't get it. I picked up a little of the conversation between Doug and Sam. It seemed that Sam had made a date with this Adam for this evening, and that furthermore, Sam had gone out of her way (she really, really could not cook) to prepare a semi-elegant dinner for two for the stupid schmuck, complete with candlelight, wine, and mood music. With timing from hell, he'd phoned just as she'd finished a quick shower.

"Stood me up, can you believe it?" In the bathroom, shaking it off, I frowned at the door. You'd have to be an idiot to stand a girl like Sam up. Or dead, maybe, but then you'd just be an idiot for dying when you had a date with her.

Sam was standing in the kitchen when I wandered out of the bathroom, lighter of step and happier of bladder. In the dining area beyond, I saw the table, clearly set for a romantic dinner.

"Called in to work?" I asked, trying to pin down some fragrance that was tugging at me.

She looked over at me. Her eyes had lost some of their puffiness, and I was glad. "Yeah, he works for this security outfit in the city, and he said it was an emergency." It was clear she didn't buy it.

"Well . . ." I said, shrugging. Beef, the smell that was nagging me was definitely beef, and it was coming from the oven. For a second I felt my mouth water, but then my stomach clenched and threatened to return what little chili I'd eaten earlier, postage due.

"We were somewhat bored," said Doug. "There isn't much happening tonight."

"Gee, thanks a lot, you guys. I'm your last resort, huh?" But at least she was smiling.

I made a little sound of disgust. "What, like you would be our first option anyway? Jeezus, get real."

"No, Lynch, I expect that robbing Social Security checks out of old ladies' mailboxes would be higher up on your list of priorities. I expect setting kittens on fire is your idea of a really smashing Friday night."

"Food stamps and puppies, Scam-I-Am, food stamps and puppies."

"My mistake."

Doug said, "How about movies?"

"Yeah," I said, grimacing, "I could stand to get *Lost Boys* out of my head."

"Sure," said Sam. "Screw it, yeah, sure."

So Doug and I went forth out into the rain again and drove to the Sound Warehouse (or Whorehouse, as we dorks called it) that was right around the corner from Sam's apartment. It took us thirty or forty-five minutes and a couple of heated discussions to pick out two movies. We got back to find Sam in jeans and a loose Guess sweatshirt, the candles gone, the china stacked, and a small but scrumptious looking London broil sitting on the stove top.

"I hope you guys are hungry, because my appetite is shot."

Doug nodded; I shook my head. Sam sliced some for Doug, slapped it on a paper plate, and did the same for herself.

"Eating when you're not hungry is my gig," I said.

"The hell," she said. "I hate to let good food go to waste."

"I let good food go to my waist," I replied, which earned me a small grin. "But I could stand for a bit of wine."

She gave me a crooked smile that you could read ten ways and be wrong twelve. "I thought you were a Coors man."

"Doug! Doug! Did you hear it? Your sister just called me a may-un!"

"It's been a rough evening for her. She's clearly not herself."

"Ah, screw you!"

I fought to open the wine, Doug went to put the movie in, and Sam wrapped up the rest of the meat. She glanced over at me as she opened the refrigerator door. "You sure you don't want some? You on a diet or something?"

I shrugged as I struggled with the wine cork.

"Well," she said as passed me heading for the couch, "at least you seem to have gotten that right."

I could only stand there like a complete buffoon and try to keep my grin from cracking my face, and be glad that she didn't see it.

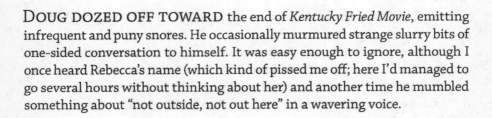

DOUG DOZED OFF TOWARD the end of *Kentucky Fried Movie*, emitting infrequent and puny snores. He occasionally murmured strange slurry bits of one-sided conversation to himself. It was easy enough to ignore, although I once heard Rebecca's name (which kind of pissed me off; here I'd managed to go several hours without thinking about her) and another time he mumbled something about "not outside, not out here" in a wavering voice.

Between movies, Sam popped a big bowl of popcorn, and she sat down on the floor next to me so we could share it as we watched *The Dead Zone*.

"I thought your appetite was shot."

"Shut up, Lynch."

I was electrified to be so close to her, like power cables had been shoved up my wrists into my arteries. The strength of this confused and scared me a little. Sam had always been my best friend's snide older sister. When had she stopped being that to me? I remembered her nagging us all the time, with her fearsome braces twinkling at us menacingly.

Things sure do change. Although seventeen never really believes that.

After the movies were over, I helped Sam clean up, taking the dirty bowl and glasses back to the kitchen while she picked up the pieces of popcorn that got away. I had to be a little extra careful, what with my light head wanting to sway everywhere. I filled the sink with warm water (as nice as this apartment was, it lacked that necessity others call a working dishwasher) and squirted soap into it. Fatigue and alcohol made me stupid; I stared at the suds rising as though it was the most fascinating spectacle I'd ever witnessed.

"Eric."

It wasn't Sam, and it wasn't Doug. The voice came from directly in front of me. But the only thing beyond the sink was a wall and a window, and the window was closed.

"You really need to pay attention, Eric. If you don't, you guys will have a real fucking problem on your hands."

The sink was full. Without looking up from the water, I turned the faucet off. My hand shook violently. I picked up a wine glass, just to be holding something—something solid, real. I wondered if maybe I was losing my mind.

I heard Sam trying to wake Doug up. It occurred to me that I should just put the glass down and walk away from the sink, just go into the living room. Safety in numbers.

"You don't listen to me now, man, it might be too late. She's getting stronger, Eric. And she's attracting attention. She won't be the only one for much longer. Her appetite won't end with you. And the things that will follow her are even hungrier."

I couldn't help it. I looked toward the source of that voice. Where my reflection should have been in the window, there was a face. The muddy memory of the incident in the bathroom at the theater rose in my mind like lake water turning over. It felt like time had doubled itself. It was still that thin, almost beautiful blond boy, face streaked with blood. God, I knew him, I did, but I did not know how.

My hand tightened on the wine glass.

"Leave me alone," I whispered.

"I can't do that. I do that, you'll suffer. Much as I'd love to let that happen, I can't. She was bad news then and she's bad news now, and she's *stronger*. Even if it was just her, it would be bad enough. But she'll bring others like sharks to chum. She can't be here. Get that through your thick fucking skull, Lynch. She'll just drag you down, she'll pull you under like a drowning swimmer because she can't help it, because she's only what she is." Pain and a desperate sincerity crumpled his youthful face. "But you need to remember what happened, you have to remember. Or you are righteously fucked, and so's everyone else."

In the living room, Doug finally awoke. I heard him mumble fuzzy nonsense.

"Who are you?" I whispered, fully aware that I was gabbing with a hallucination, which to me meant I was really gone fishing.

But the specter, or whatever it was, only shook its head sadly. He was clearly disgusted. He began to fade. Then, even as he grew less and less distinct, a wound erupted in his throat, a wet leering grin. Fresh blood erupted from this in a terrible blast of bright scarlet that almost totally obscured him.

"Eric," he said, and was gone.

My fist closed around the glass, shattering it. I looked down at the hot, sharp pain. My right hand was a confused mess of skin, blood, and broken glass. Shards stuck out at wild angles. Blood flowed out quickly, pooling in a large splatter on Sam's clean kitchen floor.

"Oh shit," I noted calmly.

Then I fainted.

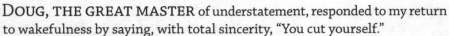

DOUG, THE GREAT MASTER of understatement, responded to my return to wakefulness by saying, with total sincerity, "You cut yourself."

Sam said, "I think he knows that, Douglas."

I nodded. Holy shit, my hand hurt. I raised my head up to discover that I was on Sam's couch. My hand lay on my chest like a dead rodent, wrapped in a thick layer of gauze. It almost looked like I'd grown a weird cocoon. Irregular blotches of red seeped through in places.

"Ow," I said.

I rolled my head, to see the sympathetic faces of the Driscoll kids. Doug was standing, he always stood when nervous or alarmed, and Sam was on one knee right next to the couch, close to me. It was almost worth the hand.

"You broke one of my glasses, Lynch, you asshat."

Well, I for sure wasn't about to start blabbing about seeing bleeding kids in the window. If I was losing my marbles, I sort of wanted to postpone letting anyone in on it as long as possible.

"I slipped against the counter," I said.

"What I get for letting a drunk do the dishes," said Sam. "What a mess. Is it still bleeding? Maybe we should take you to the emergency room."

"Bullshit you will," I said.

Sam sat back, frowning at me.

Doug asked me if it hurt. I shot him an incredulous look.

Sam told Doug to go get me some Tylenol. He obeyed like the good younger brother he was.

"Man," I sighed.

"Listen," Sam said. "Why don't you guys crash here? It's late and I don't think either of you two dweebs are safe behind a wheel tonight. I'd feel better if you did."

"Oh, *Mom*," said Doug as he handed me a couple of pills.

I frowned. Only two?

"I mean it. You're both a couple of zombies. Even more than normal. I'll get some blankets and pillows."

"You can have the floor," Doug said.

"You're all heart," I told him.

Sam gave us blankets and a pillow each. "Snore too loudly and I'll cut your throats."

"Is this the violence they promote in higher ed these days?" I asked Doug. He shrugged.

"I mean it," Sam said. "Good night."

We crashed, me on the floor on a blanket, Doug on the couch.

"Hey, Doug?"

He had just stretched out on his stomach on the couch, big feet dangling over the edge. His face was buried in his folded arms, and so his reply was muffled. "What?"

I sighed, not daring to look at him, even in the darkness, afraid of what my face might show. "None of my business and all, but is everything okay with you and Rebecca?"

I expected a simple "Great," and then I would be asleep, troubled no more by visions of dead boys or ominous pools of water. Instead there was a long pause, and this sort of sniffle that Doug always did right before answering an especially tough question, which was answer enough itself. Finally, he said, "Yeah. Why do you ask?"

"Nosey."

"Well go to sleep, nosey."

So I did.

AND THIS IS THE dream I had:

Sun, bright spear shafts down through the incomplete green mosaic of the treetops. The distant, ubiquitous sawbuzz of the cicadas. The quiet, lazy gurgles of a small stream in no hurry to get anywhere. A rope with a fat knot at the bottom, hanging down from the incredibly thick branch of the oak that guards the waterhole. A treehouse, snug and shaded far up in the wide crook between outstretched wooden arms. Across the stream, on the other bank, a pair of wild red roses, vivid red, out of place among the dusty undergrowth and stringy weeds. At the other end, the tunnel, the gaping mouth of the storm sewer that ran up under 63rd street and then shot down the length of Meridian Avenue. A half-assed oasis in suburbia.

We kids called it the Swing.

The Swing was a real place, not just a dreamscape. The old neighborhood hideaway, it was a little pool formed on a small runoff creek. It was in one of the numerous odd patches of undeveloped land that dotted Oklahoma City like patches of bread mold. It was a bowl in the land with a small gully running through it and was bounded on all sides by unusually thick tree growth, but there were paths if you were interested in following them, and what kid ever isn't? Once you got out of the trees, you found a Texaco and a couple of fairly busy streets lined with convenience stores and fast food joints. Neo-suburban Okie. But the thing was, when you were down in the sunken hollow with the pool, or in the treehouse built by our long-forgotten predecessors, all of the stores and the traffic and the bustle were gone. You couldn't hear it, see it, smell it, nothing. It was a true hideaway, treasured and nurtured by all the neighborhood kids, patched together from all the used lumber grown-ups didn't want.

We called it the Swing because of the thick rope someone had tied around a far-up thick branch of the massive oak that reached out over the waterhole. The water was typically still, and usually only about four feet deep, except after a hard rain. The creek was fed by a storm sewer, a gaping concrete mouth fifteen yards away, and once it drained out of the pool, it continued on another mile or so to Lake Hefner, Oklahoma City's reservoir.

How many afternoons had we blown wandering through the labyrinth of the storm sewer, splashing away in the pool, or lounging languidly in the treehouse? Too many to count.

I hadn't thought of the place in years.

The Swing.

And here I was dreaming of it. My dream-self found that funny and terrifying all at once.

The place of visions, the place of dreams. Or at least that's how it seemed to me in my dream. I stood on the bank and took it in. I knew I was dreaming, and felt a strong sense of security in that. The only thing I dreaded was the appearance of my specter, if that was what he was. Even in a dream, you don't like to think you're crazy.

But something was wrong. I could feel it; coldness darker than fear, that started at my back and filled my whole being.

The water. I edged down to the waterline and stared down into the murky, muddy water. The mud was the color of red clay, and made whatever depth was there impenetrable. Still, it looked like something was moving under the surface. I couldn't see it—just slight swirls and faint shadows, weak byproducts of motion.

"But it's only three or four feet deep," my dream-self said.

I knew this was true.

It didn't make me feel a bit better. I took a step back, thinking perhaps I ought to go ahead and wake up now. That seemed like a righteous idea. The dull, earthy color of that water was hypnotic, menacing.

And I was not alone.

I looked up, and straight across from me was Rebecca Connors, naked. She had a fine body. It was a body that a guy could spend a lifetime getting to know. She stared at me with deep solemnity, but not unkindly. Maybe there was something of compassion there, maybe something else. I could not define it, any more than a Neanderthal could grasp calculus. Her gray eyes held my stare; I could not look away. I forgot about whatever it was in the water. It was irrelevant, a large fish, maybe a channel catfish picked up and dumped in this pool by heavy storm runoff. It happened. Whatever it was, it came near the surface once, causing a short bustle of turbulence, then sank out of sight. I saw this from the corner of my eye. No way was I looking away from Rebecca.

She smiled. The expression filled me with light, a light that was like the peak of orgasm stretched out to eternity. It was pleasure jacked up and amplified straight through pain and heaven until it was a white-hot scouring glare.

Jesus, I thought, or said, or both.

Then I saw something that I could not force myself to deny. It shook me, even in dreaming. What disturbed me so much that I was pulled out of Never-Never Land and right back into Sam's apartment like a drowner in a cold dark undertow, was this: just above Rebecca's left breast, startling in such proximity to that perfect beauty, was a drop of fresh blood.

I gritted my teeth and tried to ignore the merrily pulsing pain in my hand enough to fall back to sleep. No dice. I looked over to the LED display on Sam's VCR: 5:13. Wonderful. I'd been asleep right around three whole hours. Sure recharged the old batteries there. I rolled and turned, counted backwards, put the pillow over my eyes to no avail. I could not successfully ignore my hand, the biting teeth of the cuts. There was nothing else to do but get some more Tylenol.

I cursed and got up. I tried to be quiet about it, which was sort of pointless since Doug slept like an old man in church. As I passed by the couch, I heard him mumble something that could have been "rose" or could have been "doze." I frowned, but my hand was really bopping to the pain beat now, so I moved away, walking like a thief. I turned down the hallway and saw a thin band of light at the bottom of Sam's door. Insomnia? I slipped into the bathroom, got some Tylenol, stepped out into the hallway as blind as a cave salamander and almost walked right over Sam.

"Jesus!"

"Oh relax, Lynch. It's just me. You'll have to wait a little longer for the second coming."

I could not locate her. My eyes were complaining about all this back and forth shit regarding brightness. They refused absolutely to do their job.

"Hand bothering you?"

"Yeah," I said. "I just got some Tylenol."

"How's it look?"

I shrugged, remembered we were in the dark, and said, "Beats me. I didn't look at it."

"Well, let's see it." She nudged me into the bathroom.

In the light I saw that she was wearing a short robe. Her legs were a good feature. Well, she maybe didn't have any bad ones, but her legs were especially good. I looked away lest I be caught, and checked out my wounded mitt. Two large dark spots stood out on the bandages.

"Sit down, let me see it."

"Aw, Ma."

"Stick it, Lynch."

"Oh, you'd like that, wouldn't you? What kinda manners they teaching you in college anyhow?"

To my surprise, she just grinned.

I sat on the toilet lid and held out my wounded hand. Sam leaned over it, frowned, and brushed back a golden strand of hair over her ear.

"If I think of them as stigmata," I said, "it's not so bad."

"Shut up." But she laughed.

"You probably should have had stitches with that," she said, looking at cuts I averted my gaze from.

"Right."

She frowned up at me. "Fine. Don't believe me. I ought to change this bandage, though."

"Okay, nurse."

She reached into a different cabinet, this one over the hamper, and found the roll of gauze and the box of sterile pads she'd used earlier. I surreptitiously watched her legs and the quick little V her robe left unguarded near her chest. Of course I wondered what she was wearing underneath the robe and of course my nasty little primate mind told me nothing and tried to show me all sorts of pictures of what that nothing might be like. I'm only human, and torture is always a private thing, the most private thing in the world.

Sam sat on the rim of the bathtub, across from me, and gently tore the first dressing off my hand. As the layers peeled away like some ghastly onion, the rusty patches grew until at the end they covered most of the gauze. The pads and Band-Aids were caked. She pulled them all off and I watched with a kind of sickened fascination. Bleeding was evidently something I did very well. The pain was a little more distant now. When she got everything off, I saw that it looked like someone in a great hurry had tried to tear my hand apart with a weed whacker. The cuts were wet and weeping a thick, clear fluid. My palm was ugly and swollen.

"Frankenhand," I said.

Sam gave me a rueful smile. "Frankenbrain, more like."

She dabbed and cleaned, and to break the silence, I said, "So, why were you up?"

She threw away the nasty mess of cotton. Sighed. Acted like she was going to try to think up something glib, something flip. Or else tell me it was none of my business. When the hell were we ever serious with each other anyway?

"I was up," Sam said, "because I had a nightmare. Bad one. I get them once in a while. Never can sleep after one of those. Hang on, let me get the peroxide."

"Oh, no, really, that's okay."

She stood and smiled at me. Her eyes, blue and sharp, held mine. "Eric," she said, "you are *such* a wuss."

As she poured the peroxide over my mitt, I gritted my teeth and, when the worst had blazed past, asked her, "So what was your dream about? Chippendales serenading you? A luncheon with Nancy Reagan? What?"

"I'm not into dream analysis, Lynch."

"I'm not Freud."

"Good. You'd make a lousy fat Austrian."

"Got the fat part down."

Sam rolled her eyes. "Oh, please. Is this pity party by invite only?"

She sopped up the excess peroxide up with a great wad of cotton balls and then tossed the soggy mess into the waste can. I blotted my hand dry with a hand towel, hoping I wasn't staining it too badly. She unwound a length of gauze and then paused, looking at me.

"You really want to know."

She wasn't asking. I kind of got the feeling that Sam was not always asked what was on her mind. If I hadn't known her half my life I might have perceived her as some kind of bimbo, too. I felt a little ashamed, to tell you the truth. I felt like a creep. But hey, I could stick the feeling up on a shelf with a whole bunch of feelings just like it, you know? I had the complete collection.

It seemed to me that she pondered over what she was going to tell me as she started the mummification of my hand.

"I found myself walking out in the woods, just out there all on my own, you know how it is in dreams. Just strolling along. I knew where I was, so I wasn't upset or worried or anything like that. It was the Swing."

I flinched, which Sam mistook for wrapping too tightly.

"Sorry," she said.

"S'okay."

"There wasn't anybody there. I remember thinking that this was some dull dream, because there wasn't a damn thing happening. Then someone calls my name from up in the tree, from the treehouse. Remember that treehouse?"

I nodded.

She went on. "I was curious, couldn't help it. I started over toward the tree, calling out for whoever it was. I knew I was dreaming, you know? It's called lucid dreaming. I figured it was my dream, I was in charge. Except I get about halfway to the tree and the bank slides out from under me. I try to twist around and grab something, a tree root, some ground, a rock, something. No good. I go foot first down into the water, no big deal, it's only three, four feet deep, right? But I kept going down and down."

She shuddered and paused. "It was so cold, that's the thing. I felt frozen, and I also felt like somebody, something, was holding me down under. I kicked and struggled, but I just kept sinking. I think once I made it back up close up to the surface, telling myself it was a dream, my dream . . . but then I was pushed back down. I was squeezed in an icy black fist, and finally, just when I was fading out or waking up, whichever, I heard that voice from the treehouse saying, 'He's mine. They all are.'"

"Then I woke up and heard you digging around my drugs." She stuck a final piece of tape on, surveyed her work.

"'Icy black fist'? What the hell's that supposed to be? You been reading Poe again? I told you about that."

"Shut up, narco boy."

"Hey, I'd known you were up, I'd have asked."

"Uh-huh."

I rested my hand in my lap and stared at it. Neither one of us said anything for a second. I had never known Samantha Driscoll to be at loss for words, ever. She was what you call high verbal.

"Weird, huh?" she said.

"Sure," I said brightly. "I told you the mushrooms were trouble. Rotten idea. Maybe now you'll listen."

"You know, telling you about it, it doesn't seem so bad. Not really. Scared the shit out of me, though."

"Laxatives are more effective."

"I'm gonna make you think laxatives."

A yawn erupted from me with no warning whatsoever. Sam smiled and stood. A rabid urge swept over me. I wanted to reach out and hold her, just squeeze her as hard as I could, hard enough to melt into her. I wanted to so badly it hurt on a level of ecstasy. I only sat there like a mouse.

"Sorry I bored you," Sam said, looking as though a yawn or two might be building up in her.

"No, it . . . no." I held up my hand. "Thanks for playing doctor."

Her smile widened. "Is *this* how you played it as a kid? Explains much, Lynch."

My glib tongue took a powder, and I was left with only a blush as my response.

"Listen, you guys don't wake me up in the morning, huh? There's Pop-Tarts in the cabinet, some cereal. Just don't wake me up. I'll see you later. 'Night."

She started out, turned back, and planted a warm, wonderful kiss on my cheek. Then, as if that were an inferior substitute for what she really wanted, she found my lips and made my heart want to burst.

"Better dreams," she whispered after.

She took herself off to bed, and after a minute of staring after her, of examining the space she left behind, I did the same. Wrung out and joyously empty, I did the same.

PART TWO: GOING UNDER

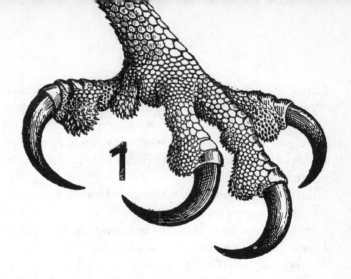

I BUMPED INTO MICK the following Tuesday, the day after Labor Day, right before geometry. Literally bumped into him. I was hustling down the hall, late like always, and I only saw Mick standing by his locker after I'd swerved to miss Kyle Sanders, who played nose tackle for the Wood Wilson football team. By then I couldn't stop, and we both went down in a tumble of books, papers, and pens.

"Jesus, man, I'm sorry, shit, I couldn't stop—"

"You broke my head!"

"Yeah, well, I'll get you another one, shit, I'm running *so* goddamn late!"

Mick rubbed his forehead and gave me grin. It was loopy, askew. "No, Eric, I'm fine, really, that's okay."

I madly scrambled my papers together, probably getting some of Mick's stuff in the process, fuck it, I could get it back to him later, and then the tardy bell went off. I looked up and watched the halls empty with uncanny speed, as though each classroom had turned into a tremendous vacuum. I gave up. Tardy a minute was the same as tardy ten.

"I'm really sorry," I told Mick. "I didn't even see you until it was too late."

"It's okay, really."

I shrugged, helped him pick the rest of the stuff up. What a mess.

"Couldn't find you Friday," he said. "And hey, what'd you do to your hand?"

"Tragic dishwashing accident. It was in all the papers."

"Yeah? Not the only thing. You hear about Monica Arden?"

"No. What?"

"Sad fuckin' thing. House fire. She burned up, along with her kid sister and her parents."

Christ. Monica Arden—dead? I stared at Mick, waiting for some punchline, but then it sank in that there wasn't one. "How'd it happen?"

Mick cocked his head. "How the hell do I know? There's the usual bullshitty rumors goin' around—she was freebasing, her bong got tipped over, somebody burned the house down because she wouldn't blow 'em. You know the fuckin' yaps around here."

I did. But I also knew—had known—Monica, and that shit made me want to knock someone's face in.

Sometimes you don't know the hole someone leaves in your life until they're not there to fill it any more. Which is shitty, right?

"So, seriously, what happened to your hand?"

I told him all about going to Sam's, having a little too much wine, getting my hand all cut up, so on. I waggled my bandaged paw as exhibit A.

"It's all that kept me from getting my ass grounded for longer," I said. Still got no end of Jesus lectures. The fifth commandment was the hot topic of the day.

"That's not bad," said Mick. Like he knew. His dad didn't give enough of a shit to ground him, didn't give much of a shit about anything. Even whaling on his ass was a matter of history, since Mick now sported enough muscles to make such an endeavor a much more dubious proposition. Mick's mom had run off several years back with a dentist. Mick's dad had been aboard a slow boat to hell ever since, pickling his liver at a steady rate.

"Mick, it sucks," I said. "So, anyway, what'd you do this weekend?"

"Well, you'll never guess who I saw."

"That would be who, Christie Brinkley? She came by and professed her undying love for you, and you had to let her down gently?"

Mick grimaced. "Not exactly."

I waited. Patiently. For maybe two seconds. "Well, who then?"

"Rebecca."

"Oh yeah? The Rebecca? The ever-charming Ms. Connors?" The supposedly out-of-town Rebecca Connors. Wasn't that what Doug had said?

"Uh-huh. And who you think she was with?"

Actually, I didn't really care. I was thinking that what she had done was kind of a shitty thing to do. But it wasn't any of my business, really, and maybe it was all a misunderstanding.

I leaned against the locker, glancing up and down the hall for the roving hall monitors. "Who?"

Mick cleared his throat, glanced down the hall. "Stan." I was going to press a little bit more—feeling like Doug's agent, like his undercover man—but then a monitor *did* turn into the hall, spotting us immediately.

"Gotta get to class," I said, trying not to scurry. The last thing I needed at this point was a detention, though, so I didn't loiter either. Mick got the hint and closed his locker door and headed off in the other direction. I did not look back at him as I headed to class. But I sure couldn't help thinking about what he'd said.

Stan. Rebecca.

My heart hurt for Doug. And poor dead Monica.

But not for long. Probably it's callous as shit, but I'm not sure any bad news had a chance against that memory of that kiss from Sam. You were ever seventeen, you'd understand.

After class I went tripping out to the parking lot, still up in the clouds. It was kind of pathetic, I admit, but I was really convinced that I'd turned a corner and something really, seriously good was gonna happen. Nothing in my experience prepared me for that.

Strolling out to the Bomb in the pleasant warm sunshine of a dying afternoon on the first week of September, a grin a mile wide on my face, even the ache in my hand gone for a while.

And as I was putting the key in the door lock, she spoke.

"Hello, Eric."

Which made me jump a foot, since I hadn't seen her at all. Yet there she stood, Rebecca, looking, I had to admit, pretty damn good in jeans and plain white T-shirt, her skin glowing in the sunlight. She smiled at me, and I thought, *Uh-huh.*

"Rebecca! Hi! What's up?"

She was on the other side of the car, standing by the passenger door. Expectantly. Those gray eyes. My heart pounded, I couldn't help it. There was no getting around the fact that Rebecca was just flat out a goddess. Maybe she could've put Helen of Troy to shame, maybe that fleet would've stayed home for Rebecca, forgotten all about that Helen two-bagger.

She said, "I thought you to me might give a ride home."

"Doug could."

Didn't faze her, did not take that cat happy smile down even a notch. "I was unable to find Douglas. He is not available to me."

What was I gonna do? Say no? Right. Maybe it was my own imagination, anyway. It had fooled me before. My heart was a zealot when it came to non-existent seductions. And I had every reason in the world to say no, didn't I? Didn't I?

I unlocked the door, got in, unlocked hers, watched her get in, watched every soft curve of her get in, feeling just a little traitorous. This was my best friend's girl, you know? Not that anybody owned her, but I had to respect Doug's feelings, right? And there was Sam. There was something there now, right?

Oh, shit, stop it, I told myself. I started the Bomb and it only protested a little bit. Kicked a tape in, Triumph, *Never Surrender*. Heard the chorus of "World of Fantasy." Rebecca still smiled.

"Where do you live?" I asked her.

"I will show you. Turn to the left here."

I did. My hands were sweaty. I, all at the same time, loved and did not care for this shit at all. She made me more than a little teeny bit nervous.

"What'd you do this weekend?" I asked, glancing over.

She shrugged. "I watched some of the television. I also read a novel. And music, I did put some music on the radio."

"Some of the television"? Who talked like that? Where was she really from?

I cleared my throat. "Doug kind of thought you went out of town."

She shrugged again. "Turn to the right at the light."

"He was kind of looking forward to seeing you."

Rebecca laughed softly. "Absence makes the heart grow fonder, this is a saying I am sure you have heard."

My turn to shrug.

We went down Meridian, past 50th, past 39th, getting a little far south, I thought, for someone who attended Wood Wilson. The Putnam City school district (named for a long-dead town) was kind of hard-nosed about its boundaries, and I was thinking that as far south as we were going, they would have made her attend PC West. But I didn't say anything. There were a lot of land mines in any conversation with Rebecca.

"Do you believe in dreams, Eric?"

"I guess. Everybody dreams."

Rebecca looked away. "No, not everybody."

"Sure they do. Some people just don't remember 'em, that's all."

"Make a left here. Of what do you dream?"

What was this, twenty questions? "I dunno, the usual I guess. Same as everybody."

She laughed and turned a little in the seat to face me, crossing her arms. "I doubt that."

We passed fast food joints, a strip mall, came up on a huge Pratt's grocery store.

"Please turn here into the parking lot," she said.

"You live at Pratt's? Maybe back in the store room?"

Rebecca smirked. "This is correct, Mr. Lynch. I sneak fruit to eat, and the shoppers late at night I terrorize. I am a night monster. Please do not to authorities report me."

"Done it myself," I told her. "Some of those old ladies can really haul ass with those shopping carts."

"Your dreams," she said again.

I sighed, Mr. Put Upon. I pulled into a spot up near the front of the store and killed the engine. We had the windows down, and a fly zipped in and promptly got trapped trying to get back out through the windshield. I watched it dive repeatedly into the glass, making tiny little dinks every time it hit. I wondered if it was tormented by the world it saw beyond the glass but could not reach.

"Okay," I said. "Sometimes I dream I'm falling. Sometimes I dream I'm naked up in front of the class, you know, trying to give a book report or something. Sometimes I dream I'm being chased by something I can't see, in a dark place." And all of that was true, I had each of those dreams once. But I was somehow sure that wasn't what she was asking for. I really didn't remember many of my dreams. The closest I usually came was waking up with some sort of shapeless longing, or some unformed dread, that slipped away with the opening of my eyes.

It was a sort of blissful ignorance, this ease of forgetfulness. I wish I had it now.

Rebecca showed that enigmatic smile again. "Have you ever dreamed about me?"

I opened my mouth to give her the right answer, the answer I had to give her because she was Doug's girlfriend. I was going to say, no, but don't feel bad, because I don't have nearly as many wet dreams as I'd like. I was going to say something clever and sarcastic like that, but her smile and the serious cast to her eyes stopped me short. What her eyes were telling me was that she already knew the answer. Her eyes were telling me that to lie to her would disappoint her terribly, and I found that I could not do that. I thought of the night we'd all gone to see *The Wall*, of the feverish scenes that had run through my head as I was passed out in the car, and even here in the sunlight far removed, it sent a spasm of pleasure through me.

To my shame, I did not think of that kiss with Sam.

I could not look away from Rebecca as I said, "Yeah. I guess I have."

She just kept up that unreadable smile.

"But, you know, so what?" My face felt redder than a cardinal, and I needed to put the air conditioner on.

She shook her head. "It is okay."

Yeah, damn near confessing feelings of lust for my best friend's major love interest, that was fine. Great way to spend an afternoon. His sister, his girlfriend, what the fuck, go for it, champ.

Rebecca said, "I must go."

I nodded. Unable, totally, to speak.

She got out, shutting the door gently, and walked around the back of the car. I watched in the rearview as I started the engine. She came around to my window, leaned down, in close to me. I felt sweat drip down my neck. Man, I sure wanted to be out of there. Or not. Something.

"Eric," she said, softly.

I couldn't help it. I looked at her, her eyes locking onto mine, so close, so close. She was even more beautiful this close in; you could feel with your eyes the full softness of those lips. I mean that, the sense was more than mere sight. I smelled a sweet, faint fragrance that I could not identify at first.

"About those dreams," she said, and then surprised me. She moved in and kissed me, easily, insistently. Her tongue flicked mine, caressed it. I made some kind of stupid little noise, something between surrender and protest, but more of the former. She kissed me for a long time. When she broke away I was almost gasping for breath. Her smile was not mysterious at all now.

"All right it is with me if you keep having them," she said.

And she walked away, toward the store, leaving me to sit there, stunned.

I was totally out of it. My mother was home, and I guess she almost saw my state, because she asked if I was okay.

"Yeah," I said, sort of shaking myself alert. "I'm just fine."

She was patting a wad of raw hamburger meat around in a bowl, and I could see all sorts of chunks of things in it, green and yellow. Meatloaf, a dish I ordinarily loved, and Mom must have been making it more or less for me, knowing that I did not work that night. Dad could take it or leave it, and she wasn't fond of cooking it. Sometimes you get so used to thinking of your parents as enemies of some sort, or as fellow prisoners with conflicting agendas, that little sparkles of kindness come out of the blue and blind you.

"Hey," I said. "Meatloaf, great!" Putting on a show of it, though, because the sight of it was turning my stomach. And I realized that I hadn't eaten that day, not at all.

"How is your hand?"

I had given it no thought. "It's better, I guess."

"Well, why don't you go get your homework out of the way? Your father might need a hand at the garage tonight after dinner, he's backed up on orders."

I shrugged. "Okay."

After dinner, before I went to help the old man out at the garage, I quietly went into the bathroom and threw up. Well, as quietly as one could blow chow anyway. At least neither of my parents seemed to notice. I washed up afterward, and didn't say a thing to anyone. Why worry them? I also weighed myself.

205. I'd lost ten pounds in, what, four days? It was like fucking *Thinner* or something.

And something else. When I unwrapped my hand, it wasn't better.

It was healed.

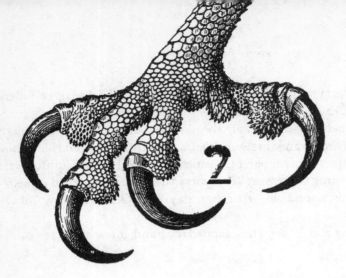

2

THE NEXT DAY, WEDNESDAY, Doug passed me in the hallway.

"Hey, Eric."

I'd been in deep thought, trying to cook up some deep excuse for not having finished up my American History homework (the simple truth, that I'd forgotten, was, of course, not an option) and so I blinked at him and went, "Huh?"

"Sam's goin' out of town this weekend. She said we could use her place."

"Hmm," I said. "Beer Patrol."

"Right."

"Out of town?"

"Ah, she's going with Adam to meet his folks. They live in Dallas."

"Oh," I said. Well, shit. Shit shit shit shit.

"So pass the word, okay?"

I agreed, not pointing out that it was just the four of us, five if you counted Rebecca, because no one else would ever come hang with losers like us. But he was already hustling away. I walked down the hall, no longer giving a damn about American History.

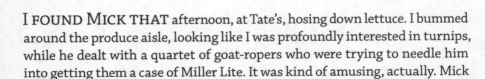

I FOUND MICK THAT afternoon, at Tate's, hosing down lettuce. I bummed around the produce aisle, looking like I was profoundly interested in turnips, while he dealt with a quartet of goat-ropers who were trying to needle him into getting them a case of Miller Lite. It was kind of amusing, actually. Mick gave them a hard time about stealing the beer, they gave him a hard time about being cool. All four of them were in boot-cut Wranglers, with these bright wide striped shirts and wide, ridiculous cowboy hats. Rings were worn into the hip pockets of their jeans from the ever-present cans of Skoal or Copenhagen. They looked like hick clones. They were trying to get Mick to boost a case of beer, stick it in a lettuce box or something, then toss the box in the dumpster out back. This was a time-honored racket, one Mick carefully managed. One of the Hee-Haw types argued with Mick while the other spat a dark glob of tobacco juice out onto the floor. Finally, Mick got them to get the idea, which was to grease the skids. The four bozos put ten bucks together, and Mick advised them on a good time to check the dumpster. The four shitkickers sauntered out in ridiculous bow-legged fashion, ready to whoop it up tonight. Like any of them would know a steer from a stirrup. Assholes.

Mick slipped the money into his pocket and said, "Hey, man, how's it hangin'?"

"Five feet. Wrapped around my leg. What are you doin' Saturday?"

"Why? You askin' me out?"

"Sure. I have suddenly succumbed to your charms, you lucky bastard. Prepare yourself for the radiance of my *luuuv*!"

"My heart's poundin'. What's up Saturday?"

"Doug's sister's goin' out of town, so we're gonna have a party at her place."

"Yeah, right, party. What you mean is you and me and Doug and Stan are gonna go get drunk at his sister's place, sit around eat junk food and rip each other, maybe have some pizza, play Risk."

"Of course. And that's not a party?"

"That's fuckin' *sad* is what it is. But yeah, I'll be there, after eight."

MY WEIGH-IN A COUPLE days before was a little panic-making. I realized that a lot of my shit didn't fit me anymore. I looked in my checkbook, saw that some of my last paycheck was still in there, and had to make a hard decision. I had enough money for some jeans and a shirt or two, which was really all I needed, because two thirds of what I wore were concert shirts anyway, and they can't get too big. But I'd been thinking about the new Maiden album. Plus, I kind of needed to set some cash aside for gas and insurance. But if I didn't drive for a while, if I bummed a ride from Driscoll, I could save on some gas, and I could always scam up extra hours next week at Tate's.

Asking my parents to get me some clothes was entirely out of the question. I'd have sooner let a blind nun choose my wardrobe. Taste in clothing was not my strong point, but when compared to that of my parents, my choices seemed sublime.

So it did not seem like a big chore. Just run over to K-Mart, buy a couple of pairs of Levi's, a shirt or two, be done with it. But since I'm bothering to tell you about it, I guess you already know it wasn't like that.

What happened was that I swung buy the Driscoll spread to grab Doug, thinking we might kill a couple of hours that afternoon. This was about two o'clock, and of course it was my luck: as I pulled onto their street and saw Doug's Datsun parked in the driveway, I also saw Sam's Fiero parked out front. I almost drove on by, but decided that I couldn't avoid my best friend forever. Besides, it wasn't Sam's fault I got all worked up over what was really nothing. Not her fault at all.

I strolled up to the front door, trying to appear jaunty. I knocked on the door, waited a second, then let myself in.

"Yo, Doug?"

He appeared out of the hallway.

"Hey, what's up?" I asked. "You wanna go hang out?"

Doug said, "Sure, we were just gonna go by Sound Warehouse."

"Ugh." I hated that place to the extent that it was possible for me to hate any record store.

"New Floyd."

I shrugged. At least I could tape it from him. We stood in the foyer like a couple of goobs. "Well, I gotta go get some clothes—" I began.

And from the kitchen, "You? New clothes? My Gawd, I don't believe it!"

Oh, Jesus please us.

"Oh yes, Scam-I-Am, even I must occasionally re-fit myself." My heart was not really in it today, but habits are hard to break.

She poked her head out of the doorway, frowning. "Sure. Jeans and Rush T-shirts."

"Hey," I warned her.

Doug said, "Don't forget Dio."

"Hey, what is it with everybody? Is this Let's Dog Eric's Wardrobe Day?"

Nobody said anything. They just grinned at me. Both of them. Apparently the holiday had been made official while I wasn't looking.

"Fine," I said, exasperated. "Then you guys come help me pick something out, you're such fashion mavens."

I didn't really think they'd take me up on the offer, which goes to show you what I know.

I lost veto power in the first ten minutes.

What happened was I got a pair of jeans and was fixing to buy a second, this time a pair of black denim, when Sam said, "No, come on Lynch, not jeans again."

I looked at Doug, as if to say, *Your sister, man, she plumb* loco.

"Why not? I wear jeans, I like jeans, and I'm gonna *buy* jeans."

She made a face like I'd just farted.

I looked beseechingly at Doug.

He said, "It wouldn't hurt you to upgrade."

"Upgrade? Upgrade to what?"

Sam said, "Come here."

By now, the frown was starting serious gouges in my face. I should have known this was a bad idea. Should have known. Never let a girl help you shop. Bad juju. And when I saw her pull a pair of Dockers off the rack, I crossed my arms and said, "Huh-uh."

"Why not?"

"Because I don't want to look like a turbo-geek."

Doug glanced down at his own pants, which happened to be a pair of khaki Dockers.

"Well, Jesus, Doug," I said. "They look great on you man, but I look mondo stupid in 'em. Besides, I buy those, I gotta buy new shirts 'cause Whitesnake tour shirts sure don't fit with 'em."

"Oh, for God's sake," said Sam, "I'll buy you a new shirt. Just relax already, Lynch. This won't hurt a bit."

"Dentists always say shit like that."

Sam got up close to me, her mouth a tight little cinch. "Quit being such an asshole," she said, her teeth never actually moving.

I scuttled to the changing room. And I do mean scuttled.

I felt like an imposter.

Sam seemed to think otherwise. "You clean up okay, Lynch. You really do."

Not as good as Adam, though, right?

"You're still a dork," Doug helpfully supplied.

"Shut up, Douglas," Sam said.

I sighed.

"Oh, Eric, you're so put upon. It's a tragedy, it truly is." She grinned as she said it, and I wanted to hate her in that moment, wanted to hate her for stringing me along even if that wasn't what she meant to do. But I couldn't do it.

Sam actually wound up buying me two shirts, and after that we wandered over to the Waldenbooks, where Doug browsed through the science fiction section, leafing through a copy of *CineFantastique*, and I watched Sam chuckle through a *Far Side* collection. She pointed a few out to me, which I already knew by heart. Maybe I wasn't the fastest car on the track, but my sense of humor took no back seat.

Finally, we swung by Camelot, which was even worse than Sound Warehouse (but what could you expect from a *mall*), so Doug could get the new Floyd album, a pompous thing called *A Momentary Lapse of Reason*. The album cover featured a lot of beds on a beach. Look up "pretentious," you get "Pink Floyd." Doug bought the cassette to listen to and the album to keep in shrink wrap. Go figure.

"Jesus," I said. "What's the theme of this one? The existential angst of sand in your sheets?"

"Well," Doug said, "without Waters, you know . . . I'm sure it'll be okay."

"At least better than *The Final Cut*. I fail to see how anything could be worse than that."

"I like *The Final Cut*."

"You would," I groaned.

"This is fascinating, you two, but I'm going to run over to Penney's to pay my credit card. If you could settle this before I get back, that'd be awesome, because, omigod, Pink Floyd."

With that, she left us sitting by the big-ass fake rubber plant.

"What do you expect," Doug said, nudging his glasses up his face, "from someone who's a fan of the Go-Go's?"

I just nodded.

I watched the front of Penney's for Sam, and when she came out, carrying a new bag, she smiled at me, and I thought, seventeen (hell, almost eighteen), twenty-one, not a big difference, not really. And to hell with this Adam creep, I could take him. Easy, I could take him.

I smiled back.

And all the while I'm saying to some part of myself, an aspect of my heart that's used to hearing all the dark shit, all the useless nattering, *this can't happen.*

But even before me, as Doug picked apart the lyrics to a stupid little album, as all these shoppers flowed around us doing their usual nothings, Sam's smile turned just that much more impish.

Just then, for a second, I thought everything might be okay after all. I thought my miserable existence might finally be taking a turn up.

"What's in the bag?" I asked her when she rejoined us.

She cocked an eyebrow at me. "Like to know, wouldn't you?"

I shook my head. "Forget it. New dishtowels, no doubt. I'm sure this burning urge came over you. It's okay. Happens when you get old."

"Well, hmm . . . maybe."

I never did find out what was in the bag. I never did.

"I've got to hear this," said Doug, holding up his new cassette. "Could we go by Taco Bell on our way back home? And could we go now?"

We could.

But on our way out of the mall, I glanced around because it felt like something was tickling the back of my head. There was nothing there, nothing like the cobweb or dangling piece of string I'd expected. What I did see, all the way down the long corridor, near the open area that was the hub of the mall, was Stan and Rebecca. Stan was oblivious, but Rebecca glared right at me. Her anger was obvious. Stan must have said something then, because the anger fell away, or was hidden as if by a mask, and she looked at him, away from me.

As we ate a bit later, Sam pointed to my hand, said, "That sure healed quickly."

I put down my water—I wasn't having anything to eat; all that greasy Taco Bell stuff was making me faintly sick just looking at it—and glanced at my hand, flexing it once.

"Well," I said, "it wasn't really so bad."

I felt the phantom pain of the wounds, just for a second or two, and remembered Rebecca at the mall. Remembered the day before when I'd dropped her off. And I wondered what the hell was happening.

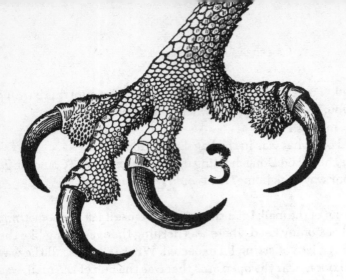

THURSDAY, LUNCH PERIOD, I was going out to the Bomb for another Lynch non-meal on wheels when she said, from behind me, "Might I join you for lunch?"

Great. Without turning around, I said, "Don't you have first lunch?"

Rebecca walked around to the passenger side and waited to be let in. I did not hurry. I was thinking of Doug, and Stan at the mall the other day, and even though the October wind had teeth with the promise of an unseasonable chill, I did not hurry.

I saw when she got in that she was wearing a Mötley Crüe T-shirt, Theater of Pain Tour, and I liked it despite myself. She had taste, at least to my reckoning. Which didn't make everything okay, not at all, but I softened somewhat.

"Where you want to eat?"

She smiled at me with that razor-sharp charm. "I'll your judgment trust in the matter."

"Shit, I wouldn't. But okay, my judgment says Sonic."

"By all means." And that smile, that twist of the lips that held a thousand meanings.

I started the Bomb and negotiated out of the parking lot. I was not sure of what I was going to say, of how I was going to say it, and for once my brain got the better of my tongue. I didn't say anything at all for maybe five minutes.

"Don't you eat with Doug?" I asked this, finally, to break the silence.

She was sorting through my tapes, and looked up at me. "No. Douglas was studying for a chemistry test."

"Yeah, that one's eating his lunch." He had complained about it to me the other day. Mister four-point-GPA was actually in some danger of flunking the class. It upset him that for all the hours of work he put into it none of it was making sense to him, and this was a guy for whom science was a snap. I felt for him, but could not bring myself to believe that he would not find a way to ace it.

Rebecca must have thought along those lines, because she said, "It will eat it not much longer."

"Oh yeah? What makes you so sure? You can see the future?"

"Parts of it."

I laughed softly, derisively.

We pulled into the Sonic, which was hopping with the lunch crowd. Cars filled most of the stalls. The way these places worked, you pulled into a stall, placed your order, then twiddled your thumbs until they brought your food out on a tray that hooked onto your semi-lowered window. I guess it was a throwback to some craze from the 1950s. Whatever, they made decent burgers and terrific onion rings. I found an empty one next to a Bronco filled with pampered preps from Putnam City North. The Bronco was brand new, and had a PC North decal on one window. I hated these assholes, gifted with money and looks through nothing more than a twist of genetic fate. They were slumming pretty far south today.

Rebecca looked over at them, at the clean-cut wholesomeness of the three guys inside and the faux fifties purity of the one blonde girl with them. The blonde, what I could see of her, was cute but looked puppy-dumb, and besides could not hold a candle to Rebecca. Not that many girls could.

But Sam?

Well, yeah, Sam. I started to feel guilty for being here with Rebecca, shit, for wanting Rebecca. Then the memory of Rebecca's lips on mine rose up and things got even worse.

Then I noticed that one of the guys in the Bronco was clearly staring at Rebecca. Staring, hell. Undressing with his eyes.

I wanted to go pound the shit out of him. Wanted to do it so fiercely that all of my other feelings were swept out in a great tidal evacuation. My hand, I swear to god, my hand was on the door handle. I was ready to do it.

The speaker clicked to life in a haze of static. "WelcometoSoniccanItakeyourorder."

I jerked. Looked at my hand clenched on the door handle. Looked at Rebecca, who was staring at me now. She seemed curious. No. *Expectant.*

"Uh," I said.

"WelcometoSoniccanI—"

"Yeah, yeah," I said, and the anger was gone just like that. I felt pale and insubstantial for a beat or two. I recovered myself enough to order a chicken sandwich for myself, a Coke for Rebecca, who shook her head at my offer of food.

She said, "I hate those guys, too."

The thing was, I hated them on general principle. With Rebecca it sounded like a personal thing. With Rebecca, it sounded like she was disappointed that I did not get out and cause them pain, suffering, agony. This blew my circuits for a second. What possible reason could she have to want to hurt them?

Because I felt threatened by them? Possibly.

Because I found the blonde a little attractive, and Rebecca was jealous? Possibly. Probably. Probably both.

The guy was still staring at Rebecca. I saw him nudge his buddy next to him, and they both ogled her. It wasn't hard to see where this was going. The only real question was how I was going to handle it. I looked at Rebecca, and that expectant look had drawn in on itself, become compact and obvious. One of my hands began to tremble.

She knew what was going to happen. Maybe even set it up that way. It was a test.

So it fell to me: Did I really want to pass it?

Oh, Sam.

Of *course* I did.

The passenger door of the Bronco opened, and the Head Ogler's buddy got out. He swaggered around the back of the vehicle and strutted up to Rebecca's window. He had on the white and powder blue letter jacket that the North jocks wore. A huge gold N was stitched on the front, like Hester Prynne's sin transmuted. Shit, who knew? Let's say it stood for Numbnuts. Narcissist. But the guy wasn't exactly small, and there was a certain confidence of strength in his walk. He had one of those stupid mullets that were in fashion then, the front trimmed close, the back a long, permed tangle of curls. I hated the guy instantly, but that did not dilute the fact that I knew he could break my fat ass with his weak hand.

He got up to the window and leaned in. I could smell Halston cologne, the stench of it slamming into me like a skunk's musk. Christ, I wanted to retch. I just sat like a gargoyle, immobile, scowling.

"Hey," said Curls, "what's up?" It was perfectly clear that he was not addressing me.

"Obviously not your IQ," I said. Oh, my wit, how it sparkled and shined! And how my mouth gaped wide, like a whale's anus, and the same product coming out.

Curls looked at me and dismissed me in a contemptuous half a second. Go away, fly.

"Where you go to school?"

Rebecca flicked a glance at me, then said, "Woodrow Wilson High School."

"Huh," said Curls. "We kicked their ass last week."

Indeed they had. Woodrow Wilson's football team, state runners-up the previous year, were sucking some serious eggs this year and had been obliterated by North, 52-2. The two came when North's third string quarterback fumbled a snap into and out of his own end zone in the last minute of play.

Which was nice, if you liked that sort of thing, but I was distracting myself.

And why not? I did not really want to die.

Rebecca said, "Is that so? I don't follow the football game. I can not see the point of it."

That ruffled Curls a little. The notion that someone did not care a sparrow's fart for his heroic and manly exploits on the honorable gridiron went pinging around the inside of his undoubtedly empty head before coming to rest in some mental dead end.

"Well, uh, what do you do on Friday nights then?"

"She knits," I told him, "in the Ladies' Auxiliary Club. Real fascinating shit. You should try it sometime, if you can figure out which end of the needle is the sharp one."

Now he sneered at me. "Whyn't you just shut the fuck up?"

Good idea. *Wonderful* idea.

And you know, I might have. I really might have, because this guy could seriously stomp my ass, and because I'd spent my whole life deferring to his type. I might have shut the fuck up just because it would have been the smart thing to do, because all we had to do was get our food and go, and Curls would be forgotten save for a few harmless revenge fantasies where I eviscerated him with a plastic spoon. This was how it worked. This was how you fucking *survived*. Heroism looks nice on paper, but it leads to a seriously diminished life expectancy in the real world.

But something like a light spring gust brushed my mind, I swear, and I saw what Curls might look like over Rebecca, his dick out of his pants and in her mouth. I saw her working on him, sucking him with vigor and enthusiasm, saw his hands grasping her beautiful black hair, heard the wet sounds of her endeavors and his fucking piglike grunts of enjoyment. And it was like a hand grenade went off in my head, and all those years of conditioning and reflex were demolished by the blast. Just gone.

I said, "Why don't you suck my dick, you fucking dipshit? No, wait, you'd just give me syphilis."

His face burned red and he started around the front of the car. I saw that a tiny little smile crept out on Rebecca's face. I was being played like a puppet, and there wasn't a lot I could do about it. There wasn't anything I *wanted* to do about it.

I was out of the door before Curls got halfway around. My body was screaming at me, nerve ends shrieking in endless electric terror. In my body, there was no fight or flight reflex. Flight *always* won the popular vote.

But that picture of Rebecca sucking him off, that was like jet fuel to my anger. Fear could come later, not now.

"I'm gonna hurt you so fuckin' much," Curls said through clenched teeth.

He was probably right. But I couldn't back down. I had a director, I was auditioning. His fist flashed out and slammed my jaw before I could see it. Hell, I didn't even hear the hit. I flew back against the Bomb, went down hard, the side of my face damn near taking the driver side mirror off. A great cold burst of light went off inside my skull, and for a long strange second I didn't even exist. Then a pounding cankerous pain set up shop on the right side of my face. It felt like someone had rammed a throbbing football under my cheek.

Curls wasted little time in grabbing me and yanking me back up. My head hit the mirror again, and I said, "Ow, shit!" Except that maybe it sounded like "Owl spit."

There was a pause of a half second while Curls cocked his arm for a haymaker, his lips pulled back in a jackal sneer, exposing teeth that were so straight his parents must still be paying the bills for it, even all these years later. I saw the carhop standing back behind him, holding my lunch. I felt absurdly apologetic. *Sorry, didn't mean to get the shit beat out of myself on your shift.* Then I saw that Rebecca's eyes were wide with excitement, and I took it all back. This was the most kicks she'd had in days, by the look of it. I also noticed, in that weird rubber second, that lots of other people were craning their necks out of their cars to see the mauling. Some of them dispensed with the pretense of decor altogether and got out of their cars to have an unobstructed view.

Sorry folks, I thought, *this one's gonna be short.*

And how.

Curls swung. Hard and fast.

I surprised my dazed self. I launched at him, maybe out of desperate fear as much as out of sound tactics, but the result was the same. It was like Curls was giving me an overly emphatic hug. His fist popped my back with most of the momentum spent. The top of my head, meanwhile, cracked into the jutting prow of his jaw. I felt his teeth click together. He grunted, and we both went over, him backwards, me on top. I think he took the worst of that one, although I would not want to repeat the experience. One of his knees caught me in the side, which didn't tickle. My paranoid brain said I'd broken a rib, but that was bullshit. It only felt like I had.

Where was Rebecca?

That light touch in my mind again. Her red lips, sliding back and forth . . .

"Oh, you fucker," I rasped. While he slapped at my head, sending jolts measuring, oh, 4.5 on the Richter, I grabbed his head and bashed it on the concrete three times in quick succession. The slaps stopped, Curls wised up, and he sent a punch into my face that almost turned my nose inside out and had it peeking out the back of my neck.

That was pretty much it for me. I toppled to one side, blood spraying from my pulped proboscis. I dimly noted that I'd showered the Neanderthal's jacket with a chaotic spray of red. Well, one for the Gipper, I guess. Whatever.

I sprawled against somebody's tire, thinking, *Oh shit this hurts more than anything I can remember.* If I was really thinking anything at all.

That filthy image reared in my mind one more time, like some kind of mental cattle prod. Curls got up, swaying. I saw with a tiny spark of satisfaction that his own nose bled, although surely not like the deluge coming forth from mine. He looked a little dazed, and I wondered how hard I'd hit his head on the concrete.

On the concrete?

That question cleared my head, and it made room for incredulous shame. Christ, I could have *killed* him doing that. And for what? Now I could barely remember what started all this.

I saw, behind Curls, a tall guy with a receding tangle of red hair and a bushy mustache running up toward us. The guy had a grease-stained apron on, but under that he had on a white shirt and the sort of tacky tie I wore to work. The manager no doubt, running out here to put a stop to this trouble.

What's the rush? I thought.

Curls drove one of his Adidas into my balls, and my attitude underwent a complete change. I curled up into a fetal position and wondered why the fuck the manager couldn't hurry the hell up.

"Stupid motherfucker," slurred Curls. "Open your stupid fucking mouth, see what you get?"

Oh yes. Lesson learned.

Well, apparently not.

"Fuck your own mother, weasel dick," I gasped, and under the circumstances, I suppose it was the best comeback I could reasonably hope for.

"What the *hell* is going on here?"

Well, it wasn't me, and it wasn't Curls, so I figured it was the manager, and I said a silent thank you and closed my eyes. It was turning into a really long day.

"You two little dipshits take this someplace else, you ain't gonna fight in my establishment, you got that?"

I opened my eyes and looked up at the guy. His eyes were wide and his mouth was cinched into a tight little frown that was almost perfectly camouflaged by his moustache. His nostrils flared in and out like a winded horse's. I saw that his hands were balled into fists, and my, what big fists they were.

Adult authority had reasserted itself, and the compact storm that had blown up was now dispersed. We lost our audience as fast as we'd gained it. Curls wiped blood off on his hand and stared at it in surprise. He glanced over at the Bronco as if to say, "You see what this punk did to me?" The manager glared at him until he shuffled back over to his side of the truck and got in. There was a dead moment, and then the Bronco roared to life, the stereo pounding out some Bon Jovi song at ear-crushing levels. I closed my eyes again.

"I see you back here I'll call the cops, you worthless shits!"

Huh, he thought they started it. I wasn't going to disabuse him of the notion. No way was I going to do that.

Soft hands moved over my face and lifted under my arms. I looked and saw Rebecca, trying to stand me up. I got the drift and contributed to the effort. It hurt like hell. I tried to read something out of her face, and couldn't. Certainly there wasn't the concern I was looking for.

That I got from the Sonic manager. He stood before me, took off his apron, and handed it to me to hold against my fountain of a nose. It stank to high heaven, like onions and half-cooked beef, but it beat just bleeding all over the place.

"You okay?"

I nodded, wincing at the way my brain banged against my skull when I did it.

"You sure? You want to go inside, sit down, maybe call somebody?"

"No thanks, really." My voice sounded completely fucked. I smiled a little because the carhop was still standing there with our lunch.

"I guess, um, I guess we'll pay for that now." I pointed at the tray the girl held.

"I don't like it those punks come in here and start crap like that. Gettin' tired of it. Don't worry about the food, it's on me. I hate to have shit like that happen here."

I was struck by the way he kept assuming it was the guys from North who started it. It never occurred to him that I could have been the one to pick the fight. I looked at him, somewhere in the neighborhood of forty, gut pooched out over his cheap work slacks, the awful tie stained in a half dozen places, stress wrinkles climbing halfway up his forehead, and I saw myself in twenty some-odd years. My God.

The carhop, at a loss in the whole situation, did the only thing her bubblegum brain could tell her to do. She hooked the tray onto the car window, looked at the manager like a lamb at a shepherd, and scuttled back up the walkway when he nodded.

"Thanks, Mr. . . ."

"Jon, and don't worry about it. Just eat up and get yourself taken care of. You look like you got hit by a truck."

He held out his hand.

I blinked, and then realized he needed his apron back. I handed it back to him, shocked at how much blood was on it, and gave him my best sheepish grin. It hurt. My face felt like it was falling off.

"Sorry for the trouble," I said. I could barely understand myself, I can only imagine how I sounded to him.

He waved it off. "Just go on."

And since he had a lunch rush to deal with, he headed back inside, no doubt replaying a dozen instances of being bullied in his formative years.

I looked at Rebecca, who finally smiled.

"Let us get you cleaned up."

I left the food on the tray, the tray on the holder. It was a three-dollar meal. I left a ten under the bag, and would have left more if I'd had it.

AT FIRST, I WASN'T sure if I could walk, much less drive, but somehow I found myself in the Bomb, heading out of the Sonic. My head felt like a steady chain of depth charges were going off inside it.

"Turn left here," Rebecca said. We drove down 63rd, heading west toward Rockwell. She pointed at a large apartment complex called Lakeside. It was one of the biggest apartment complexes I'd ever seen in my life. I knew a guy who worked there, summer '83, on the groundskeeping crew, and he'd told me the thing covered like fifty or sixty acres. The year he worked there, a good chunk of the place burned to the ground, one of the most spectacular fires Oklahoma City had ever seen, killed a whole shitload of people. For a long time the company that had owned it had tried to sell it. At one point the city had been planning to buy it and turn it into a massive park, but this was Oklahoma City, and the city in those days had as much ambition as a tree sloth on Valium. So the holding company just built a new complex on top of the gutted one.

Rebecca said, "Turn in here."

So I did. She guided me down the parking lot toward the building she said she lived in, while I was thinking that this was a long way from where I'd dropped her off the other day. I did not pursue this line of thought. I was incapable of it. I looked all fucked up in the mirror. Aside from all the dried blood, the right half of my head was swelling like overripe fruit. The lumps were an ugly purple-red color. My right eye was incredibly bloodshot.

"The building at the end, I'm in the last apartment."

"Okay." I nosed the Bomb into an open spot directly in front of the door. I wanted to hop on out of the car and rush around to her door, be gentlemanly, but wires were crossed.

She got out and came over to my side to help me out. I needed it. My balls pulsed like grapefruits of pain, and my side ached ferociously where Curly's knee had hit. Maybe he hadn't broken anything there, but he'd for sure bruised it, I could feel that. Rebecca guided me up the sidewalk while I took little shuffling old man's steps. I waited while she unlocked the door, or at least I thought she did. I cannot actually remember if there was a key involved,

The door opened and Rebecca led me in. Circe's cave.

It was a small two bedroom, nothing fancy, but just scant furniture leftover from the seventies, full of that decade's lack of color understanding. No paintings, no photos, no decorations. No television. No books. No personality.

I could see through the living area to part of the kitchen. It looked neat and unused. Everything there was in place.

Rebecca led me past a closed door (the other bedroom, I presumed, and then I realized that I had no idea if she lived with one parent or the other, or both, or neither) to her bedroom. I followed, something like a zombie in my bruised state.

Her room was dark, calmness, and order. The room was small and dominated by a large bed that looked sinfully comfortable. There was a small closet to one side of the bed, a dainty dresser, mirror atop it, to the other. And next to the dresser was a stool and a pretty nifty looking Yamaha keyboard. Even in the walking wounded stage that I was in, I took notice of the keyboard. I said nothing about it, mainly because speech really, really hurt. Rebecca took my hand and towed me to the bed, lowered me onto the bilious softness. I surrendered. There wasn't even any thought to it. The pain was so bad now that I was kind of phasing in and out. So this was what it was like to have the shit beat out of you. I now had a deep understanding of that phrase. I thought *everything* had been beaten out of me.

Rebecca lowered herself on top of me. I thought it would hurt but it didn't. My breath caught and held. She straddled me, atop my stomach. She touched my brow with her index finger, traced it along the swollen area on the side of my head, came back to my lips. Current ran from her skin to mine. I sighed, and she leaned down close. All I could see was her eyes, it seemed; my world was that cold beautiful gray. Did I drown in it? Did I slip under and give in to that icy comfort? I did. I didn't. I don't know.

"Eric," she whispered, and I knew then, with certainty, with absolute assuredness, that this beautiful creature loved me. I was not sure what she was, too much girl for woman, too much innocent for seductress, and yet all of these. I didn't care. Let her be the very devil. I did not care. I was going under and that was fine. Someone would be owned, and whether it was me or her, what difference did it make?

She opened her mouth as though to kiss me, but her tongue came out and licked my cheek, my chin, my lips. A small, quiet moan escaped her as she did this. I shivered, thinking that it was all right that some of my blood went into her. It was, maybe, a more intimate exchange than sex. She kissed me, and the taste of my blood was everywhere. My heart tried to punch out of my chest.

Sometime, an eternity later, Rebecca raised up again. Faint red smears decorated her lips. I could scarcely catch my breath. She looked like a vampire. I knew better; it was only what coated my face, but the illusion held. She stared at me with naked hunger. I was so hard I thought I would explode, and Rebecca shifted herself against me, and we both shuddered.

"I need you," she whispered.

I nodded, weakly, afraid of any motion too severe or pronounced, afraid that this moment was like a bubble drifting among pins.

I wanted time to slow, to crawl, to stretch out forever.

Rebecca peeled off the Mötley Crüe shirt. I was not surprised that she wore no bra. She leaned over me, guided herself to my mouth, and I suckled on her right breast. Her skin was the softest thing I'd ever encountered, as though she had not existed through nearly twenty years of life but had been born mere days ago. I bit her gently, and her nails dug into my head, her rush of breath hot against my forehead. I let my hands drift down her back, luxuriating in the silky terrain, and slide down under her jeans. No underwear there either, and no surprise. Oh, Christ, but she was everything I'd ever dreamed of, and I almost could not believe it was real, and if this was what I got for passing her test then it was a steal. I bit her again, harder, and her hoarse encouragement was electric on my ears.

"Yes," she said. "Do that again."

Instead I kissed it, kissed the swell of her breast, kissed the hot skin between them. Her taste was exotic and inscrutable. I wondered how the rest of her tasted. I ached to find out. She sat a little and I rose with her, and her hands deftly undid the buttons to my Levi's. The stars sang in my veins. I felt part god, part child.

And she tilted her head down, her eyes caught mine, that unearthly, incredible chipped-ice gray seizing me, and she said, "Make me whole, Eric."

I did the best I could.

SHE SHOOK ME AWAKE, how much later I don't know. Maybe seconds, but it could have been days for all I knew. Her shirt was back on, to my disappointment, and I was dressed, too. Could it all have been a fever dream? I had aches that said otherwise.

"Can you drive?"

I looked over at the mirror, examined the wreckage of myself. My head was filled by a steady high pitch tone—a late reaction to my pummeling? I turned to Rebecca, grateful for her expression of concern and sympathy.

"I don't know," I told her. "I guess, yeah."

She kissed me, hard and with a glorious sense of appetite. "I won't let anything happen to you. Ever. Remember that."

I held her for some time, like a child in the dark, and I do not remember leaving.

When I got home, my mother, of course, almost had a stroke, a coronary, and a set of triplets in the same instant. She set the spoon she was holding down with a loud crack the second she saw my face.

"What happened to your face?"

"Would you believe I fell down the stairs?" I smiled, which didn't feel too good, but at least it didn't feel like someone was cleaving my skull with a rusty axe the way it had earlier.

She stared, mouth agape, until I said, "Well, there was a fight, you see . . ."

Then she rushed to me, clucking, checking, was I still bleeding, was anything broken, was I okay, until I thought I'd die. She was all set to run me up to the emergency room, and it was only by major effort that I talked her out of that one. A few aspirin, I told her, I'll be fine.

And I couldn't just go telling my mother that I'd had my ass kicked for being an asshole, so I made up this whole thing about some guy really messing with Rebecca and how I had to stop it because it was getting really ugly, and the guy just went nuts on me, and no, I didn't know who he was, just some guy.

"Who's Rebecca?"

"Um, Rebecca Connors, this girl I know from school."

"Is this a girlfriend?" As in, "Have you become unclean before the eyes of the Lord?"

"Umm . . ."

"And why haven't we met her?"

"Well, see, um, she's really kind of Doug's girlfriend. We were just, you know, having lunch."

Fine, except Rebecca wasn't really kind of anybody's girlfriend, maybe never would be. It wasn't like that. I wasn't sure what it was like, but it sure wasn't like that.

I washed up and got ready for work, and once I got some of the dried blood off, it wasn't nearly as bad as I'd figured. A couple of bruises, my nose a little swollen and sore, but not so awful.

But it had been, that was the thing. I could remember the pain quite clearly, and it had been pretty bad.

I looked at my hand, only the faintest of scars left from the broken wine glass. I shook, and it took some effort to control myself. Rebecca was starting to scare the hell out of me. It didn't make me want her any less.

4

STAN AND I GOT to work at the same time that Saturday. We walked in the front door and I saw that the manager on duty was our old nemesis, Roger Craw.

"Uh-oh," I said. "Look who's on today."

Stan followed my gaze. "Aw, man, it'd have to be Craw, wouldn't it? This day's gonna suck mightily."

It would. Roger was the King High Lord Weenie Assistant Manager. Our mortal enemy. And Craw watched the beer like a hawk. You could still get it out from under him, but oh boy, you had to be careful.

"Shit, shit, shit, shit."

We got to the time clock. "Livingston, calm down."

"Oh, shut up, Lynch, you know I hate that."

I knew. I punched in, found Craw's card and punched him out. Craw wasn't an hourly, but he still had to punch in and out, and everybody screwed him up on it.

Stan said, "Power to the people!"

"Seize the means of production!" I said.

Stan looked at me like I'd spouted Esperanto, so I shook my head and went to get my till.

There was never much difference from day to day at Tate's. Same shit, another day. Usually. Tonight felt different. No Monica, a Saturday night fixture. And when I thought of how permanent that hole in the routine of things was, that she was dead and not just moved on to another job, I wanted to fucking bawl. Not that we had any bonds, you know, but to know that she wasn't out there somewhere made the world a little more dim, a little more dirty.

We got the usual assortment of working stiffs, Saturday afternoon football drunks, family food caravans. You could time the rushes by halftime of the OSU and OU games. I checked at my usual mercurial rate and Stan the Man rushed from check stand to check stand. Things were crazy since three of the six sackers had called in sick, so he was sacking groceries madly if not always sensibly. Stan had a high rate of attrition when it came to eggs and bread. That wasn't important, though. The important thing here is that Mick was in produce that night. On my break, I tracked him down and greased his palm. I told him anything but Coors or Busch. Standards were important.

Once my shift was over and we had the store closed, I waited for the parking lot to clear out, chilling out to some Honeymoon Suite. When the coast was clear-ish, I drove around to the back of the store and waited for the two cars ahead of me to get their business at the dumpster done. Busy night for Mick.

My turn came up. I got out of the Bomb and scrambled up the side of the dumpster and cautiously settled on the trash. I was not eager to turn an ankle, or wind up hip-deep in some noxious shit. Then I groped around for my box. It didn't take me long. Stench is a great motivator.

Someone pounded on the side of the dumpster and I just about shat myself. "Yo! Police!" Stan yelled

"Stan," I called, "you fucker, I don't think that's how it's done."

I heard one of the sliding side doors scrape open and saw his eager face appear. "Hey, get my box while you're in there."

Leave it to Stan to figure out how to get me to do his dirty work. But I found one last produce box with a case of fucking Busch in it. Busch. I was inclined to leave it.

"Take 'em," I said. I handed him the two boxes one at a time.

Stan grinned when I gave him the boxes. "Phew. Get outta there, man, you *reek*, man."

"You too, nosebag."

"What'd you get?"

"I dunno," I said. "We'll check."

Stan shook his head. "Hope it ain't Bud. Shit's horse piss, man. Fucking horse piss."

This from a guy who'd stolen Busch. Jesus.

I clambered out, almost slipping because of the muck on my sneakers. We opened my trunk and stuck the beer in. I was curious to see what was in the third box. Bud Light. Oh well. I was too tired to climb up and put it back.

Stan started to close the trunk lid and I stopped him.

"Hang on."

I grabbed a Busch, warm though it was, and popped it open.

"Hey, that's mine!"

It was lukewarm, scummy, and thick going down. Tasted like shit. I stood there a second and then let loose a huge, ripping belch.

"Aw, was that necessary?"

"Yeah," I said. "I feel a hell of a lot better."

"HORSE PISS! THIS IS fucking horse piss!"

Doug, glazed-eyed and grinning, raised his arm and promptly gave the middle finger salute to Stan. Stan responded by scarfing a handful of Doritos down his throat and scowling, and washing it down with the remainder of his Bud Light. Finished, he belched loudly. I thought he sounded like a barfing brontosaurus.

"No one made you drink it, dweeb," I pointed out to him.

Four of us were at the absent Samantha Driscoll's tiny kitchen table. Aside from Doug, Stan, and me, Mick had made it. While this did not qualify as a full tilt wallbanger of a party, it was good enough for us, our quorum. I guess at this point we'd been chugging pretty hard for an hour or so. Mick wasn't keeping up with the rest of us, but he kind of liked to be able to stand up at the end of these things, and we respected this odd inhibition. Restraint was not a common affliction among us. Restraint was, in fact, for losers better than us.

Mick, unlit cigarette dangling from his lips (Sam had a zero tolerance smoking policy, and he knew it), leaned forward and grabbed the red attack dice.

"Ukraine to fucking, uh, um, whatever the hell that is there."

He was pointing to the Risk board. For all I could see, he was pointing to the South Atlantic. Mick was going to invade the South Atlantic from the Ukraine. This was a pretty good trick in my book. I was a big supporter of amphibious operations. I belched my approval, and reached down for my Bud.

"That's Mongolia," said Doug, "and you can't invade it. Stan nuked it last turn."

Mick glowered at Stan. "You fucking nuked Mongolia? What was your problem? What did the Mongols ever do to you, you brute?"

Stan stared back at Mick. "It was there."

Mick sat back to ponder what he might do instead. Figuring this could take some time, I got up to go get another beer.

Doug groaned to the heavens as his country was overrun by the barbarian hordes from Ukraine. "Nothing but a bunch of illiterate communists!"

Doug had found a bottle of Ketel One in one of Sam's cabinets and now he assaulted it with astounding speed, putting away some sort of awful Kool-Aid and vodka concoction. His eyes were red and teary, and his hand kept making really absurd gestures that had nothing to do with anything. When he rolled dice to defend or attack, they usually shot off the table and into the kitchen.

As much fun as this was to watch, my bladder started issuing militant demands. I mumbled some sort of excuse me—something along the lines of "mgonnapiss"—and sauntered off toward the bathroom. I was already to that stage of drunkenness where sauntering was the only form of walking left.

As I got to the bathroom, I heard Doug snap at Mick. "Jesus, not again!"

World conquest reduced to meaningless bickering between drunk dorks. Maybe not that far removed from real life, actually. I smiled, shook my head,

Sam had a one-bedroom apartment. I was quite familiar with the bathroom, living room, and the kitchen/dining area. Never, however, had I seen the bedroom. I stood before the bathroom door and considered this. It seemed unfair to me that I had never seen it; after all, I knew the rest of the place so well. What could it hurt to explore the rest, anyway? Never mind that she made it strictly *verboten* to us.

With a surreptitious glance down the hall, I stole into her bedroom. Well, if any movement in the condition I was in could be described as "stealing." Probably more like "stumbled idiotically."

I shut the door and flicked on the light. The taste with which the room had been decorated struck me immediately. When one is strongly lacking in an attribute, one recognizes it readily in others. The furniture was white and quietly stylish, slightly feminine, and it was all meticulously clean. Her bureau was neat, with a jewelry box and a couple of framed snapshots atop it, none of the scattered makeup or hair crap I would have assumed would be there. There was also a mirror on the wall over the bureau, and a small photo was stuck into a corner. I leaned in and squinted at the picture, but I didn't recognize the muscular young man in it. He wore a tank top and shorts and had a tan to end all tans. I guessed him to be a couple of years older than myself.

Adam, probably.

I decided that he was an asshole. His mother was a bearded lady in a second-rate circus in Mississippi somewhere. His father was a convicted pedophile, or possible a German Shepherd, depending.

I snarled at the picture. My bladder was suggesting perhaps I piss on the photo, but the image of a dog marking territory occurred to me, and my venom drained out.

"Man, you are drunk." Extending my streak for pointing out the obvious.

One of the framed photographs was of me and Doug, striking a typically stupid pose that we must somehow have found funny at the time. It was about a year old, taken the previous February at Doug's seventeenth birthday party. I knew that she kept it up because of Doug, but I was absurdly touched that she had chosen a picture of him that had me in it.

I turned away from it before I started to get real maudlin. I tended toward that when skunked. I tended toward a great many ugly things when skunked.

The walls were decorated with framed art prints, including one that I somehow recognized as a work by Georgia O'Keefe. Art history not being my thing, I was awfully impressed with myself. There was also a beefcake calendar, which I naturally took to be an uncharacteristic lapse in taste. This, despite the two *Playboy*s and a *Penthouse* hidden underneath my mattress.

A bookcase, by the bed. Hmm. What dark, secretive insight could I glean from the titles of the tomes on these shelves? As if I hadn't known her all these years, as if I didn't have a pretty good take on her personality, as if. Still, because it seemed the sleuthy thing to do, I read the spines. Lots of poets: Keats, Sandburg, Whitman, Shelley, names I did not know from squat. Novels. *Catch-22*, that one I recognized because Doug had threatened to disown me if I didn't read it, rightly so. And *The Catcher in the Rye*, ditto. Otherwise, nothing that I recognized. Rock bands were my realm. I could tell you that Rick Wakeman played keyboards on a Black Sabbath song, I could name, in order, the various incarnations of Deep Purple, I could with some authority state that Pink Floyd had once been known as The Screaming Abdabs and that Blue Oyster Cult every so often appeared in clubs as Soft White Underbelly. Poetry and novels, especially if they had some meaning or value, were beyond me.

Also on the shelf were some texts, history stuff, and what appeared to be every *Far Side* book to date. Finally, something I could relate to.

I stood still for a moment, reveling in a sort of mushy sentimental respect for Sam. Gawrsh, I hardly knew you, Sam, Sammy, Samantha dear.

I slipped back out of her room with a strangely pleasurable pain in my chest. "Jesus, Lynch, took you long enough? Whatdja do, piss out Lake Hefner?"

"Piss this," I replied to Stan, popping open a Bud.

"Your turn," said Doug.

"To what?"

Mick tapped me gently on the shoulder. "The game."

I looked at the Risk board, at the scattered black, blue, green, and red armies spread over the jigsaw-pattern map. "Uh, um, I'm blue, right?" I grinned.

Stan, Doug, and Mick all stared at me.

"Oh," I said. "Well, there you go."

"Your turn, Eric."

"Can we take a break from this, maybe order a pizza? My head hurts."

"I'm gonna go have a smoke," said Mick, "but Canadian bacon would be okay by me."

"Pineapple," muttered Stan. His head was drooped now. He appeared to be edging into a siesta. Stan had these brief downtimes when he got smashed. He would doze five, maybe ten minutes, and then come to twice as ready to go.

"Yeah," said Doug, "Pizza. But to hell with pineapple. Hey, Eric, would you get me another beer?"

"Let it all hang out, man," said Mick, pausing at the door. "Anyone seen my jacket?"

Doug showed him where it was while I found a phone book. Doug had to help me read it—Christ, was I already up into the latter half of my second six pack? We found a Domino's nearby and took giggling turns trying to get the order straight with the guy on the other end. We hung up completely unsure of what we'd just bought, and completely not caring. I'd have eaten anchovies at that point. Shit, I might not have even realized they *were* anchovies.

Stan swayed into the living room. He was pale. His mouth was pressed down in a tight little line. His bleary eyes stared fixedly ahead.

"C'mon, man," I told him. "You need some air."

I nudged him for the door. "We can wait out there for the pizza, 'cause they might not be able to find us."

"I'm coming," said Stan.

"Yeah, well, use a Kleenex for a change, huh?"

"Go to hell, Eric."

Mick, being by far the most sober, was tagged to count out our money. He had to practically horsewhip Stan for it. Stan, freshly awake from his snooze, only coughed up when we assured him he would eat only exactly what he paid for. He started to argue, but then whatever social account that resided in Stan's head must have informed him that he needed the few friends he had, and that he might want to ease up on the asshole pedal. He forked over, cursed once, and went off in search of a bush to barf in. Mick sat on the grassy little rise and lit up another coffin nail. He was staring up at the sky. I looked up too, at the chill winter sky, at the almost preternaturally bright stars. To the south lay Oklahoma City, and the night sky there was washed pale by the city lights. I tried to pick out the constellations, although by now I was far too gone to hope to recall any of their names. Once, when still a child, I had wanted to be an astronomer. This was before junior high and the realization that this involved math and physics. No Eric Lynch, Junior Rocket Scientist.

Doug sat on the other side of Mick and joined our stargazing.

"Hey Doug," asked Mick.

"Huh?"

"How's it goin' with you and Connors?"

Doug frowned at him. "What do you mean?"

Mick raised an eyebrow at Driscoll. He shrugged.

"Nothin'. Just askin', that's all. Nothin' major."

I plucked a few dead grass blades, ground them between my fingers. I thought back to that long, unreal afternoon in Rebecca's apartment. How much did Doug know? How much could he guess? And what about Stan? I glanced at him, but he seemed to be intently looking for just the right bush to puke in.

"Everything's okay," said Doug.

I feared I was too drunk for this shit. I wished I was a lot more plastered than I was.

"Is it really okay?" I should have kept my goddamn mouth shut.

"Yeah," Doug said, lolling his head around to look at me. "Why wouldn't it be?"

"'Cause you're awfully toasted, man."

Doug grinned, but it looked like the teeth-gritting grimace you get when something painful is lanced. He took off his glasses and acted like he was cleaning them, this seemed desultory to me.

"Yeah, and you're so fucking dry and sober."

"Yeah, well." What I meant to say was that it was expected of me.

Doug stood up. "Man, it's cold tonight."

"I think she's jackin' with you," said Mick.

I sighed heavily. *Fuck, here we go.*

Doug whirled at Mick, fists clenched, and my mouth dropped, because it was the first time in my life I had ever, ever, seen Doug act like he was about spin someone's head.

"I don't care what you *think* she's doing to me, it's none of your business!"

"I was talkin' to Eric."

Doug whipped that red-eyed glare over to me. I stared at Mick.

"Do what?"

"You heard me."

Doug said, "Hey, what's going on here?"

"Dunno," I said, playing stupid, something at which I do not normally have to pretend. "Mick, what're you talkin' about, man?"

Mick laughed, and took a long pull on his cigarette. "Ya'll are like a pack o' horny little puppies paddin' along behind a bitch in heat. Fuckin' Rebecca, she cocks her ass just right, you guys all cream yourselves. I bet you all lie in bed at night pullin' your monkey and whisperin' her name and she just loves it that way."

"Why don't you shut the hell up," Doug whispered. He shook and swayed, like a man caught in an earthquake.

Mick pitched his cigarette butt off into the parking lot. It bounced with a burst of sparks. I wished Mick *had* just shut up. Stan, by now, had weaved his way over to us. I could see that he was trying to assimilate the odd situation here, and was failing miserably.

"Why don't I shut the hell up? Shit, 'cause I'm *stupid* and 'cause ya'll are my *friends*. And I hate that this shit's goin' on."

"Nothing's going on," said Doug.

Mick stared at him, reached into his pocket for his pack of Marlboros, and said, before he lit up, "Christ, okay. Look, I'm sorry I said anything. I'm just drunk, okay?"

But Doug didn't believe it and, though his face was quickly obscured by a stream of smoke, I could see that Mick did not mean it.

Stan said, "Pizza's here!"

I hung back while Doug went with Stan to get the grub.

Mick regarded me with no trace of amusement whatsoever.

"What was that all about?" I tried to sound pissed but only came off as scared and desperate.

"You fuckin' her yet?"

"No. She's Doug's girl, man."

Mick sighed. Then he coughed, a hard and extended hacking. "Eric, she ain't nobody's girl. She's the queen of all the nightbirds, she's anything. She's flat fuckin' *trouble*."

"You said that before."

"Yeah," he said, standing, "but now I *know* it."

A little Toyota pickup truck with a Dominos sign on top of the cab idled in the parking lot. The headlights cast long shadows from the figures standing before it. I walked over toward it with exaggerated and careful footsteps, saying nothing more to Mick. It pissed me off that he was so high and mighty about all this, but it pissed me off more that he was probably right. I wasn't sure what I was going to do about any of it; shit, I wasn't sure I wasn't going to blow chow in a few minutes. I was only barely sure that Ronald Reagan was president and would not have bet the farm that the sun was due to rise in a mere seven hours or so.

Doug was helping Stan count out change to the delivery girl. The girl was smiling, and as I got close enough to smell the pizza, I noticed that her teeth were slightly uneven, a little crooked. She looked kind of plain to me, not ugly or unattractive, just a little . . . plain.

She was patient enough while our resident brains did their best to get the money together. "You guys havin' a smooth time tonight?"

Oh sure, I thought, *if we don't wind up killing each other it'll be a wild time.*

"Yeah," shrugged Stan, "mostly."

"Cool. Puttin' the beer away?"

"Each and every one of us is twenty-one and a half," I said, and I only slurred it a little bit.

She laughed. "Oh, uh-huh."

Mick took the money from Doug and recounted it, losing track a time or two, stopping to straighten out a bill now and then, adding a couple of bucks from his pocket as a tip.

The delivery girl watched this with interest. Or I thought she did. After a silent moment or two, in which I could hear the radio in the truck playing a Whitesnake song, I realized she was not watching Mick count the money, she was watching, less discreetly than she thought, Doug. A hint of a smile, damn near invisible in the pale light from the parking lot lights, tugged at one corner of her mouth. Douglas, the great imbiber of vodka, he of the red-rimmed eyes, was oblivious to it. Probably just as well.

Stan, always cautious and aware that he was a minor, had a can of beer with him. He popped it open and took a swig. Doug, aghast, popped him in the ribs and forced beer out his nose. The delivery girl found this amusing. Everybody loves clowns, don't they?

Mick handed her the money, which she stuffed into her money pouch, and tried to take the pizzas from her. She handed them to Doug. I still had no clue what we'd ordered, but it smelled good.

She flashed a smile at Doug, and for half a moment, she appeared rather pretty after all. Smiles are so often the real light of beauty. Had I seen Rebecca smile? I couldn't remember.

"Well, ya'll have yourselves a good one, enjoy the food."

Stan tipped his beer can toward her. "Want some?"

She laughed again, and I thought it was a laugh you might get used to in a hurry. "No thanks, gotta drive."

Mick grabbed Livingston by his arm and steered him toward the apartment, while Stan muttered, probably to himself, "The pizza, I meant the pizza."

We started back, hearing the truck door open and close, but the girl said,

"Wait." She came toward us, brandishing a pencil.

Doug looked at me, confused. His eyes were like those in a mounted animal. The girl came up to him and started writing on the top pizza box.

"Uh . . ." said Doug.

Done, she looked up at Doug, smiled, and hustled back to the truck. I decided right there that I liked her. Doug squinted down to see what she'd written. He laughed.

"What?"

"Nothing. Let's get back inside. I'm sobering up."

"Not fuckin' likely. What'd she write?"

He sighed, then slid the top box over so I could see it.

It read: Eva Galli 555-8715 CALL ME!!!!

"Huh," I said. "You gonna?" Knowing he couldn't.

He didn't say anything until we were halfway up to the apartment. Stan and Mick were at the door, Mick pitching off another cigarette in the parking lot.

"I don't know," he said at last, almost a whisper.

Stan went inside, and a second later, I heard him say, loudly, "Who the fuck are you?"

My skin was three sizes too small as I stepped into the apartment. I suppose I knew who it was going to be before I even got a look at him; not that knowing was any comfort.

The kid from my visions stood in the hall leading down to the bedroom, same Adidas T-shirt and jeans. Same blond hair.

And everybody saw him.

"Holy shit," I whispered.

I stumbled back, not wanting another one of those visions. A second later it struck me that this time, I was not the only one having one. Mick looked confused. Stan was pale, drained. He leaned against the table like a man having a heart attack. Doug looked at me with an expression approaching dread, like it was just dawning on him that something was about to seriously go off the rails.

The kid said, "Hey guys, how they hangin'?"

Doug dropped the pizzas on the table, on top of the saltine crumbs. His face was still, carved from flesh-like stone. He looked a lot calmer than I felt.

Stan groaned.

Doug said, "I'm not dreaming this."

"Nope," said the kid, "and neither is Eric, or Stan, not even you," he pointed to Mick, "whatever your name is."

"Mick." But he wasn't looking at the kid. He was scanning the rest of us, trying to figure out what the hell was happening.

"Right. Well, I guess maybe you're caught up in this too, although I don't see how. You really don't like her, do you?"

Mick shook his head. Stan sank a little lower.

I smelled roses.

"You got that right, Eric. You guys remember the roses, huh? No? I don't guess any of you remember dick. And I gotta tell you, I'm hurt."

"Who are you?" Stan's voice came out in a pathetic whine.

"Somebody you used to know. Maybe your guardian angel. Somebody's got to be, 'cause you guys are in for a world of hurt, and you dipshits may cause a world more."

The kid smiled, and a thin rill of blood trickled from the corner of his mouth.

"You made something you couldn't unmake. I did too, I guess, but it's a little late for me to be worrying about it. My dreams are done. You need to stop yours."

I stepped forward to grab him, because my fear, finally, finally, had been plowed under a great wave of anger; I'd had just about enough.

I did not reach the kid. I slid down a loose slope of earth, hit a scrawny bush, and tumbled awkwardly into a shallow pool of muddy water.

The Swing.

5

I'M TWELVE AGAIN AS I stand, feeling the bright summer sun cook my
skin. I'm looking over at the treehouse, that Frankenstein stillbirth of a shelter
perched up in the tree. It's early afternoon; the sun sits high up in the sky. I
can't see any clouds up through the gaps in the leafy overhang.

I breathe in, now doubled in my body, me at seventeen a passenger in me
at twelve. I think for a moment that this could be a dream, but then there
is weight, heat. When I breathe, I catch the odor of tobacco, coming from
somewhere above me, coming from the treehouse. Then a burst of music
erupts from the treehouse: April Wine, "Enough is Enough."

I grin a little, tremble a little, and walk over to the trunk of the monstrous
old oak that cups the treehouse in its twisted arms, find the rising series
of lengths of one-by-twelve nailed to the tree, and climb. The treehouse is
perhaps twenty, twenty-five feet off the ground, but it squats safely in the V
of two fat, huge branches. I think of the weather this thing has survived as I
approach the trap door in the middle of the floor: heavy snow, torrential rains,
and the common Oklahoma windstorms. Not to mention the blast-furnace
summers. It could probably hold up a couple of hundred years without a lick
of maintenance.

The aroma of cigarettes kicks in like a slap when I poke my head up into
the treehouse. It's dim inside—the thing never gets much light—and the
shadows have helped to keep it relatively cool despite the heat outside. My eyes
adjust and I see Stan sprawled in one corner, inhaling deeply on a cigarette.
His eyes are squinted shut with the drama of inhaling, and so it's Doug who
sees me first.

"Hey, Eric," he says.

"Yo," I say.

Doug, who sits across from Stan, with Stan's massive boom box and a pile of cassettes between them, raises a hand in greeting. He's carving his name in the wood floor with a butterfly knife that I recognize as Stan's, who thinks it makes him tougher or some shit. What a joke. We're all about as tough as Charmin tissue.

I ask the obvious. "Whose smokes?"

Stan says, "My brother's."

"Cool."

I come all the way in, the thick boards creaking under my weight. At twelve, I am already almost one-eighty. The first great love of my life is food. Just lately the idea of girls (well, more precisely, GIRLS) has been making headway. I have discovered the twelve-year-old's fascination with *Playboy*, Vaseline, and self-pleasure. It has occurred to me more and more that at some time these two pleasures, food and girls, are bound to conflict. I postpone these thoughts when possible.

I duckwalk over to the boom box. The treehouse is really tall enough to stand up in, but there's something about being this far off the ground in a structure that's this patchwork that makes one feel like hugging the ground.

I look at the tapes: obviously April Wine, some Styx, Asia, Van Halen, the Police, some old Black Sabbath, a new band called Zebra.

"Man," I say, "it's *hot* out today."

Doug points behind me and I see the little cooler.

"Just Dr. Pepper." He shrugs.

While I'm digging one out, Stan hands me a cigarette. I pause long enough to feel the wildness; we are twelve-year-old middle-class white kids. This is as rebellious as we get in 1982.

Stan shifts to a cross-legged position, and starts in on this band he's hot on, Night Ranger. I ignore him as I light up and grab a cold drink out of the cooler. The smoke burns in my lungs, and I let loose a dying cat cough.

It's great to be twelve. It's great to be alive.

I WAS ON THE floor in front of Sam's couch, curled up and quaking. My cheeks were wet with tears and after a second I realized that the sobs I heard were at least partly my own. Partly. Someone in the kitchen—Doug, I think—was crying and saying, "Oh shit, oh shit." Stan, had to be Stan, shrieked from somewhere in the apartment.

"Jesus," I muttered. I uncurled, got to my knees with an effort of will that left me drained. Worse than drained, full of despair. Fuck that. I stood, sucked in air. And there was the kid again, the kid with the voice from the treehouse. He looked at me with a kind of terrible pity.

"Fuck you," I spat. My hatred was black and animal. I started around the couch for him.

The kid said, with considerable astonishment, "You think this is *my* fault?"

I screamed and ran for him.

I—

I LOOK TOWARD THE trap door. "Hey, Randy, what's up?"

Randy Crawford pokes his head up through the hole in the floor, his blond hair painted to his forehead with sweat. He smiles at me and it's the smile of an angel. Randy is the only one among us who already draws attention from the girls. We're all jealous of him, of course, and he's drawing away from the group because of it. We can't handle the fact that the girls find him attractive; he won't be held back by a bunch of geeks who can't cut it. But none of that really matters on a hot summer day, a day made for hanging out with your friends and being a wastrel.

Randy struggles on in. He has to do this because of the olive green backpack slung over his shoulder. He barely squeezes through. With a grunt, he heaves it over onto the floor. Sweat stains the armpits of his Adidas shirt. Something inside clinks, a muffled glassy sound. Randy hauls himself in, brushes splinters and dust from his white Adidas shirt, sniffs the air, and grins. "Shit, you guys are bad!"

None of us disagree. We as bad as it gets, fer sure, fer sure.

"Watcha got?" I ask.

"I got your mama last night."

"Eat me."

He unzips the backpack and pulls out a bottle of Coke.

"Oh man," says Stan. "You're really being dangerous. You get caught with that, you could be in bad trouble. I mean, a bottle of Coke, wow!"

"Yeah? Then what about this?" The bottle he hands to Doug is full of a rich amber liquid.

Doug looks at it, shrugs.

"Rum, dickhead."

"Cool," I say, "but we ain't got no cups."

"No sweat. Here." He pulls out a sleeve of Solo cups. Also a couple of his father's skin mags. Randy is a constant source not only of skin mags, but also X-rated tapes and cigarettes. Finally, he brings out a much abused sketch pad.

Randy's got this ongoing comic that he draws, that he only lets the three of us read. It's a lot better than he thinks it is. It's called "The Guardians," and it's about these people in this little town who all get psychic powers from an alien ship that smacks down into the town and wipes most of it out. The style is crude, but he can tell a story, and we're all hooked.

I'm already pouring Coke into a cup and eyeing the unmarked bottle with rum in it. This is how we occasionally fill our summer days, trying to adjust our age with booze and hollow, enormous yearnings, building emotional voids and then lacking the means or the ability to fill them.

A breeze blows in through the crudely cut square that serves as a window. Leaves whisper against each other, passing on secrets. Randy starts drawing on his comic, flips a few pages up, lets his hand wander aimlessly, pregnant with creation but without point, purpose. The four of us bathe in the silence, something waiting to happen. I am twelve. I am seventeen, and I am remembering this while I experience it again, but this is not a memory. This is real. I am here. This is real. And I can no more stop it than I can halt time, than I can be God.

SAM'S APARTMENT AGAIN. I was on the floor, dazed. Mick shouted, "What the fuck is this?"

Doug screamed out my name.

Hey, compadre, I got a few troubles of my own. I blinked, looked around, my head swimming from the distortion of time. Hadn't I just been going for the kid . . . for Randy? What happened? Now I was in the kitchen. I looked and Mick was over by the front door, gripping the doorknob so tightly, I thought he might crush it in his fist. His eyes were bulging almost comically. He was wheezing for air. He was like a rock in the maelstrom for me.

"Hey, Mick," I rasped.

His eyes sought me, found me, and he blinked. "Eric, what's *happening*?"

The end of the world? "Fuck me, I don't know. Where is everybody?"

"That kid, he . . . he was right there," Mick pointed to the hallway, where I had charged Randy, maybe minutes, maybe hours ago. "And then he was just gone."

"You're drunk man, you'll be all right."

Something shattered in the bathroom. It sounded like the mirror. Stan screamed. I stumbled down the hall, looked in and saw Stan leaning over the sink, reflective shards and pieces scattered over the countertop, blood dripping from his hands, splattering everywhere.

"No! I don't want her," he shrieked. "I don't want her, it ain't right!"

Mick was right behind me. "Fuck," he whispered.

I nodded. "Pretty much."

"And who do you blame for all this, Eric?"

I turn to face Randy, the ghost of Randy.

"Like we *knew*."

"Like she can help what she is. No creature creates itself."

Randy stood before us and a blossom of blood opened on his shirt. It ran down over the Adidas logo like a bright red tear.

"But sometimes, we undo ourselves, Eric. Sometime we do that, and you know it."

The things I knew anymore could be packed in a thimble with room to spare.

"CHECK OUT THESE TITTIES," says Stan, leaning over to show me and Doug a badly shot photograph of a statuesque redhead on a bed with her ass stuck in the air and her admittedly huge breasts hanging down like gigantic fruit ready to plummet from the vine.

"Nice bazoombas, but I bet they'd smother ya," I tell him. "Besides, look at that face, bow-wow."

"Eric," frowns Stan, "you don't do it to the face."

"Yeah? Well, *you* don't do it to nothin'."

That hangs there for a second. It's too hot to run with the putdowns for very long.

"Who says it's all about sex?" asks Doug.

"Yeah," I put in. "What about love and all?"

Stan makes a farting sound. "What about it?"

"So you're saying you'd hide your salami in a chick even if she was an asshole?" I'm sort of surprised to be taking Doug's side in this; hell, there are times I'm pretty sure I'd screw a knothole if I didn't think I'd get splinters; not a lot of those times, mind you, but I do experience them. I'm not proud of it.

"Well..." says Randy, pausing to sip down some rum and Coke. "Maybe not, but that whole personality thing, no way man. Overrated."

"C'mon, dude," I said. "She'd have to be a saint to let you put it to her, I mean with all those zits."

Randy kicks me in the thigh just hard enough for muscles to knot. I wince and rub the spot. "Faggot."

"I don't know. I mean sex is great and all, but if you have wait until you're married and—"

Stan laughs. "No one waits 'til they're married, Doug. I bet my brother does two different girls a week." Stan's older brother is a tight end for OU. Backup. Nineteenth string.

"So," I argue, "there's nothing special about it, huh? It's all just 'wham bam thank-you-ma'am'?"

Doug says, "Why not just get a prostitute?"

"'Cause you catch shit, that's why." Stan, who would not in a million years be able to tell you exactly what one might catch. Just stuff. Public school sex education is failing us all miserably.

"I don't know," says Doug. "I think, I always thought, that I would wait for the right girl. I think there's a real love for everyone out there. I think it's like fate, or destiny. I have dreams about a girl like that—"

"Woo-hoo! Wet dreams!" cries Stan. "Dougie's wet dreams!"

Doug blushes but presses on. "Sometimes I have these dreams where I'm all out on my own in the dark, and I hear her call my name, she's so close. I reach out for her, to find her, and I can't. I know she's there, I know it, and then I touch her fingers, just barely, and it always ends there. It always ends there."

Randy taps his pencil against the sketch pad.

"My dream girl . . ." Randy begins, and then stops, thinking, staring at his sketch pad.

Doug ejects April Wine, looks at the scattered tapes Stan has brought, and switches over to the radio. He finds a rock station, in the middle of Zeppelin's "D'yer Mak'er." He turns the volume down low.

"What?" asks Randy.

Doug nudges his glasses up the bridge of his nose with his index finger and squints at all of us. "I don't know. She'd have to be, you know, smart. I'd want to be able to talk to her."

"Before or after?"

"Both, Livingston, both."

Stan grunts. His cigarette is done, and he taps another one out of the pack, only three of them spill out. Trying to look cool and being a bigger dork for it.

"So, smart, that's all?" Randy leans on his knees now, and his eyes are sparkling and animated. He loves theoretical bullshit sessions. He's the dreamer of our little clan, always a step outside of everything. "Man, maybe more than that. She'd have to be cute, green eyes and black smooth hair."

"Oh," I chirp, "like Alma Mobley." Alma Mobley is this totally hot ninth-grader at Central Junior High, which is where we all go.

He doesn't deny it.

Randy's hand moved across the sketch pad, the graphite whispers across the paper. He stares at it like it's a rebellious child.

"She'd have to love rock 'n' roll," says Stan.

"Uh-huh, Joan Jett."

"Aw, screw you, Eric."

"Eat me."

"Legs," Randy says, a dreamy expression on his face. The pencil is furious in his hands. "Long, strong legs. Wrap around you."

I close my eyes and think about it. My dream girl. Whatever that means. Man, I like all kinds.

"I like big titties," says Stan.

I don't even open my eyes when I reply. "You like any kind you can get, which is none."

"Shut *up*, man, bite me."

My dream girl: yeah, maybe smart like Doug says, but not a brainiac, a girl with smooth lines and soft porcelain skin and beautiful curves, the raven hair and gray eyes, the full red lips, the gentle, exotic hands, sharp wit, sharp mind, heart of desire . . .

We're all silent, and I don't have to open my eyes to know that everybody else's are closed as well. The pencil still hisses and scratches like a small creature against the paper. Warmth envelopes me like a soft breath, and, embarrassingly, I have a hard-on to end all hard-ons. I can see her now, though, this beauty of my imagination, this ethereal angel of my heart's dream; I can smell her, a smell like that of a wild rose, a scent that sets my heart racing. Even now, I don't open my eyes. There is a spell here, I feel it, all of us feel it. It is as though something has descended on us, and the day outside is distant, removed to another plane.

REBECCA WAS THERE.

I could feel her. She was there in Sam's apartment, and it felt very much like the desecration of a temple to me.

IT'S HOT IN THE treehouse, the previous cool now driven out, away, and the air has a slight metallic undertaste to the sweet smell of flowers. I open my eyes, feeling faint, light, almost nauseated. Randy sits up and leans out of the "window." Nobody speaks. There is the feeling, at least from me, of having slipped through a membrane and come back, of having been strained somehow. I feel like I've run ten blocks, ragged, exhausted. Stan's eyes blink open, and he stares up at the plywood roof of the treehouse, seeing nothing, seeing everything maybe. We all want to ask the same thing—"What the fuck?"—but no one does. Randy's sketchpad has fallen near his feet. I see the figure he has sketched and my heart skips a beat. Words collide into meaningless fragments in my head as I reach over to pick up the pad.

Randy has drawn my dream girl. Almost as though he had burrowed into my most profound fantasies. He has drawn her.

"She's beautiful," I whisper.

Doug looks over at the pad, his mouth an open gateway to panting little breaths. He nods once, pauses, nods again.

Our dream girl.

Doug says, at last, "Let's get out of here. Let's go down to the tunnel. Too hot."

The tunnel is the massive storm sewer that feeds into the creek. It's easily nine feet square, built to handle all the water that channels down into Lake Hefner. The body of it runs for two and a half blocks under 63rd Street and Meridian Avenue, eventually splitting into smaller branched-out tubes. It is common for us to make ridiculous homemade torches out of two-by-fours and old T-shirts, rags, towels soaked in kerosene lifted from my father's garage and wander through the tunnel like characters from the Dungeons and Dragons games Stan sometimes talks us into playing. We also like to set off Thunder Bombs and Black Cats hoarded from the Fourth of July and listen to their loud, flat, reverberating explosions. Roman candles are great too, and bottle rockets are not to be turned down.

On the really hot summer days the air in the tunnel is moist and cool and a blessed haven, except for the occasional snake. Sometimes we find dry spots not far inside the mouth of it and sit in the faint light and waste days bullshitting eleven- and twelve-year-old bullshit, kick the radio up loud and blast music through the odd acoustics, until the batteries wear down or the afternoon wears on.

Stan gathers up his cassettes, Doug gets the radio, and the rest of us follow them down to the tunnel. We are not ourselves. Nobody says anything. It is as though we are a troop of shell-shocked warriors trudging off to the front again. I carefully climb down, just clearheaded enough to worry about losing my footing on a step and breaking an arm or my neck. As I step away from the tree to make way for Randy coming down, I look over to the swing, the watering hole, and I see an odd sight: a wild rose bush, blooms the color of bright fresh blood. At least I know where the smell was coming from.

It's cool in the tunnel, wonderfully, abnormally cool. Doug sets the boom box down, fine-tunes the station again, and Randy pours another rum and Coke, and we listen to a Boston song fill the tunnel.

And she steps out of the darkness.

Our dream girl.

"YEAH," THE GHOST OF Randy Past said. "All coming back, isn't it?"

I stared at him, beyond him. Down the hall, near the front door, stood Rebecca. With tears on her face. She was still beautiful, and terribly, terribly desirable. What the fuck did it say that some part of me still wanted her so desperately? I stepped around, or through, Randy. I trembled as I approached her. What could she mean to me? Everything, probably, everything I could think of and then some. Christ, I wanted to kill her, I wanted to fuck her, I wanted to shrivel and die. All at once.

"What *are* you?"

She did not answer me, just speared me with those gray eyes like ice.

THE FIRST SHOCK IS that she is there.

The second, and more delightful one, is that she is stark naked. And what rapturous nakedness it is. We stare at her as one, four kids on the cusp who have suddenly hit what appears to be the ultimate jackpot.

"Oh man what is this?" asks Randy. His eyes are wide like headlights on a Mack truck, but more with disbelief, I think, than surprise. Randy is holding up his sketchpad and looking from it to this beautiful woman/girl before us, his eyes flicking back and forth as though he's watching some kind of hyper-fast tennis match. I'm looking my friends over for their reactions because a part of me is afraid to look back at this girl, this fantasy come to life. Part of me is afraid I will lose myself in it forever, drowning in some kind of syrupy ecstasy. And she exudes a strong sensual desire, a kind of megawatt sexual beacon, and I feel like a moth near a searchlight. It's like something has dumped not mere not hormones in to my body, but the originators of the pale ghosts that they are. Pure eros shoots wires of energy through my veins. This is contact with the bare power and electricity of being, and the raw force of it is intimidating, terrifying. And I am only twelve. I can no more voice these thoughts, pin them down with words, than I can sprout wings and soar.

But there is no way to not look at her. Her trim, athletic body is full of fruit and promise. Her face is everything I would ever desire, and to break it down to components is to demean it, but the one thing I can't get away from is her eyes, the incredible, rare ice-gray color of them. She is some kind of loveliness too perfect, too rarified to exist in this, or any real world.

And the spectral, older me within me, the prisoner in this memory or vision, knows her very well of course. Say hey to Rebecca Connors, fellas, or the being that will later call herself that.

She steps toward us. Her eyes are wide, and it seems as though she is seeking to communicate, to bridge some vast gulf between her and us.

Doug moves to meet her, and my first impulse is to stop him. *She's mine!* But that's not right. It's not even true. He holds out his hand, an offering, a supplication, and she reaches out to take it.

"Shit," says Stan. "What goin' on with this?"

"I dunno," I whisper, and I realize I'm scared.

Hey, when I got out of bed this morning, the most I'd envisioned was blowing a hazy hot July day down at the Swing, sneaking those guilty bad boy pleasures of stolen booze and cigarettes, farting off with my geeky friends, you know, hanging out. Instead, my first true sexual experience flies up to meet me, unprepared, and it's something as weird as this. It seems like a bizarre kind of failed joke as it is. For a second, I imagine trying to tell my folks: *Hey, Mom, Dad, went down to the water hole today and here was this nude chick; she followed me home, can I keep her?*

I'm glad to see that Randy, at least, seems to be having as much trouble with this as I am. He keeps shaking his head, and his mouth is like a little bloodless wound. Randy's a true-blue Catholic, despite his inclination toward chemicals and foul language (he will probably grow out of this stuff anyway; it all kind of seems like an act) and frequent talk about getting laid, and I think this is not sitting very well with his view of the world. The Bible does not say a whole lot about stuff like this. Not a whole lot of good stuff, anyway.

She kisses Doug.

Well, now I'm embarrassed. "Um, Doug?"

The girl grips his shirt, pulls it up over his head, disengages from him long enough to get it off of him, and then she's back on him. Doug hesitates for a minute, and then gives in to the inevitable and decides to enjoy himself. Maybe he thinks of England, the seventeen-year-old me muses.

I look at the others. Stan shrugs, says, "We could wait outside."

This is too weird.

Randy says, "This ain't right."

He is not addressing any of us.

I take the boom box from Stan, nodding, "Yeah, c'mon."

What else is there to do? I glance back at Doug, and he has moved off down the tunnel, has found a large dry area free of the slime and broken glass so prevalent here, and she is working his jeans off of him. This I do not want to see.

Stan leads Randy, who is starting to babble. "This ain't right," he says in a monotone. "This ain't real."

Maybe he's right. What do I care? If this is a rum dream, it's the best I've ever had.

Except that it's not.

We step carefully through the water, ignoring the sounds and sighs coming from back there. I hit this slick patch of green scum and almost go down on my ass, and Stan shoots me this look that informs me of the damage he will inflict upon me if I should, God forbid, drop his boom box.

Outside, in the bright sunlight that seems disturbingly unreal now, I set the radio down, put on KATT again. An old T. Rex song is on: "Bang A Gong." How appropriate. Dirty? Yep. Sweet? I don't know. I giggle and am alarmed to find that I almost can't stop.

"What is she?" I ask. Stan shrugs.

"Lilith," says Randy.

"Aw, bullshit," Stan says. "She's just, you know, some chick from PC." Meaning Putnam City High School. Meaning get back down to earth.

"Whore," Randy says, and now he's just staring at the tunnel, his mouth hanging open, and I'm suddenly sure that his mental train has jumped the tracks, that his little red caboose is flying about wildly. "The Great Whore."

Stan asks, "Do you think we maybe imagined her real, man?"

Our dream girl. I stare at Randy. The late Marc Bolan sings urgently about gongs and getting it on, as though large percussive musical instruments have much to do with the beast with two backs.

Stan finds a big thick stick, takes his butterfly knife out, starts whittling. I can tell this is all a bit much for him too, but I think he has just dealt with it the way he deals with everything he doesn't understand. He just accepts it. I envy him. He sleeps well most of the time. His sky is always full of puffy little clouds.

"I don't know," I finally respond to Stan. "I don't know what she is, but I don't care. She's a goddess!"

He nods.

"And I think she wants us all."

He nods again.

"And I don't see no reason to look a gift horse in the mouth, do you?"

He just grins.

What the hell. I grin right back at him.

It seems the right response.

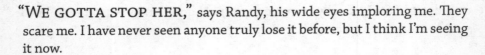

REBECCA SHOOK HER HEAD.

"Oh don't give me that shit!" I wanted to control the note of tight panic in my voice, but did a lousy job of it. My head was still swollen with vision, the bare metal taste of memory filled my mouth.

"What do you *want*?" Was I begging? Well fuck it if I was. Because I already knew what I was reliving. The memory was all the way back.

Rebecca stepped toward me as if to put her arms around me in an embrace. I backed away.

"Eric," she said, "I don't know what's happening here, but you have to believe me—"

Randy's ghost, off behind me, snorted derisive laughter. I refused to look back at him. I could not look away from Rebecca. Christ, was I in love with her? Was that what all this was? I thought maybe it was. It made all of my little puppy-dog infatuations vanish by comparison. They were blades of grass before this giant redwood. And yet what I felt I loved was no more real, no more substantial, than a wisp of steam rising off a lake on a winter's morning. She was a conjuration, a vivid fantasy made momentarily whole by the collective lust of four boys.

This did not matter.

Randy said, "Remember it all, Eric."

But I already did.

Rebecca stepped forward to kiss me. I saw my tiny frightened face reflected in her gray eyes, and I stepped back myself.

I remembered it all.

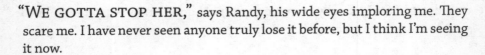

"WE GOTTA STOP HER," says Randy, his wide eyes imploring me. They scare me. I have never seen anyone truly lose it before, but I think I'm seeing it now.

"Chill, man, hang loose," Stan says.

"Stan's right. Probably the last time any of us gets any for a long time."

A Boston song comes on the radio, "Smokin'."

"We gotta stop her."

Stan whirls on Randy. "Listen, why don't you just shut up and sit the hell down. I'm not about to have you screw this all up for us, okay? If you don't wanna, go home. Just don't tell anyone. Okay? Okay?"

I look to the tunnel, but it's far too dark in there for me to see what's going on. My erection's back. My stomach is pinched and nervous, the cold sweat on the back of my neck has little to do with the heat. I wonder if I'll be next. I wonder what it's going to be like, going up inside a girl. Will it be hot, wet? Most of the sleazy skin mags Randy gets talk about it like that. And the crude, almost violent terms they use: cooze, cunt, slit, snatch, twat, honeypot, a million and a half others. I shiver, once, half from expectancy, half from stage fright.

From the tunnel, Doug: "God. *God!*"

Stan gets to his feet. I start toward the tunnel.

And Randy screams.

The two of us freeze for a second and that's all it takes. Randy knocks Stan to the ground, into a scrawny, thorny bush, and Stan yelps in surprise. He drops the knife. Apparently, this is what Randy is after, for he snatches it up and takes off for the tunnel.

"Oh shit!" I chase him, trying to catch him but I'm heavier and can't run as quickly. I'm not quick enough. Neither of us are.

***

"Jesus," I said. "It was a sacrifice. You were a goddess and it was a sacrifice!" I turned away and there was Doug, in the hallway, staring at me, shocked, stunned.

"Rebecca," he asked in a trembling little voice. "Eric?"

I shook my head. "Doug, she . . . I . . . what the hell did we *do*?"

"I can't believe you'd do this to me."

Clearly, we were not on the same topic. Hell, we might not have been on the same *planet*.

"What? Look what she's done to us. You, me, Stan. Christ, Doug, don't you *remember*?"

He stared at me with naked, suspicious anger.

I pointed at Randy's bloody shirt. "This is what she made us do. Don't you remember?"

We all froze as Stan moaned out of the bathroom.
"Don't you remember, Doug?"

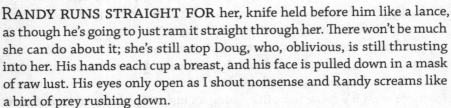

RANDY RUNS STRAIGHT FOR her, knife held before him like a lance, as though he's going to just ram it straight through her. There won't be much she can do about it; she's still atop Doug, who, oblivious, is still thrusting into her. His hands each cup a breast, and his face is pulled down in a mask of raw lust. His eyes only open as I shout nonsense and Randy screams like a bird of prey rushing down.

I'm close, so close, but I can tell that I won't be able to stop Randy in time.

I don't have to.

One second Randy is bearing down on her like a freight train, like a shrieking missile, and then his feet go out from under him in the muck. He skids crazily, looks like he's going to spill onto his back, then overcompensates wildly, too much, too much, and slips forward, face down.

And lets out a hoarse, strained grunt.

I try to stop and slip onto my back. I wince as my head cracks on the pavement. I lie there, trying to be cool, but it hurts like hell and I'm thinking that my mother will kill me when she sees this crap on my clothes, and then I notice that Randy's right arm is under him.

He's not trying to get up.

Stan splashes in behind me. "That stupid dork, what the hell's his problem, what'd he push me—"

"Stan," I say in something between a moan and a sob, "shut up."

"What—?"

"Shut the fuck up!"

Stan says wonderingly, "Shit, I think he's hurt."

But Randy's breathing. As I crawl near him I can hear him crying, sobbing, in a series of ragged little breaths.

Oh fuck, I think, *the knife, Stan's* fucking *knife.*

Stan kneels down, saying Randy's name over and over, and he tries roll Randy onto his back. I help him, and we get him over. Randy's fist is clenched around the metal hilt of the butterfly knife, that stupid pointless thing that Stan carries around to be cool, and the blade is gone, all the way in, disappearing into Randy's stomach. Randy's eyes are wide open, darting, not seeing much. His mouth quivers and works with every sob.

Doug sees it, says in a dull monotone, "Oh shit oh shit oh shit." He crawls over to us, naked but forgetting all about it. The girl, our fantasy, stares at us with wide eyes, stands perfectly still.

"We gotta get that out," says Stan.

Doug shakes his head. "He'll bleed if you do that."

"He's bleeding now."

"Fuck that," I say, and now I sound like the truly terrified twelve-year-old that I am. "He's *dying.*"

Randy's frantic eyes settle on me. "Screw you, Eric." He breathes this out, pausing between each word, working for it.

"We gotta get it out," Stan says again.

"Yes," says the girl.

We all turn and stare at her.

MICK SAID, "I TOLD you she was bad news."

Rebecca turned on him. "Shut up. This has nothing to do with you. You should leave."

"Yeah," said Doug.

"No," I said. "No, Mick, hang around for a while, man. You may not want to after a bit, though. We're all kinda poison now, aren't we, Rebecca? After what we did that day?"

I wasn't looking, so I didn't see the blow that knocked me over Sam's couch. Hurt like a sonofabitch, though, and I knew who had done it. Didn't blame him a bit either. My head was pierced by a high pitched tone as I lay there and waited to recover a bit. Doug loomed over me, face red with rage, glasses askew, his breath snorting in and out.

It had to be said.

"I fucked her, Doug," I said. "We *all* fucked her."

He screamed then, as raw an expression of pain as I have ever heard.

"YES," SHE SAYS.

"Oh man," Stan wails. "Oh man."

"Stan," I say, "you gotta, I can't, I just can't."

Stan looks at me, grief and terror distorting his face almost beyond recognition. We both look down at Randy, who is quickly panting now. Bright red blood runs down under his clenched hand, soaks his white shirt.

Stan grips the knife, sobs once, and quickly jerks it out. There is the small sound of meat coming together. Then Randy howls, his body jerking as though electrified. The blood, which had been a creek, becomes a flood.

"I DON'T GET IT," said Mick. "What's all this shit going on about, this slut puppy?" He pointed at Rebecca.

"Pretty much," said Randy's ghost.

"Huh."

Doug couldn't decide if he wanted to pound me or if he wanted to pound Mick. It had been me, I'd have left Mick alone. Mick was buff. Doug turned toward him anyway.

"Shut up, asshole."

Mick seemed to have regained his composure somewhat; at least he wasn't freaking and trembling the way he had been earlier. But his hand shook when he took a cigarette out and lit up. "Hey, chill, I'm leavin'. You might want to go check on Stan, though. He mighta hurt his hands with that mirror."

I'd forgotten about the mirror. Hell, I'd forgotten about *Stan*. I looked back toward the bathroom and hoped he was okay.

Rebecca stepped away from the door, as though to allow Mick to pass through unimpeded.

Mick looked at me, looked at Doug. "This ain't about me, guys. Am I wrong?"

"No," said Doug. "It's not about you." He looked at me when he said it.

Rebecca smiled, and it seemed to me the most cruel, cutting smile I'd ever seen. Was I like some bottom-feeding fish that had been lured out of his depths by some bright, shiny thing, only to find a hook attached to it?

She said to Mick, "It couldn't be about you, could it?"

He froze.

"I'm not your type, am I?"

"Why don't you shut the fuck up, huh?"

"'Fuck,' now there's an interesting choice of words, coming from you."

Mick paled.

Stan came into the living room. Each of his hands were wrapped in large towels. I almost let a bitter laugh burp out. Hands were always getting cut in Sam's apartment. Otherwise Stan looked okay, alert. He saw the little drama unfolding and his mouth hung open, his astonished face asking what Rebecca was doing here. But he knew. His eyes made a lie of his face.

"What Mickey can't bring himself to tell you guys is—"

Mick leapt at her. He hit her and drove her back into the door before any of us could react. Rebecca did not seem particularly surprised. Or frightened. She did not try to defend herself as Mick put his hands around her throat and squeezed, shouting incoherently as he did so. Doug and I were on him in a second, pulling him away, but even as I did so I wondered how much harm he could really do to her. I looked into Rebecca's face as I fought to get Mick away from her, and I saw an almost alien, incomprehensible hatred and loathing distorting her features. As though being touched by him was almost more than she could bear. Maybe if she couldn't charm it, she didn't want it.

"Goddamn it, let me go, let me go!" Mick was almost sobbing. "I'll kill that bitch!"

Rebecca squirmed free of him, and slid sideways along the wall, away from him. "Don't touch me, *faggot*."

I could feel Mick tense, and dismay shot through me.

Rebecca sneered. Her loathing was palpable. "He's queer, did you guys know that? He is. Gay through and through. Ask him how much he likes it up the ass. Ask him. Ask him how much fun he has at the rest stops."

My God, she was so *ugly*.

Mick sagged, the fight going out of him, and we let him go.

"Jesus," Stan whispered.

I looked back at him, and was alarmed to find that an expression of loathing much like Rebecca's on his face.

"I can't believe it. Mick?"

Mick would not look at him. He stared at the floor.

"Goddamn," Stan muttered. "Goddamn." He absently wiped the back of one towel-wrapped hand on his jeans.

Mick walked to the door. He opened it slowly. He turned once to look at us, all of us, and none of us stopped him, not a single one of us stepped forward and said to him, "Jesus, man, wait." None of us put our hand out. We were rooted and mute, like dead trees. He stepped outside and closed the door gently behind him.

Rebecca watched him go, and now the loathing was gone. Her look of victory was even worse.

When the door clicked shut, she looked at us. Smiling. "I heard you guys were having a party."

I looked around for Randy, but he was gone.

I said to Rebecca, "What, you didn't want us to kill him for you?"

I don't think she realized until that second that any of us remembered it *all.* Her mouth dropped and her eyes gaped wide.

And a tiny breath escaped her.

THE BLOOD SPURTS OUT. Randy whines, clutches at the wound. Doug babbles nonsense in an increasingly shrill tone. I can almost taste his panic; it is the flavor of my own. Stan peels his shirt off and quickly, frantically folds it into a compact square.

"Press this on it!"

He is shouting at me. I take the shirt from him numbly, and do as he says. I look at him. He's in Boy Scouts, unlike the rest of us, and has some notion of first aid. He nods at me. There is blood all over my hands now, and Randy has stopped thrashing. He is limp, conscious but dazed, weak.

"It hurts," he says in a tiny voice, a five-year-old's voice. "It hurts so bad, oh God, oh, it hurts."

Stan holds his knife, staring dumbly at it.

"We gotta get him outta here," I say to Stan. He's the only one of us with his wits left, I think. I'm uselessly freaked and Doug's off somewhere else. And I don't think our mystery girl will be of much assistance. I'm twelve. I don't know how to keep people from dying. My brain keeps wanting to fly off in a crazy circle. But if that happens, Randy will die for sure.

"No," Stan replies. "We move him, he'll only lose more blood. I'm gonna go get help. You have to keep that pressed tight to him, Eric. It'll slow the bleeding down enough until an ambulance can get here." He breathes out and it is quaking, scared.

He stands and turns and is at the mouth of the tunnel before she speaks. "No."

Stan turns, and I follow his look to the girl.

"Stay."

I stare at her. Jesus, is she crazy? Randy is *dying.* She is irrelevant just now.

"He'll die anyway," she says, and her voice is the way I would have wanted it, always; I wonder if what I see, what I hear, matches up in any way with what the others see and hear.

"I can only be here for a while," she says. "Already I am fading. But there is a way for me to stay."

"Stan," I say. "Go. Now."

"Eric, oh God, help me," Randy pleads.

The T-shirt is sopping and hot. I can smell the blood now, like the stench of a butcher's shop, with a faint scent of hot metal beneath it.

The girl, Rebecca, steps forward, and I realize as she comes more into the light that she is insubstantial, not altogether there. Like a wisp of smoke that has attained cohesion. Like a cloud wrapping into a familiar shape. A dream striding into reality. She stands before me, and I am overpowered by a flowery miasma, a palpable rose scent.

"Tears," she says, and until she touches my face I do not realize that I have been crying.

She looks at Doug. "Seed."

And then she looks at Randy. "Blood."

Randy stares at her. "Not . . . right."

Randy is correct. This is wrong, all wrong, and every bit of me knows it.

She catches Stan's eye. "Lifeblood," she says.

Stan shudders, and like a zombie, lurches back to us.

"Yes," she says.

Stan kneels. He looks at Randy, and a coughing, choking noise that might be something like a sob bursts from him. "Randy," he whispers.

A second too late, an eternity too late, I realize what is happening, but by then Stan has driven the knife deep into Randy's side, angling up under the ribs.

"Jesus CHRIST!" Randy screams. He spasms wildly, and I can't keep the compress on him. Blood jets over me.

Randy bucks free, and he unsteadily gets to his hands and knees and tries to crawl away from us. He wobbles, and except for the blood raining down into the water, would appear drunk.

"Christ! Oh God! Ah God!"

Who'd have thought he had this much fight in him?

Stan gives the knife to Doug.

"Yes," says Rebecca.

Doug stumbles over to Randy. I do not stop him. Stan does not stop him. I'm not sure I could. Doug retches, steels himself, and his scream uncannily matches Randy's when he drives the blade into his back. Randy collapses into the water, his feet kicking without rhythm, his right hand clutching with idiot strength on a broken shard of glass from a long shattered beer bottle. The knife protrudes from Randy's back like some bizarre mutation.

Doug falls against the tunnel wall, sobbing.

Randy, incredibly, rises from the water. He crawls, again, for the light. He is crying for his mother. He begs for his mother to come get him. He wants his mother to make the hurt go away.

"I can't," I say.

Rebecca smiles at me. "You must."

"No, no, please."

"I will never leave you," whispers Rebecca, "and his pain must end."

Pain? Christ almighty, *agony*.

I'm scarcely breathing as I step around Stan, who is on his knees, weeping silently. Oh, we're all damned here. I close my eyes, I cannot believe what I am about to do to one of my friends.

"Stop this," I whisper. I open my eyes, catch hers.

"I want to live," she tells me. "I want to live in the light."

We stare at each other as Randy's shrieking dies down to a wet choking sound.

"Now you," she says, gently. I stare into her gray eyes. She is not unkind. There is pain in their frozen beauty. There is love there, desire. I understand that she was not making empty promises. She will not leave. She will be with me always. I will not lack for love. Ever. What will a person not do for love? Nations have been razed for it. Innocents die in the name of it. Love is an extreme before which no other can stand.

Randy is choking, gagging. I should end his pain. His agony. No one should go through this.

I pull the knife from Randy's back. It is warm and slick. A faint vibration comes off of it, or maybe I'm imagining that. The radio is still on outside. It's playing Al Stewart's "Year of the Cat." The piano work is beautiful. Randy's eyes are wide, but moving. He has rolled onto his back. Blood has painted his face, a pink froth bubbles at his lips. He is moaning the same word over and over. *Mama*. Blood is spattered over his blond hair in patterns that hold no meaning. He is a twelve-year-old boy. The death of a twelve-year-old boy is stupid and meaningless.

I am a twelve-year-old boy.

I do not stab Randy.

I pull the blade's edge across his throat.

I put my back into it. I strain and grunt. And hot, bright, wet blood sprays me weakly. There are already too many leaks for any real pressure. Randy's eyes stop moving, fix on a spot, and the only noise now is a soft gurgling from the unnatural mouth in his neck, a wet hiss like spilled cola.

Rebecca moves me aside and places her face in the maw. For only a moment. When she stands again, and turns, her face is clean. And Randy is dead.

I drop the knife. It splashes and clatters at my feet. I do not speak. What is there to say now? Rebecca smiles, opens her arm to me as for an embrace, and something in me stirs, but it is not, I think, what she expects. I am overcome with horror and repugnance. At myself, at her, at all of us. Randy died so we could get laid? This monstrosity is more than I can bear. Numb, I step back from her, shaking my head.

"I can't."

Whatever magic we have brought into play today, whatever unnatural power we have tapped into, is fading. I feel it. So does Doug, so does Stan. What we have just done is the slap of icy water against our faces, the waking of moral dread in the presence of conscience. I, Eric Lynch, have just taken a human life. I am a murderer. It is a fact so huge that I cannot think around it. So I run.

I run.

I turn and stumble from the muck, stagger out into the pool of muddy water underneath the rope swing. The water is not clean; it will serve as no baptism. I wade out to the deepest part, making no sound, knowing only that I have to get away. I climb up the bank, soaked from my chest down, scramble up to higher ground. I trample the wild rose bush I'd seen earlier, thorns biting into my hands. This is almost beyond my notice in my wild flight; away, I have to get away, from her, from the deed I have just done. I race through the copse of trees and the high grass and weeds, run out into the asphalt behind the Texaco station, barely slowing down when I hit the wall. I collapse against it, slide down to a sitting position, and sit, blinking stupidly in the hot summer sun.

After a while, I wonder what I'm doing here.

After a while, I wonder why I'm sweating and breathing hard, why there's sweat on me, why there's blood on my hands and arms. I panic and see if I'm cut anywhere, but nothing hurts. While I'm checking myself over, Stan comes out of the trees, carrying his radio, Rainbow's "Street of Dreams" belting out, and I raise a hand in greeting to him.

"Hey," I tell him. "What're you doin' here? I didn't see you down there."

He shakes his head. "I just got here. I was looking to see if any of you guys were hangin' out. I didn't see you though. I thought I heard Doug. But I couldn't find him. Man, you're a mess. You got clay all over you."

"Yeah," I say, "I thought it was blood or something. I better get home and change 'fore my mom sees all this, or she'll have a cow."

"I'll go with you. Lemme get my bike."

Stan gets his bike, and we walk over to my house, which is not too far away. It is a bright summer day, and the cicadas are buzzing in their amber shells and the birds are singing.

I LOOKED AT DOUG. "You remember any of it, Doug? The tunnel, Stan's knife, each of us takin' a turn? You remember any of that?"

"It wasn't real."

"Oh yeah, I think it was."

"It was an accident," said Rebecca, "and there is not a thing you can do about it now. It was horrible. It was a tragedy. But it was an accident. I would never hurt any of you. I love you all."

"See, Doug, I told you so. This is a genuine USDA certified clusterfuck."

"Shut up, Eric."

"Shuttin' up," I said, and I left them all to go into the kitchen. I knew that bottle of Ketel One that Doug had been sampling from earlier was in here somewhere. I passed the cold, uneaten pizza. Yummy. Where the hell was that bottle? I found it on the counter behind a confusion of empty beer cans. Two-thirds full. Good. Time to drown. This is Eric, going under. Don't bother signaling the *Carpathia*.

"I am going away now," I told everyone. "You may do as you wish. I don't give a tin shit. Just leave me alone."

I went outside, found a nice dark, quiet spot. And began drinking. If I had my way, I wasn't ever going to stop. Maybe, maybe this time I would forget again. Hell, maybe I'd die, maybe that would be the ultimate forgetting.

I don't know how long I sat out there. At some point, some numb, destroyed point, the bottle became empty, and I tossed it aside. The act of doing so caused me to empty the contents of my stomach violently, and my guess is that maybe this saved me from alcohol poisoning. In typical fashion, I couldn't even successfully kill myself. It was damned cold though. I hugged my knees and rocked back and forth on the ground. With luck, hypothermia might get me yet. I was probably thinking of this when I blacked out. Probably.

But I got back inside. She helped me. Take from that what you will. She needed me alive.

Whatever dreams, whatever nightmares I had, they remained hidden to me.

PART THREE:
TERMINAL FROST

A DOOR SLAMMED.

Severe pounding in my head discouraged me from opening my eyes to see what was going on. I did move slightly, and this proved to be such a disastrous idea that I decided to take up a new vocation: mannequin.

Another slam of a door, a cabinet or a drawer.

I slid my head under a pillow, groaning softly.

Something somewhere rattled and fell onto the floor with loud tinny racket. Beer cans, from the sound of it.

I huddled down farther. I would have burrowed into the bed itself, had I been able. I would have become one with it. Hangover metaphysics. What is the sound of not getting up for anything? If Eric does not get up, and no one is around to see him not getting up, does he make a sound?

A woman's voice yelled, very loudly, "Shit!"

I was *up*.

A moment or two passed before I was able to orient myself. The previous night's hellish festivities swarmed in on me in their full detail, and I moaned again. And moaning, let me tell you, really hurt. Plus I could smell my own breath, which would have gagged a corpse. It felt like smog, and the inside of my mouth was lined with pond scum. My eyes refused to focus properly, out of sheer spite. Nothing was functioning according to design.

And Sam was home.

"Look at this goddamn mess!"

"Oh fuck," I mumbled. My jaws ached for some arcane reason. The inside of my skull felt like someone had scrubbed the reverse side of my cranium with steel wool and then replaced my brain with soggy, pulped newspaper.

The idea of standing was starting to occur to me. My body, alarmed by this, took a vote, and was tallying the results when the bedroom door flew open and in rushed Sam, eyes slitted in anger, mouth clenched so hard her lips were white, and—I'm not making this up—angry orange licks of flame shooting out of her nostrils. She halted and glared at me, chest heaving in and out, raising her fists as if to batter me more senseless. I scrambled to my feet. I became acutely aware of my own mortality. Sam had experienced a total psychotic breakdown and was about to peel the flesh from my living body.

Inexplicably, she paused just as she was about to launch the Rant That Would Destroy Worlds, her eyes widened, and she burst out laughing.

I only stood there. "Uh . . ."

She laughed and pointed at me. She laughed so hard she staggered back against the doorframe and almost slid to the floor. Say this for her, she knew how to shore up a guy's sagging ego.

"Christ," I rasped. "Keep it down, will ya? And what's so funny?"

"The way your mother dresses you, that's what."

I glanced down. I had managed to get my Levi's on backwards some time the night before.

I looked back at her with what I am sure was haggard stupidity.

This provoked a fresh round of giggles. She clapped a hand over her mouth and clutched her stomach with the other. I admit I did not see the humor in it.

Doug shambled up behind her, and he looked like something out of a George Romero flick. Not one of the good guys either. At least he had all his clothes on right, although his glasses were slightly askew.

"Uh, Sam," he said, with the proper note of contrition in his voice. "You're home early."

Sam stood again, her laughter subsiding. She wiped away a tear that had dripped out of one eye. "Yes I am. And you are dead meat." She socked him in the arm to punctuate this.

Doug winced and protested, "You said—"

"That you could use my place for a night. I did not, and I remember this very well, O Brother of Mine, I did *not* give you permission to hold a demolition derby, nor did I suggest that you detonate explosives. What the hell did you guys do? And what slobs drank up my bottle of vodka?"

I raised one hand, quietly. It was not easy.

Sam blinked at me. "The whole bottle?"

"Um," I said, quietly, "largely."

"What'd you want to do, Lynch, kill yourself? A whole *bottle*?"

I nodded, slowly and (you see a pattern here) quietly.

"Could I go someplace less noisy, please?"

A cold front had moved in sometime the night before. I hugged my arms around me to keep myself warm. The cold air helped me regain myself a bit, and I thought for a moment about my decision last night to sleep outside. I really *would* have killed myself, and that realization chilled me far more than the early winter air. Worse: I deserved it.

My watch said that it was ten-thirty. I had missed church, and would pay hell for it, but that seemed a small thing now. I was not the same person I had been the day before. Memory had recast me. I was a murderer. I rolled the word around on my mental tongue. It tasted awful.

My legs took me down behind the apartment building, down to the pond. The slightest puff of breeze was stirring, and the cold air whispered through the branches, nudged the dead leaves on the ground. Two weeks before Halloween, and the icy heart of winter not far behind that. I looked up at the trees, with the mix of green and dead leaves. Crooked as the branches were, they looked like gnarled hands pleading to heaven for life.

Randy had begged for life.

I swallowed and closed my eyes. How could such an event have hidden in my mind all these years, without betraying any sort of clue to its existence? Was it one of those repressed memory things someone had been blabbing about on Geraldo? I didn't know. Maybe it was nothing more than an elaborate hallucination.

Who was I kidding? I knew better.

My head ached horribly, and my stomach was acting as though it had grown to like vomiting, so I sat on a log and watched the water. Flat grayness, like cotton dipped in used paint thinner, obscured the sun and made the pond a lifeless gray-green color. I still liked to watch it, watch the tiny waves made by the breeze, the ripples caused by the pebbles I lazily tossed in.

I heard the footsteps behind me, and assumed it would be Doug, probably coming to rip my ass about Rebecca.

"Hey, you lush, mind a little company?"

As if I would ever turn down her company. I patted the log next to me and Sam lowered herself down.

"What's the idea of downing a whole bottle of vodka, pilgrim?"

"Doug had some of it."

"Much?"

I shrugged.

She looked out over the water. "What's eating you?"

"Nothing."

"Yeah right. Do you know just how much booze you put away last night? You know what alcohol poisoning is?"

"Yeah, I know what it is."

"A person who's fine doesn't do that. A person who has their shit together doesn't do that. C'mon, Eric, what's up? Talk to me."

"I don't know."

"Okay, if you're going to be an asshole—" she began, rising.

"No! Please!"

She looked at me, with those whip-smart blue eyes that I never did feel worthy of. We were both quiet for a minute.

"Doug made a mess with the crackers, huh?" I said.

She laughed, a little. "Yeah. But you're ducking, Lynch."

I nodded and looked away from her. I could feel her staring at me. I wanted to tell her everything; I wanted her to be my confessor. But the truth was that I didn't know exactly what was happening, and I was scared that I might be crazy, that Sam might think I was. What could I tell her that wouldn't sound completely insane? And what if it was true, that I'd helped kill someone? What would she want with me then?

The prospect of not having Sam around scared the shit out of me. It wasn't love, I knew that, but it would serve in a pinch.

"I just . . . Sam, I can't grab the right words."

She sighed. "Okay, you don't want to talk about it, we don't talk about it. You decide otherwise, I'll listen, okay?"

I nodded. Fair enough. "When I can, I will, I promise. I mean that. And no more booze either. I'm really not trying to kill myself. There's just something I have to work out."

"So long as it's not something involving dogs and Valvoline, that I don't want to hear about."

"So where'd you go last night?" Like it was any of my business.

Sam smirked at me. "What's it to you?"

"Not a thing." Did I squeak when I spoke? I assure you I did.

She nodded and absently picked up a long twig from the ground before her. Her hands worked the stick over and over. Almost a minute passed, and she didn't speak or look at me. I didn't mind. I was in no hurry for anything this morning, and every minute I spent out here with her was a minute away from the hell the rest of life was rapidly becoming.

At last she gave a little sigh that trailed off into a brief chuckle. "I guess you know that there's this guy I've been seeing for the last six months or so."

"Yeah." The guy in the picture on her dresser. Adam. "Doug pointed him out to me on a post office wall."

"Well, he talked me into having dinner with his family in Dallas last night."

"Ooh," I said, "Sam-I-am, are those wedding bells I hear in yon distance?"

"No. You've gone psychic, and you're hearing the sound that's fixing to be in your head when I clock you. Will you for the love of the sweet feathery Jesus shut up for at least the briefest of moments? Is that possible?"

I mimed zipping my lip.

"Adam wanted me to meet his family because . . ."

I hoped she didn't hear me gulp. Her grin said she had.

"He was going to propose."

I held fast to her use of past tense.

"We . . . weren't on the same page there. This girl isn't ready for that just yet. And not with him."

"He's a studmuffin."

Sam's eyes narrowed. "How do you know?

Shit.

"Were you in my room, Lynch? You *were*, you little creep!"

"I took a wrong turn."

"I'm about to make your head take a wrong turn."

"Would it help if I said I'm sorry? And that I really mean it?"

She sighed. "It'll do, I guess."

"So you said no?"

Now her look was pure evil. "Wouldn't you like to know?"

I sighed, threw my hands up in surrender. "*Que sera sera*, right? I'll read it in the papers, I guess."

"I said no. Just friends. That's all."

"Sam-I-Am, no guy on Earth wants to be 'just friends.' That phrase is poison."

"So is that attitude."

I nodded. Probably she was right. And all men are brothers in a world that is filled with peace and light. Sure thing. "Well, did you at least get to see the ring?"

"The ring?"

"The guy was gonna propose, did you at least get to see the ring?"

She shook her head as if clearing it. Her smile returned, crooked and sardonic. "No, dammit, I surely did not. Needed you there to remind me, I guess."

"I'm there, I usually make people think of hiding the snacks."

She shook her head. "So how did you guys manage to so *thoroughly* trash my apartment?"

"Dumb luck, I guess. Sorry about the mirror."

She sighed. "Sorry, my ass. You know how much my apartment manager's going to charge to get that fixed?"

"No. But I'll pay for it."

"Did you break it?"

"No. But I'll pay for it." And I let my tone tell her I was not going to argue with her on this one.

"Okay. Suit yourself. What happened with it, though?"

"Stan slipped on some water and put his hand through it. What a klutz."

"Cut himself?"

"Looked worse than it was. I mean, it was kind of like mine, bled everywhere, but it really wasn't that bad."

Which was bullshit, of course. It had been that bad, and mine had been, too.

"At least he cleaned it up," Sam said, and she was looking out at the sky, so she missed my worried expression. I knew that Stan had cleaned nothing up. He had been in no better shape than I, and after the events of the night before, cleaning up that mess would have been the last thing on anyone's minds.

"Speaking of cleaning up," Sam said, rising from the log, "I think you better get in there and pitch in."

She offered her hand to help me up. "And Lynch?"

"Yeah?"

She touched the tip of my nose with her finger, and her face was still and serious, her blue eyes wide and piercing.

"The next time you feel like you need to down a bottle of booze, call me first. Okay? I mean it. You really and truly could have killed yourself, and the last thing I need is to lose you that way. Promise me that, will you?"

I tried to make some stupid wisecrack, and couldn't. All I could say was, "Okay. I promise. No more. I'm done."

"Now get your ass up there and clean up my home."

DOUG WAS RUNNING THE vacuum, and the expression on his face suggested that he was going through a most unorthodox brain surgery at the same time. Like with maybe a Waring blender. I could certainly sympathize. The screaming noise that Sam's old Hoover made was like a Greek chorus of demented banshees in my tiny little skull. I walked past him with a hand waved in greeting, to find Stan in the bathroom, sweeping up the last fragments of the broken mirror. His hands looked fine. This did not surprise me.

"Hey," I said.

"Oh, hey, man. Somebody fucked up this mirror big time, man. Doug's sister was pissed. I mean big-time pissed."

"It's cool now. I took care of it. How you feelin' this mornin'?"

Stan gave me a grimacing smile. "Like I been skullfucked with a bowling ball. How do you think I feel? Shit, you drank more than I did."

I wondered how much Stan remembered. "What about the Swing?"

His expression was baffled. "What about it?"

"Nothing." Jesus, Stan didn't remember a thing.

"Oh. Well. When you gonna pitch in, *kemo sabe*?"

I sighed. "Right now."

Sam came up behind me. "What kind of donuts you guys like? I'm heading up to Winchell's."

The thought of eating anything made my guts churn ominously. Stan, however, said "Glazed chocolate, please."

I faced Sam, digging in my pocket for some cash. Only then did I remember that my jeans had been on backward the whole morning. I grinned sheepishly.

"Forget it," Sam said. "And stop thinking you can bribe your way out of the doghouse, Lynch."

"Sorry, ma'am."

She gave me a sour look before leaving to get breakfast.

"What's up with that?" asked Stan.

"Livingston," I told him, "that is absolutely none of your business."

Doug had finished vacuuming and I found him in the kitchen standing before a sink filled with sudsy water. He wasn't washing anything, though. It seemed to me that he was only staring at it with obvious melancholy.

"Hey," I said.

He looked over at me, and his air of sadness turned bitter. He breathed hard but said nothing.

Given that Stan didn't remember anything, who knew what might be swimming around in Doug's mind. I apparently had forgotten nothing. (Of course, how would I know if I had?) This was probably not the time to go probing around.

But I had to know.

"Okay, what's up?" I spoke more loudly than I had intended and it hurt my head.

His lips clenched. He said nothing.

Okay, safe to assume he knew about me and Rebecca that one time. Oh boy. Like I had even *wanted* that. Well, I hadn't. Much. And I really unwanted it now.

"Talk to me, man!"

Doug stared at me with raw, naked hatred.

I stepped toward him.

"Don't you fucking come near me." Mostly I got that from reading his lips; I could barely hear his whispered warning. I held out a hand in entreaty and it trembled. Doug was my main man, my bud since graham crackers and milk in kindergarten. He was the one who told me all the weird, cool stuff in the world. He was the one who made me read *Catch-22*, which had maybe saved my life. He was the one accepted me as the fat dork I was. Naturally we had disagreed in the past, even had a fight or two, but nothing like this. Nothing like this meltdown. I truly am not exaggerating the sheer rage in Doug's face. He wanted to kill me in that moment. That much was clear. And if the nightmare from the night before was at all true, he was capable of it. We all were.

So what was I to say in the face of this?

"Doug, I'm sorry." Oh yeah, that was going to get it.

He said, "You fucked her."

I could not deny it. Forget that she started it. Forget that it was the last thing I wanted now, that it made me feel dirty and untouchable. Yes. We had screwed.

Stan stepped into the kitchenette and stared at us.

"How could you do that to me?" Anguish warped his face. *"How?"*

"I didn't," I said. His frank disbelief unhinged me. "I didn't do anything to *you*. I didn't even have a *choice* in it. She raped me, Doug, and she's raped all of us. Still doing it. Might as well wake up to that, man. You might as well remember what happened at the Swing."

"I don't know what the hell you're talking about. Leave. Right now. Just go. Don't talk to me again."

"Hey . . ." said Stan.

"What, are you screwing her behind my back, too? Is that it? Well, fuck you, too. Fuck all of you."

I glanced at Stan, and from the paleness of his face, my guess is that, yes, he and Rebecca had done the nasty. Well, good Christ, who *hadn't*?

"Doug," I said, "will you listen to yourself? You sound so paranoid. We're your friends, man."

"If you don't leave I'll beat the shit out of you."

I froze. "Okay. I'm gone."

Stan stopped me at the door. "Eric, man, what's happening here?"

I glanced back at Doug. His hands were balled into fists at his sides. "Call me, we'll talk. Or ask Rebecca. Tell Sam I'll call her tonight."

I left before I began crying. He didn't have the right to my tears, dammit.

I SHOULD HAVE GONE home. I was hungover, frazzled, slipping gears. The prudent thing to do would have been to get my ass home as quickly as possible. Promptness might lessen the severity of any punishment headed my way. And even if I wasn't in hot water I was certainly in need of it: a good steaming shower would help my world view immeasurably, not to mention getting rid of the stale stench of vomit and sweat. Food usually helped too, but I was still queasy enough from the excesses of the night before that eating might well be out of the question for today.

So, I should have gone home immediately. I didn't.

Instead, I drove down from Edmond and cruised the nearly endless backstreets of northwest Oklahoma City, through numerous suburban wet dream houses. Trim lawns starting to yellow with the imminent onset of early winter, two-car garages with big Ford and Dodge pickups or Chevrolet or Chrysler gas-guzzling family cars obediently heeled before them. Smoke curled from the chimneys, a thick Sunday Oklahoman newspaper lay neatly before each front porch. Mostly tidy brick homes, low slung ranch style houses, a bicycle lying in a yard here, a basketball there. A world of middle-class comfort, and it seemed so cold and remote to me as I wandered through it all that I wanted to stop the car and scream. I knew someday I would be forced into that world, as relentlessly as a caterpillar is driven towards brief colorful flight. Did the butterfly ever look back and wonder how it got there?

Then I was crossing MacArthur Avenue, heading southwest, and I realized where I'd been going all along. Just taking the scenic route, was all.

Mick lived over near Bethany. It was not the richest of areas, to be diplomatic. Mick lived with his father in a little post-World War II tract house that was far removed from the suburban splendor I'd been in only a few minutes before. This neighborhood had seen better days, mostly around 1955. Now the driveways were full of old, abused Ford pickups and trashy, worn-out sportscars, old Trans Ams and Camaros. Also, one saw the occasional Patton tank masquerading as mid-seventies Pontiac or Buick. On many lawns, if there were toys abandoned outside you couldn't see them for the unmowed grass, the tall clumps of dead weeds. This was even more depressing than what I'd seen earlier. All of these houses were cracker boxes with siding, and many of them were about a decade past the need to be put out of their misery.

I'd only been to Mick's house twice before, and was unsure if I could find it now. I went down several streets, staring at damn near every house, trying to remember if that was the one. No doubt some paranoid old fart was on the line to Bethany PD reporting my suspicious behavior.

Finally, I saw his Camaro. It was parked in front of a house smaller than many garages I'd seen. I pulled up in front of it, and noticed that at least the Cornwells tried to stand out, to distinguish themselves from the rest of the pack. Their lawn, instead of being overgrown, had more bald patches than a cancer patient undergoing radiation therapy.

I parked behind Mick's car, shut off the engine and very seriously considered what I was doing there. As I thought about it, I felt at first that I was there to show Mick that he was still my friend, despite what Rebecca had said. I had never before known anyone who was gay, and now that I did, I found that it did not much matter. This was something of a surprise to me. The worldview of my parents included the notion that homosexuality was the biggest abomination there was, short of murder, although if you murdered a queer, who knew? But it just didn't matter to me. Mick had always been cool. He was cool now, as far as I was concerned, and this sort of explained why he had a lot of first dates but not a ton of follow-ups. But hating him because he was gay? It made no more sense to me than disliking someone for the color of his or her skin, or the fact that he or she chose to eat peanut butter and banana sandwiches.

Well, actually, I questioned the sanity of anyone who ate those things.

So I sat there and began to get a warm fuzzy for myself: here I was, Eric Lynch, the ambassador of decency, Doing a Good Thing, reassuring a friend that his "alternative lifestyle" was fine by me. I was going to be a righteous man and proclaim that everything was okay. Was going to be above it all.

But that was bullshit.

I was there because Mick was the only one who could tell me if I was losing my mind or not.

"Fuck this," I muttered, and got out of the Bomb, slammed the door shut, and strolled up the sidewalk to the unpainted and weathered front door. I pushed the doorbell but heard nothing from inside. So I knocked. No answer. I knocked again. I waited. No answer. No sounds within. I raised my hand to knock again as the door flew open. My hand held in the air, suspended mid-knock.

I only vaguely remembered the potbellied wretch before me, since I'd only been here twice before. I had some doubt that this ogre could even be related to Mick, much less be his father. The first thing I noticed about him that morning were the enormous sweat stains under the armpits of his less than pristine T-shirt. Hygiene clearly was not a priority for the senior Cornwell—a short man with a firm beer gut, as though he was deep into the third trimester of a terrible pregnancy. His face was shot through with broken capillaries, and

I could smell the rich fruity fumes of Jim Beam tainting his breath.

The bloodshot stare he bestowed on me was not kind.

"Um, is Mick home?" Right, like this was a home.

Mick's father scowled at me. The only thing missing from his B-movie bad guy, wino boss caricature was a stub of a cigar protruding from his mouth. And I bet there was at least one in the house. I did my best to appear contrite for disturbing Mr. Cornwell's early morning tranquility; it looked to me like he was nursing a brain-sucker of a hangover. I knew how he felt. We were all brothers under the skin.

"Yeah," he mumbled. "C'min."

I followed him into the house, wincing as he broke wind.

"Mick!" he bellowed, contorting my skull. Monasteries were invented for hangovers.

I heard Mick from back in his room, voice muffled by the closed door, "What?"

"One o' y' friends is here."

A pause. "Fine."

Mr. Cornwell looked over his shoulder at me. "Make y'self at home." He left for where I think the bathroom was. The haze of vapors he left behind made my head ache even more savagely.

I sat on a saggy old brown and orange couch and let my gaze wander over the living room while I waited for Mick. My eyes were drawn to the carpet in particular. It was a thick shag that might once have been some demented emerald color but now was more the shade of decomposing limes. It was impressively ugly. It was the sort of carpet that made you respect anyone who could live with it on a daily basis. I gleaned new insights into Mick's character. The paneling was no great shakes either, and was made appreciably worse by the fact that the two windowless walls were largely bare. Two walls of empty ugly. Shit brown paneling, rotten fruit carpeting. This was one of the most depressing rooms I'd ever seen. There was, for a touch of decorating class, a Coors clock next to one window. It was the kind that hang in liquor store windows, with the airbrushed mountains behind the clock hands. The clock was slow. Then also, there was the TV, directly opposite the only other furnishing in the room aside from the couch, a patched-up Naugahyde recliner. Although the rest of the furniture bore a late seventies thrift store feel to it, the TV was a nice new Sony. It fairly sparkled. Amazing.

Mick came out of his room, interrupting my *Southern Living* critique of the Cornwell abode. "Hey," he said.

"Hey."

"What's up? Hardly ever see you here."

"Thought you might want to talk, after that horror show last night."

He shrugged. He reached for a cigarette, but was halted by a wet, nasty coughing fit. He paused, examined the back of his hand, the wiped it clean on the black jeans he wore.

"Jesus," he said. "Maybe I ought to cut these things out." He lit up the cigarette anyway. "Let's go outside," he said.

I followed him out. We stood in the bitter air, my breath trailing off and mingling with the smoke from Mick's Marlboro. He wore his snakeskin boots and black Levi's and a shirt that I knew was far too thin for this cold. I wasn't exactly dressed for it either; someday I would learn to check weather forecasts like a normal human being.

"Okay, Eric, what do you want?"

The edge of antagonism in his voice startled me. "What do you mean?"

"You come over to rub my face in it a little, maybe? Or maybe I borrowed something off you once I forgot about and now you want it back?"

"That's a load of horseshit."

He glared at me and took a long drag on his cigarette. A moment went by, and then he arrived at some kind of decision. "Okay. It's horseshit. So why are you over here, anyway?"

"What did you see last night?"

"I was drunk."

"That ain't what I asked."

"Fuck off, I know that." He stomped his boots against the cold, threw the half-smoked cigarette down and ground it out with a boot heel. He studied the cig the whole time he did it.

Finally he brought his gaze up to mine. "Yeah, I saw the kid. I got no idea what it means, but I saw him. I guess it meant something to y'all, huh? The way y'all freaked out?"

I sighed. Well, that was that. The question was settled. No more *Is it live or is it Memorex?* "Oh yeah, it means something, okay. It means we're in some deep shit. The rest of us, I mean, not you. It's got nothing to do with you."

"This is about Rebecca?"

I nodded.

"Then it's about me. You saw what she did to me. I could kill that bitch. . . . She's playin' you guys."

"Yeah, that's sort of sunk in now."

"To you, maybe. I bet Doug's acting like nothing happened. Stan, too."

"Well, Doug's got a pretty good idea I banged her in the not too distant past."

Mick looked at me with some disgust. "Jesus, you didn't!"

"It was a moment of weakness. What do you want from me? C'mon. I know what she's about now. I don't want it."

Mick nodded. "So what do you want?"

Sam. "I don't know."

"That'll make it hard to find."

"No doubt."

Mick had another protracted coughing fit. This time I saw flecks of blood on his fist.

"Shit, man, you okay?" He doubled over with the effort of hacking, and didn't look like he might be able to stand. He managed, though, reaching out against the wall of the house to steady himself. He feebly grinned up at me.

"Fuckin' bronchitis," he rasped.

Yeah, right.

He straightened, wiped his hand off, dug out another cigarette. Christ, he hadn't even finished the last one. "So what are you gonna do about her?"

I shrugged. What *was* there to be done about Rebecca? I didn't even know what she was. Christ, I was just some dipshit. What was I supposed to know about this kind of stuff? Enough to get myself into it, I suppose, and enough to drown in it after that. The prey only had to be clever enough to figure out the bait.

We shivered in silence for a minute or two. Finally, I said, "Mick, you won't take this personally or nothing, will you?"

His eyes narrowed at me. "Depends."

"Well, I mean, shit, I don't even know how to ask this, but, um, you never wanted to hit on me, did you? 'Cause, you know, I hate to be a heartbreaker an' all."

He stared at me for maybe a full minute, and I thought with a leaden feeling that he was indeed going to take it the wrong way, when his face broke into an enormous grin. "Eric, man, rest assured you are in no way my type."

"Oh," I said. Then, "Well, what is your type? I mean, you don't mind me asking."

"Joe Elliot."

"From Def Leppard Joe Elliot? That Joe Elliot?"

"Yep."

"Huh. Joe Elliot. Wow. Huh."

"You look like you just swallowed a bug."

I shrugged. "I'll get used to it. It's not a big deal. Just different is all."

"You're not telling me anything new."

We both tensed as Mick's father yelled something inside. Mick glared at the front door with undisguised hatred. Maybe now I had a better idea of why his old man laid into him so much, and why Mick worked so hard to get into shape. Maybe someday he'd smash the old fucker in the mouth. Maybe. Hope sustains us—I read that somewhere.

"Better go," he said.

"Yeah. Listen. I'll think of something about this Rebecca business."

He nodded as he opened the door. He smiled feebly as the house swallowed him.

I turned away, toward the car, knowing what his smile had suggested: I wasn't going to think of any kind of solution at all to the problem of Rebecca. What was there to do, anyway? Give her the bum rush? Call the cops? Tell our parents?

Kill her?

I WAS DRIVING DOWN 39th street when a voice behind me said, "Coelacanths."

After I pulled the Bomb back into the correct lane of traffic, after I forced my heart to stop doing a Mick Mars drum solo against my ribcage, after I was able to coax my lungs into accepting air again, I glanced in the rearview and saw Randy staring at me.

"What the hell was that all about? You almost gave me a coronary! Don't do that shit! Jesus!" I paused for breath. "No offense, but I'm not ready to try out your condition yet."

"Good. It sucks. The hereafter doesn't live up to its press. Just drive, I'll talk. I suppose you remember last night pretty well, huh? I mean, you can see me this morning, so you must."

"Huh?"

"You're dense, Eric. Every time you've seen me until now, you've been drunk, or at least getting there."

I thought about it, let's see, there was The Wall, Sam's apartment, the party . . . he was right.

"Yeah, well, it's enough make me find an AA meeting."

"What?"

We stopped at a light. I wondered if people thought I was talking to myself. What the hell, it was a crazy world, wasn't it?

"Never mind. So I never saw you unless I was drunk—what's that mean?"

"I don't know. Maybe just that your brain wasn't working as well, maybe you were closer to remembering what happened at the Swing. I think you would have remembered it on your own eventually. You or Stan. But I think eventually would have been too late, so I forced the issue last night."

I found a commercial park oxymoronically named Perimeter Center and pulled into the empty employee parking area. No way was I going continue this conversation while driving. I shut the engine off and turned to face Randy.

"Why don't you sit up front? This is gonna kill my back."

Before I could blink, he appeared in the front seat.

"Better?"

"Uh, yeah. Jesus, that's weird."

Randy shrugged.

"So, um, you made us remember all that last night?"

"It wasn't hard. You were all pretty tanked. I'd have hoped for it to stick a little better than it did."

There was no problem with that on my account. I could not forget one moment of that horrible day at the Swing. I could still hear Randy wailing for his mother, blood choking his voice, I could still see him crawling through the muck, his hand making a fist around a shard of glass. I did not think any of this would ever leave me.

But it had once, hadn't it?

"So I'm the only one who remembers it?"

Randy looked thoughtful. "Sort of. Stan thinks it was a dream. I can't reach him except through his dreams, and that won't be enough. Doug I can't get to at all." Randy turned a most serious expression on me. "I'm very worried about Doug."

"That would make three of us then."

Randy said nothing.

"Let me ask you something. What's in this for you? Why are you running around trying to save us from ourselves?"

"You were my friends."

I snorted bitterly. "We killed you, unless I'm mistaken."

"Don't you ever say that again! Listen to me, Eric. Listen *good*. You guys did not kill me. *She* killed me. Maybe she didn't mean to do it at first. Probably she didn't mean to do it. But blood and semen are powerful hooks separately. Together they're incredible. And she wanted a hook worse than anything."

"A hook."

"Yeah. She is a heavy creature, and cannot rise to the surface on her own. Think vampires and succubi. Think coelacanth."

"Think what?"

"Coelacanth. It's a fish. For a long time, they were thought to be extinct. They were found only in the fossil record, ranging anywhere from 60 to 350 million years ago. Fossils. Dinosaurs, essentially, and thought to be just as gone.

"Three days before Christmas, in 1938, a fishing trawler pulled into a port in South Africa, with an ugly blue fish that weighed over a hundred pounds. A coelacanth. Caught live. A creature thought gone for millions of years. My point is, the world, the universe, hell, reality is like a big deep ocean, and there are some things swimming in it that haven't seen the surface for a long, long time."

"And that's Rebecca."

"The thing that calls itself that, yes."

I thought of her, of her body in all its softness and sorrow, and how even though I despised her, I ached for her, and could not bring myself to think of her as an it. No matter how much I might come to hate her, some small part of me had always been and always would be hers. The best I would be able to hope for would be to make that part as small as I could.

"So how'd she get here?"

Randy smiled, although it was more full of sadness than mirth. "We were like a big giant lure, man, all shiny and bright. Desire can be a beacon. And it just swam up out of that starless depth and took the hook."

"Why'd she kill you?"

"I don't think it was going to do that at first. Semen might have been a strong enough hook on its own. It's a precious fluid, and often enough it'll do the job. Pain works, lust works better, because lust always *calls*. But then I freaked and fell on the knife, and the blood was more than it could pass up. And by having you guys finish me, it linked my blood and death with everything and made the tie holding it here almost unbreakable. Believe me, you guys had little say in what you did."

"Little say." Not "no say." Meaning maybe at some level we wanted to do whatever it took to keep our Dream Girl around. Maybe we were willing to pay just about any price for ownership of her. Or to be owned by her.

"And then she went away for over four years," I mused, "and we forgot the whole thing."

"Maybe it was a kind of hibernation," said Randy, and for a moment the incongruity of what appeared to be a boy of twelve educating me on the nuts and bolts of the supernatural realm struck me. It was a surreal second, one of those pauses where a part of me stepped outside of myself to assess my grip on reality.

"Or maybe," he continued, "it was a sort of acclimation, the way a diver has to come up in stages to avoid the bends. Who knows? It's back, though, and we need to figure out what we're going to do about it."

I sighed, rubbed my numb face with hands that felt like cold cuts of meat. "Who says we have to do anything?"

Randy stared at me as if I were crazy.

"Look," I told him, jabbing the dashboard for emphasis, "she's not my problem anymore. I don't want her. The spell's broken, far as I'm concerned. I've got my own problems, I got something really good going with someone else now, and I'm trying to work through that, I got troubles at school, and my best friend ain't talkin' to me anymore. If Doug wants to keep makin' googlie-eyes at Rebecca, there isn't a lot I can do about it. I don't care. What's the problem, anyway?"

Randy let his gaze wander out over the empty parking lot. It was after eleven o'clock now, a crisp, cold day, the wind picking up steam. Dead leaves and light debris scuttled across the parking lot, fleeing on the wind.

"Okay," he said quietly, "but keep this in mind. You can walk away, great, but this thing will destroy any competition for its . . . affection. It's hooked, but it wants to stay, and you guys are what keeps it here. Rebecca. She'll do anything in her considerable power to stay. And can you blame her? It? Because coming up out of that dark void was like being born, and this is the joy of being alive, and just like every other living thing, it will do everything it must to keep living."

"Bullshit."

"Bullshit what? She won't do it, or she can't do it? Either way you're wrong, Eric. Listen, after I died, she wiped every trace of my existence away. My own parents have no idea they ever had a son named Randy. I'm sure they have nightmares once in a while, I'm sure that incomprehensible snatches of memory dart through their minds every so often, but, effectively, I did not exist. Check it out. No birth certificate, no social security number, no doctor who remembers birthing me, no teacher who remembers an essay I wrote, no girl who can still feel a stolen kiss. Maybe there are little scraps here and there, a yearbook I signed or a lost receipt for something I bought or maybe I'm in the background of some stranger's snapshot. That's it. Consider what it might have taken to do that. Think about it. She could do that to just about anyone. It would be an enormous effort on her part, but she could do it. And she will. Sooner or later, she'll have to, because sooner or later her mere presence is gonna remind you guys of what happened, and it'll all unravel."

I stared at him. "I don't think so. It's a good scare story, but I don't think so."

Randy looked stricken. "I hope you don't mean that, Eric. If the three of you get together, you can get rid of her. It won't be a piece of cake to do so, but it can be done. You can cut the line that ties her here. If you just walk away from this, you're only making it worse. You bought it, you own it. And if you don't do something about it, everything you love will be swallowed whole."

I closed my eyes and leaned against the steering wheel. I was tired. I was nobody's savior, nobody's knight errant. I only wanted a little sunshine, a little warmth, some respite from the black clouds. I didn't think that was too goddamn much to ask. And besides, if this morning was any indication, my friends didn't want any help.

I opened my eyes and my mouth to tell Randy this, but he was gone.

"Be that way," I said, starting up the engine. I sought a tape, shoved it in the stereo. It was the most recent Queensrÿche album, "Rage for Order."

Whatever. I relished the noise, even with my headache. I waited before shifting into gear, pausing as a cloud of dread settled over me, and then I turned the Bomb around and headed for home.

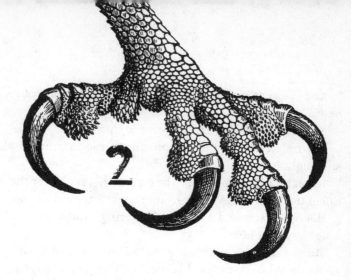

2

"YOU DIDN'T INVITE ME? You had a party and you didn't invite me? I'm wounded. Deeply. Truly."

Rebecca folded her arms and let a little smirk show to let all of us at the table know that, hey, she was only kidding. What little was left of my cafeteria meal immediately lost any appeal it might once have had. Doug and Stan were not affected. Stan shrugged and chowed on as usual. It was as though nothing had happened the other night, and I guess I was the fool for thinking otherwise. I had skipped my fourth-hour class to try to talk to these two, and it was going balls up thanks to Rebecca's arrival.

"Well," said Doug, stumbling over his own tongue a little, "we didn't think you'd be interested in watching the bunch of us make asses of ourselves."

"Yeah," agreed Stan. "Extremely large asses. I got *so* sick."

I had mentioned the party earlier. Neither of the two remembered a thing about the Swing, about Randy. I had not been able to find Mick, and I'd scoured Wood Wilson trying.

"What," said Rebecca, pulling a chair out to sit and join us, "you didn't think I would have enjoyed making an ass of myself, too? See if I invite any of you to a party. Ha."

Stan, sitting right next to her, looked as if someone had just handed him a dime bag of weed: he couldn't wait to try the stuff but he was scared shitless of being busted.

And Doug noticed it. His knuckles whitened as he gripped a fork, and I'm only guessing, but I think for a second there he wanted to stand up and jam it through Stan's throat.

Hello, I thought, *look where this shit's getting us. Before long, we'll* literally *be at each other's throats.*

And Rebecca was eating it up. I wondered which of us she was planning on fucking next.

"So was it fun?" She was asking me this.

I stared at her for a long moment, trying to think of all the myriad ways she might be meaning that.

"It was an experience not to be repeated," I said after the silence had become uncomfortable for everyone. "It brought back old memories."

Her eyes narrowed. She ran a fluttering hand down the front of her T-shirt; a sigh escaped her.

Stan said, "We sure made a fuckin' mess out of Doug's sister's place. Took about three hours to clean it all up. Not that we had any help from putsky there."

I turned to him. "I was asked to leave, so I did."

"Was someone angry at you?" asked Rebecca.

I looked back at Doug. "Oh, you could say that."

Rebecca smiled, completely absent of humor. "Perhaps that fence can be mended. Harsh words can be forgotten."

I returned her smile with the same chill. "What about harsh deeds?"

Stan said, "What are you two talking about? Everybody had a great time, we should do it again sometime."

I stood and gathered my tray. "Not me. I'm grounded until Armageddon. Guys, gotta go, talk to you later." If I didn't get out of there immediately, I was going to regret it.

No one seemed too upset at my leaving.

After class, I went straight to the restroom and lost lunch. Like some kind of bulimic. I was in one of the stalls whoopsing my cookies when Blake Hardesty, starting offensive lineman for the winless Wood Wilson football squad, stuck his head into the stall, down near mine, and said, "That looks pretty fuckin' gross, huh?"

Who was I to disagree?

STAN CAUGHT ME ON break that night at work.

"Hey man," he said, dropping into the chair across from mine. "What was up with lunch today?"

"I wasn't feeling very well."

He nodded, taking this in, and opened up the chocolate Yahoo he'd probably snagged off the shelf on his way to the break room. He put it down and picked up the crummy tin ashtray on the table.

"Yeah, you were acting kinda weird," he said.

"Something I ate."

"No doubt."

Something was up. Stan was far more fidgety than usual. He kept turning the ashtray over and over in his hands. His gaze held on the table, not looking up at me, so I knew something big was on his mind. There was nothing to do for it but wait him out. Sooner or later he'd blurt out whatever it was.

Sure enough, he finally said, "Listen, some guys asked me to join a band."

My first reaction was that whoever had asked him must have never heard him play. I mean, we sucked. I hadn't even touched my bass since . . .

Since Rebecca.

I knew what was making him nervous. We had talked for years of starting a group. Now I was being cut out of the picture, and he felt badly about it. Thing was, I found, to my surprise, that I didn't really care.

"Man, that's great! Anybody I know?"

I could see the tension drain right out of him. "Uh, well, sort of, yeah. You know Stacy Alciatore?"

"No."

"Um, well, he's a sophomore, he plays drums, he's got an awesome kit. He's got a friend from West who plays bass, and, uh, well, it turns out Rebecca can play piano and keyboards and stuff."

I had to be careful. I didn't want Stan to think I was hurt: I wasn't. Like I said, so someone else played bass in his band, big deal. But this bit about Rebecca being in it, it made me uneasy. She was in too many places, and I was not able to forget everything Randy had said about her.

"That's cool, man. You guys actually rehearsing or anything?"

"Just jams, you know. I got some ideas for some original songs. I don't know, we'll see."

Stan, writing originals? This was hard to believe.

My break was up; I told him I'd come by and hear them sometime. A heaviness persisted in my chest all the rest of that night. We were almost nothing more than acquaintances now, and it had happened in a matter of days. Or worse, it had been happening all along—we had been becoming strangers due to some hidden tectonic drift, and I just never knew it.

THE FIRST MONDAY IN October was an in-service day, meaning the teachers got to get together and talk shop and we got stay home. I had no complaint with this arrangement, particularly since my parents had no clue about it. Their ignorance, my bliss. I drove over to Denny's and picked at a breakfast and chugged a pot or two of coffee, reading the paper. I thought maybe it was the coffee, but I was even less hungry than I had been lately. I wondered about that, a little. I'd always been a real chowhound, but over the last month and a half, I'd been eating like a bird. This was not something to complain about, mind you. I was down under 180 for the first time in a million years, and even the newer clothes I'd bought a month ago were getting a little big on me.

So I asked myself when I'd starting losing all this weight.

Right around the time I'd met Rebecca, of course.

Which really killed my appetite.

After I paid up at Denny's, I went on a record crawl. Five hours, six record stores, and twenty bucks later, I decided I'd gotten my fix, and wondered how I was going to kill the rest of my day. Here it was only two o'clock and I had nothing else to do. Couldn't catch a flick; nothing was showing before five on a weekday. Didn't want to go home yet, since I was still in the doghouse and it would look suspicious if I showed up too soon.

So I drove up to Edmond. With nothing better to do, I thought I might see if Sam was through with her afternoon classes. I had meant to call her the night before anyway, and felt this was a good way of living up to my promise to do so.

All the way up the Broadway extension I marveled at the mild weather, at the unusually good quality of music KATT was playing, at how well I felt, for a change.

I hit a Sonic a few blocks from Sam's apartment and picked up a couple of cherry limeades. This was my attempt at a belated peace offering to her for trashing her apartment. Sam had a jones for cherry limeades.

I was delighted to see that her car was in the customary slot. It was all I could do to keep from bounding out of the car and sprinting up the front walk. I restrained myself.

When I knocked on her door, she yelled from the kitchen to come in.

I let myself in and set the drinks on the kitchen table. Sam was perched up on the counter, one sneakered foot banging gently against the cabinet door. She had the phone mashed against one ear.

"Uh-huh," she said into the phone, "I know."

I cocked my head inquiringly. She rolled her eyes and mouthed "Adam."

I made a sour face, and with an exaggerated flourish, presented her with a drink. Her face lit up.

"Thank you," she mouthed.

I shrugged and sat at the kitchen table and tried not look like I was paying too much attention to the conversation she was having. As if. I looked around at the apartment, and was relieved to see that it showed no lingering effects from our apocalyptic soiree. I remembered the broken mirror, though, and dug out my checkbook.

"Listen," Sam said, "I know that. I know all of that, Adam. This is not a reflection of you. I'm not rejecting you. If I'm rejecting anything, I'm rejecting the relationship."

Well, that was a variation on the just-wanna-be-friends line that I'd never heard. Surely he wasn't *that* stupid. Of course she was rejecting him. But so what? I was the king of the rejects, and just like in medicine, it signaled little more than a bad organ transplant.

Of course, I was always pissed off about it, too. I guess that just meant Adam and I were similar idiots. The human kind.

"Yes," Sam said. "Yes. Yes, it did. I'm not cheap. Okay, okay, I know you didn't mean it that way. I'm sorry."

I wished I'd brought a book or something.

Sam sighed. I looked over at her and saw that she was frowning and holding the phone about two feet away from her head. She shook her head bemusedly.

"Should I go?" I asked quietly.

She shook her head and brought the phone back to her ear.

"No, look, we've been over this. We talked all about this last night. I'm not mad at you, this isn't about that Saturday night. This—*what?*"

Her voice tightened on the last word. I could hear shrill buggy noises coming out of the earpiece of the phone. It sounded like an angry ant was trapped in there. I winced, knowing it must really be ugly, knowing of a time or two when I had sounded just like that.

"Yeah, well, I'm seeing someone else now, so don't fucking bother me again!" And she slammed the phone into the cradle so hard I thought it would pulverize into powder.

I stared at her. She stared right back.

"Yeah," she said. "What?"

"I brought you a cherry limeade. I'll just be going now. Really can't stay. My, look at the time."

She laughed and leaned back against the upper cabinet. "Stick around, I'm over it. I'm not going to let that schmuck screw up my day."

She took a long pull from her drink and sighed in bliss when she was done. "Thanks, Lynch. You made this girl's day."

"I kinda figured I still owe you something for the mess we made the other night. And I need to know how much the mirror's gonna set me back. Hope your landlord wasn't too upset."

Sam waved a dismissing hand. "Whatever. I borrowed some money off Dad, they fixed it already."

"I'll still pay for it."

"Are we suddenly turning responsible?" Her grin made it impossible to take offense. "God, I hope not. I don't know if I can handle you with character, Lynch."

"So that was Adam."

"Most definitely so. I believe he is now out of my life."

"Oh."

"Ah well, I tried to keep it civil." She polished off the drink with a hearty slurp. "So what brings you here?"

"In-service day. I went and blew all the money I could really afford to, so I figured I better get to a safe place. Plus give you a check while I still know it won't bounce."

Sam hopped off the counter and threw the now empty Sonic cup away into the trash. "So why didn't you stay home?"

"Are you out of your mind? My parents think I'm in school. If they knew there weren't any classes today I'd be cleaning up at the shop. They grounded me for—"

Sam giggled. "I'm sorry. I still can't get over you being *grounded*. My God, you're *seventeen* years old."

"Almost eighteen."

"Almost eighteen."

"And you know how my folks are. As long as I'm living there, I will be subject to being grounded. I could be sixty for all they care."

"No, they'd just cut off your Geritol then."

"Well, I kind of see their point," I admitted. "I was off the straight and narrow there for a bit." To say the least.

Sam cocked her head, frowning. "Let me get this straight: You're siding with your parents?"

I shrugged.

"Are you *maturing* on me, Lynch? Damn. But grounding? Couldn't they just, you know, register their displeasure with you?"

Now it was my turn to make a face. "And when has that ever had any effect on me?"

"True. Persuasion of nearly any sort is wasted on you." She grinned at me.

I could only take it for a couple of seconds. "What?"

"Nothing. Grounded, huh? And here I thought you'd been hiding out from me. Well, that's your loss I guess."

"Why?"

"No, no point in it now."

"Oh, come on, I hate it when you do this!" Ever since were kids running around on the elementary school playground, it had driven me absolutely nuts.

"Well . . . Okay. I was going to ask you out Saturday. Guess it's moot now, huh?"

It was horrible, blackly dreadful. After years and years of half-serious bantering and verbal dart tossing between us, I had almost lost the ability to take anything Sam said on face value. The fact that she was now showing that smirking, mirthful, bemused grin did not help. Was this another Samantha Driscoll sarcastic bon mot?

"C'mon, don't tease, all right?" I said. "It's kind of been a bad month, and I'm feeling just a little oversensitive along those lines."

Sam nodded. Nibbled at the corner of her mouth for a second, mulling something over. "You hungry?"

I wasn't, hadn't been, but why tell her that? "Sure."

She came over and got her purse off the table. "C'mon, I haven't had lunch yet."

It was three o'clock. I glanced at my watch to confirm it.

"Yeah, well," she sighed, "I'd been on the phone with that schmuck since *noon*. So I need to eat. And we need to talk. Let's go. Up, *kemo sabe*."

"Okay," I said, standing, draining the last of my cherry limeade in a loud, obnoxious gurgle.

"And Eric?"

"Huh?"

She smiled at me. "I'm teasing you, you'll *know* it. Okay?"

I got a stupid lump in my throat. "Okay."

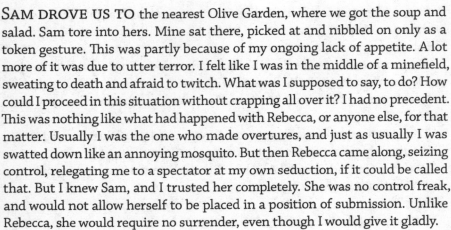

SAM DROVE US TO the nearest Olive Garden, where we got the soup and salad. Sam tore into hers. Mine sat there, picked at and nibbled on only as a token gesture. This was partly because of my ongoing lack of appetite. A lot more of it was due to utter terror. I felt like I was in the middle of a minefield, sweating to death and afraid to twitch. What was I supposed to say, to do? How could I proceed in this situation without crapping all over it? I had no precedent. This was nothing like what had happened with Rebecca, or anyone else, for that matter. Usually I was the one who made overtures, and just as usually I was swatted down like an annoying mosquito. But then Rebecca came along, seizing control, relegating me to a spectator at my own seduction, if it could be called that. But I knew Sam, and I trusted her completely. She was no control freak, and would not allow herself to be placed in a position of submission. Unlike Rebecca, she would require no surrender, even though I would give it gladly.

I was at a total loss.

Our conversation wandered lazily at first, meandering among the usual first-line-of-defense topics that had the emotional charge of tap water: school, politics, the continuing downfall of the likes of Jimmy Swaggart and Jim Bakker, Iran-Contra, stuff like that.

But sooner or later, the spiral had to wind down to the center.

I was the one to broach it, more out of a searing need to end the suspense than out of any kind of bravery.

"So," I said, looking down at my plate full of salad, too much the coward to risk eye contact while I asked her. "You were really going to ask me out Saturday?"

"No."

Did the collapse of my heart show in my face? Does a bear do his business in the trees? I glanced at her, and saw that she was smiling.

"I was going to ask you out today for a date on Saturday. You have this problem with grammar, Lynch."

I could not help the gasp of exasperation. "Jesus, that was a mean, mean thing to do."

"Lighten up, huh? I know you've got a better sense of humor than that. It's your most charming characteristic."

"So you mean it?" I had to force my hands to quit kneading the napkin, and

I hated the meek little display I was putting on, but get this, *chew* on it: I had known this beautiful, intelligent girl—woman—for maybe a dozen years, had grown up with her as a virtually constant presence in my life, and I had never even dared dream that she might harbor any feeling other than a cheerful tolerance for me.

And now she sat not three feet in front of me, telling me that there was a romantic spark.

How could I help but feel a little cowed, a little intimidated? I hated it, but there it was.

She leaned back in her chair and brushed back a stray wisp of her golden hair. Her smile faded a bit, replaced by a more inquisitive expression.

"Has it been that bad for you?"

I chuckled with just a little, a smidgeon, of bitterness. "C'mon. Has it been so great for Doug?"

Sam shrugged.

"Well," I said, "the truth is it hasn't been great for any of us, you know? Me and Doug and Stan, we're all kind of hitless at the plate."

"What about this Rebecca that Doug's dating? He hardly shuts up about her."

Could you call any kind of experience with that creature dating? Many other things, yes, but *dating*?

"I don't know," I said. "I'm not sure what's going on there."

"Hm. Well, I hope it works out for him. Gotta watch out for my baby brother."

"Let's not forget his baby friends."

Now she leaned forward, her eyes locking onto mine, her expression serious and, I think, a little concerned. "Is that going to be a problem?"

Was it?

"No," I said, almost a whisper. "Not for me. It's just that, uh, well . . ."

"Yeah?"

"I don't know, I . . ." I fumbled to a stop, hesitating to open myself up like this, wary of dragging something out into the light, something that I'd have to name and kill.

"Look," Sam said, "how long have we known each other? A long time, right? I've always liked you. Oh, you were, and are, a little crude sometimes, a little thickheaded sometimes, sometimes you made me want to bash your brains in, sometimes I doubted you had any *to* bash in. But I always liked you. Doug's a good judge of character, hah, better than me. You're a putz, occasionally, but you're a *good* putz. Eric, you're a really *sweet* putz. When you're not being a misogynist creep, which has been less lately."

"Um, thanks for the compliment. I think. That was a compliment?"

"You bet your ass it was. I've hardly ever known you to be mean to anybody, you're generally decent, you hardly ever pick your nose—these are worthy traits, my friend. Besides, you're cute."

"Cute?" I choked—and damn it, she was enjoying every second of this.

"Did I stutter?"

I did not want to know what the blush I felt looked like. Horrendous, no doubt.

Sam pointed to my plate. "You on a diet?"

Yeah, the Rebecca Connors Starvation Plan. Some kind of perk for being her chosen, I guess. It's great. No appetite at all, ever. "Yeah," I said. "I got tired of being a fat little curly-headed kid. I got tired of looking like that guy in the Doritos commercials."

"I'd say you've lost, what, thirty pounds? Am I close?"

I tried to remember when I'd last weighed myself. What was it, 178? Jesus, it had been *more* than thirty pounds. I nodded.

"Well, Lynch, you're takin' care of yourself. A girl's got to be impressed by that. The other morning being an exception, of course."

"Of course."

"So what do you say?'

"Huh?"

"Next chance you get, why don't you take me to dinner and movie, something like that?"

I spread my hands. "It might be a couple of weeks."

She smiled. "I think I can wait that long."

"And you won't be embarrassed to be seen with me? You know, cradle robbing and all?"

"Eric, dear," Sam said, accepting the ticket from the waiter, "three years ain't shit."

I smiled so hard I thought my head would crack. "No, guess not."

ON THE WAY HOME, I had to stop in a Seven Eleven parking lot to vent a little excitement. I cranked the stereo so loud the back window of the Bomb bowed out, the slamming percussive beat of "Owner of a Lonely Heart" blasting out. I pounded the steering wheel and let out a victorious whoop.

I had a date with Samantha Driscoll.

It was almost enough to make me believe in God again.

And almost enough to make me forget about the devil we'd unwittingly invited into our lives.

4

THAT FRIDAY, I WAS sitting in the Bomb before class, grooving on Maiden's "Somewhere in Time" and for a change thinking about nothing in particular when Mick rapped on my window. I reached over and unlocked the passenger door and cleared off all the crap from the seat so he could sit down, and turned the Maiden down to a dull roar.

As soon as he got in, my hair stood on end. Mick did not just look bad; he looked like something that might have crawled out of an intensive care ward, and should have been crawling right back in. His hair was a mess. Black caves were scooped out under his eyes. And he looked to have lost maybe ten, fifteen pounds since that last time I had seen him, less than a week before. I didn't even try to hide my shock; it wouldn't have been possible.

"Fuck, man, you okay?"

He smiled weakly as he pulled the door shut. "Yeah. Bronchitis. No big deal."

Looked like a big deal to me. Looked like an awfully big deal.

"Listen," he said. "I saw Doug with Rebecca this morning. I tried to talk to him, you know, about the other night. Tried to tell him what she was doin'." He ended this with a loud, wet cough.

At the moment, I really could not have cared any less about Doug Driscoll. "Man, are you sure you're okay?"

Mick's grin was lopsided and rueful. "I ain't dyin', that's what you're askin'. I'll be fine. Anyway. He wasn't havin' any of it, like that's a surprise. He called me, what was it, oh, yeah, he called me an 'ass-fucking queerbait who didn't know shit about shit.' I quote."

I wrapped my arms around the steering wheel. "Christ. Doug said that? *Doug?*"

Mick nodded. I was amazed to see that his eyes were watering. "Yeah. Doug. I mean, I knew he never liked me *that* much. I'm from the wrong side of the tracks, you know, and I don't think he can handle that. I think he always kinda thought poor meant stupid. And I always knew Stan's about as homophobic as they come, and he almost can't help it, that's just Stan, but I, uh, shit."

He stopped for a second to get himself together. "I always figured Driscoll was a little smarter than that. *Damn* that hurt. And that bitch just grinned while he said it. Grinned."

"You're a threat."

He stared at me blankly.

"Don't look at me like that. There are two people on Earth who have even the slightest idea what's up with her. And they're both takin' up space in my car."

Mick nodded. He placed a hand on his chest and tried without success to suppress a rumbling cough.

"You oughta see a doctor about that."

"Fuckin' quacks, forget that shit."

I noticed that the stream of people heading toward the front doors had increased, and glanced at the clock. I'd have just enough time to get to first hour to avoid a tardy, more of which I did not need.

"Yeah," Mick said. "Gotta get goin'."

As we walked to class, I said, "Listen, you really ought to just kind of lay low about all this. There's no need for you to get all caught up in this shit."

Mick shook his head.

"I mean it. She's got her hooks in Stan and Doug. It's their problem. Let them screw with it."

Mick opened the door and looked at me angrily. "Is that how you fight for your friends? Man, she is real trouble. Is that how you try to fight for 'em?"

His righteousness pissed me off. "No. Only when they don't want it, and believe me, they don't. Piss on 'em, man, Rebecca's their problem."

Mick did not say anything more as we went to our separate classes, but he didn't have to. His disappointment was almost physical.

But here was the thing: If the other two did not remember Randy's appearance at the party, how come Doug for sure, and Stan maybe as well, remembered Rebecca's outing of Mick. And yet did not remember Rebecca being there at all? What kind of fog were they wandering around in?

I GOT SOME IDEA of that a couple of weeks later. It was unseasonably warm for the last week of October, and I was helping my dad out in the shop, putting up supplies, cleaning up, generally being a gopher for him. He was grateful for the company, and I was even a little happy to be there. It was nice for a change to be in an environment where there was no friction, where everything was laid out clean and neat. We had a good morning of it, chatting about the cars we worked on or the people who drove them, the weather, just stuff. And miracle of miracles, not a Bible verse one popped up.

Around lunchtime, my father left for McDonald's to grab us some grub. I stayed behind to tinker around and hold down the fort on the off chance a customer wandered by.

No customers did, but Doug pulled up about ten minutes after my father left.

"Oh man," I muttered. "What now?"

He got out of his Datsun, and walked up to me, slowly, his hands in the pockets of his Dockers. I waited for him, still holding the broom I'd been sweeping with, clutching it almost like a weapon.

He stopped maybe ten feet in front of me. "Um, hey."

"Hey, Doug. What's up?"

"You, uh, you got a minute."

"Probably."

He looked down at his feet, scuffed around some of the gravel. "I think I owe you an apology."

This was not what I had expected. "For what?"

"Well, I've been acting like a rectum lately, to tell you the truth."

"Right."

He looked up at me, frowning. "I thought you'd been sleeping with Rebecca."

Well, let's be blunt about it. "And what changed your mind?"

There was no question about it. She had, of course.

"Rebecca asked me what my beef was. So I told her what was eating me, and she . . . she put my mind at rest. I just jumped to the wrong conclusions."

Now I was confused. Because he still didn't seem to remember that Rebecca had been at Sam's that night. "What gave you the idea that I was, you know . . ." I almost said "boinking her" but for a change discretion won out.

"Just suspicions, you know. I'm not sure how I got the idea, actually. . . ." He looked off down the street, seeming to try to find something in the distance.

"It doesn't matter, does it? I was wrong," he continued. "That's all. I'm sorry. I just . . . I've never had anyone like Rebecca before. There's never been anyone who was so open and total. I feel like I've been wandering around my whole life incomplete, and she's some part of me that was separated during my childhood, and now I'm all one again. That sounds crazy. I know. But I just got this suspicion in my head, and then I couldn't get it out. And I was an asshole. I'm sorry."

I was shaking. I was not sure which of us was losing his mind. Maybe both. "It's okay," I mumbled.

His eager relief was so palpable it was painful.

"Maybe you owe one to Mick, too."

Doug cocked his head. "Mick?"

"Yeah Mick. You kinda shat all over him this week."

He struggled to recall what he had done. I could see him wrestling with it. "I . . ."

"Never mind, I'll tell him."

"Well, there was another thing I came by to ask you. What are you doing Thursday the 14th?"

"Working, probably."

"Get it off. We've got tickets to Floyd."

I was blank. "Huh?"

"Pink Floyd. Dallas."

"Dallas? I can't go to Dallas, especially on a school night. I'm already grounded until forever."

Now he grinned. "Come on, we're all going. Get someone to work for you, we'll leave about three, see the show, and be back by about four in the morning."

"You're crazy."

"So?"

I was suddenly glad my dad had stepped out to get lunch. I could just imagine him overhearing this.

"Who's going?"

"Me, Stan, Rebecca. You."

"I don't know." Actually, I wanted to go, but not with Rebecca.

Then again, what could happen? And how many chances was I going to get to see Pink Floyd? And maybe my overactive imagination was putting way too strong a spin on everything that was happening. This is the way we sell our souls.

"Yeah," I said. "Okay. But I'm gonna have to bum some money for a ticket, I'm broke."

Doug grinned and shook his head. "Already taken care of. Rebecca bought 'em for everybody."

Well wasn't that nice? It seemed her generosity knew no bounds.

I was about to ask him whose car we were taking when my father pulled into the drive. This put an abrupt end to our discussion of the matter, since my father made it clear that my being grounded included no visitations at the shop. I sometimes thought this was a little harsh, but what the hell. All I had to do was remember that I'd once slit the throat of a friend, and I found I had no problem with being grounded.

But it was getting harder to remember what I'd done, and harder for it to not feel like some dark fairy tale someone had cooked up.

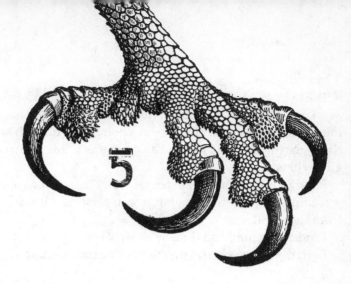

5

ON HALLOWEEN, HAVING TOLD my parents I was working a long shift at Tate's, I picked Sam up after her last class and we took in a triple bill of horror movies: *The Hidden*, *Prince of Darkness*, and *Near Dark*. It was the most fun I'd had in forever: cheap cheesy chills. We sat in the dark and held hands, and when the credits rolled on the last flick, Sam leaned over and kissed me and it was the sweetest thing I've ever known.

I CHECKED MY OLD yearbooks, looking for Randy Crawford. No dice. I went to the library and looked up back issues of *The Daily Oklahoman* for the whole summer of 1983 looking for a news item about the murder of a kid behind the Texaco. Nada. One night, as I sat back from the microfiche and rubbed my eyes, Randy appeared beside me, and said, "She disappeared me good, huh?"

"Yeah," I said. "She did at that."

"I don't think it was easy for her to do. I think that's why she hibernated—I think it drains her."

"Could be," I told him.

He grinned that bloody grin at me. "I didn't think you cared."

I sighed and shut off the fiche reader. "I don't," I said, and got up to leave. One of the reference librarians looked at me oddly as I left.

REBECCA WAS OUT BESIDE my car again one afternoon. I didn't say a word to her, just got in, started the Cherry Bomb, and backed on out. To my mind, hitting her would have been a bonus, but no such luck. She just stood there glaring at me as I pulled away. It was a free country. She could glare all she liked.

Randy stretched in the passenger seat. "This can't go on, you know. I know you think it's peaceful now, but it won't last. She'll start cutting you all off from the world soon."

I snorted at him, and then he wasn't there.

Even my ghost was starting to become routine now.

MICK DID NOT SHOW up at work, or school, the week of the Pink Floyd show.

Rebecca was out as well Monday, Tuesday, and Wednesday, and for those three days it almost seemed like old times. Stan hassled me a couple of times about coming by some night to listen to his new band—they were calling themselves Serpent's Tooth, and Stan could not say why—and maybe sit in on a jam. I made vague noises about doing so, but to be honest, I was wondering how much I could get for my bass at the pawn shop. A decent wardrobe was now beginning to seem important. I really, truly did not want to give Sam any pause whatsoever to be seen with me.

We all went out to lunch on Tuesday, diving into the buffet at Pizza Hut. I was soundly dogged for eating only salad, and only a little of that. Doug suggested that my ribs could be counted, even through my sweater. This was all fine and well. I was actually quite pleased with my new slim figure, and piss on 'em if they didn't like it.

We kicked around the Floyd show and decided to take Doug's Datsun because, even though it would be a tight fit, it was far and away the most reliable vehicle any of us possessed. Doug was about to explode with anticipation, unable to believe that finally he was going to get to see his favorite band, something he had long ago given up hope for. Hell, even if it didn't include Roger Waters.

And what neither of them said but I know they thought: Rebecca's going, too.

Myself, I couldn't have cared less. The biggest reason I was going was that Doug so obviously, so badly, wanted me to, and I was desperate to find some way to mend our friendship. I was not thrilled at the idea of spending almost eight hours in a car with Rebecca.

I TOLD MY FOLKS I had to stay late at school to work on a project for my American History class, and that I'd be going straight from school to work. They had no problem with this; lately, things had been good between us, my grounding aside. Their religious fervor had entered a quiescent period, and I had learned to keep my mouth a little shut. They took my sudden scholarly industriousness as a positive sign that finally, at last, all their Christian parenting was paying dividends. And I figured they'd be safely asleep by the time I came in that morning.

I had Stan follow me to Tate's before classes that morning so we could drop the Bomb off in the parking lot. Verisimilitude, I felt, was the key here. Stan then ferried me back to school, where we endured the slow, dragging day.

Doug was waiting by the door after lunch, grinning manically and ready to roll. I crawled into the back seat.

Stan yelled, "Shotgun, losers!"

As I was already in the back seat, I would have shrugged if the room inside the Datsun had allowed it. I tried anyway, and it came off more like a squirm. "Maybe the queen here would like to sit up front. With Doug."

Doug said, "Yeah, I—"

"I am fine back here, with Eric."

Ugh.

"Or maybe," I said, "you'd like to sit back here, Livingston."

"No. Don't call me—"

"Right."

"I could drive if you want, Doug, and you can sit back here with—"

"I am *fine* back here with Eric."

I did that stunted shrug-squirm again. "I just thought you might like to sit with your boyfriend. Just a thought."

She glared at me, something in her eyes glinting light sunlight off a glacier. "I have my own thoughts, thank you."

Doug cleared his throat. "I, uh, I guess that's that. Can we roll now?"

I settled in for the ride. Not looking at her.

We stopped for some chow at the McDonald's in Gainesville, taking fifteen minutes to stretch our legs and eat. While we were there, a stunning redhead came in wearing a pair of the tightest jeans I have ever seen and a clean white T-shirt. She was not precisely statuesque, but she was very, very beautiful, with wide green eyes and soft hair that swept down to her shoulders. Stan and I both watched her from the moment she came in to the second she left. I heard Stan mutter, "Wow."

I grinned and turned to Rebecca, who was glaring at both of us. "Aw, just a little competition, Becca. Can't you handle it?"

Stan cleared his throat, and I saw that he was blushing. Jesus, did they all think they were so discreet? He was paying attention to her now, and a puzzled frown creased his face. Doug was off in the restroom, or I think it might have been really ugly.

"Eric," she said, with a smile that was covered with terminal frost, "believe me, there is no competition."

I shrugged. But she was wrong.

She didn't say another word to me until we got to Reunion Arena.

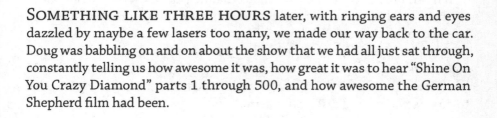

WE GOT THERE MAYBE forty-five minutes before showtime. Rebecca pulled four tickets out of her hip pocket and dispensed them like communion wafers. Doug studied his by the glow of the parking light.

"Yeah, it's real, geez, Doug."

He grinned at me. "Oh yeah."

There was a huge mob still moving inside, and of course we had to detour by the T-shirt stand. It seemed like Doug bought two of everything. I felt this was a bit hypocritical, since he was on record as being far more pro-Roger Waters than Pink Floyd, in fact, having said at one time that he did not even consider this to be Pink Floyd. "Pink Fraud" I think he called them. Yeah, but here he was coming to see 'em anyway.

Somewhere around "Money," Rebecca abruptly disappeared. I tried to tell myself she'd just gone to the bathroom, but she was back a couple of moments later, too quick for Reunion's restrooms. I stared at her.

She mouthed the words to me: "Took a little trip."

And then she smiled. Like a shark.

A well-fed shark.

SOMETHING LIKE THREE HOURS later, with ringing ears and eyes dazzled by maybe a few lasers too many, we made our way back to the car. Doug was babbling on and on about the show that we had all just sat through, constantly telling us how awesome it was, how great it was to hear "Shine On You Crazy Diamond" parts 1 through 500, and how awesome the German Shepherd film had been.

I had kind of felt any film that featured dogs with glowing eyes chasing some slob through an airport in a hospital bed had to be suspect, but maybe that was just me. I was mostly tired at this point, and was not really that impressed by the show. I'd seen Triumph pull off better gigs, for crying out loud. With fewer musicians, and at half the ticket price. I was beginning to regret coming, because I knew I would be getting no sleep on the way back. This was because, at some point in the show, maybe during "Learning to Fly," the aging hippies sitting next to us had pulled out a baggie full of joints and lit up with merry abandon. As is usually the case with pot smokers, they began to feel terrible about not sharing, or else maybe they were worried that they would be the only ones around smoking themselves stupid. Whichever, a steady procession of doobies came our way. I passed: weed just gave me a headache.

Stan and Doug showed no such compunctions. Any weed that went their way would not be heard from again. And a whole ton did.

Consequently, that left me and Rebecca as the only two sober members of our party by the show's end, and Rebecca firmly insisted that she could not drive.

"Jesus," I said, "that's great. Doug, man, I need your keys."

Doug chuckled, and even in the bad light, his eyes looked like they belonged on a teddy bear. "I can drive okay."

I stuck out my hand. "Hand 'em over."

Doug shook his head. "You'll wreck my car."

"Fine," I said, and turned to Stan and Rebecca. "You guys hold him, I'll go through his pockets."

"You will not!"

"Doug, man, you're drooling on yourself and your eyes look like marbles. You ain't driving for a while."

Rebecca said, "He's right."

Doug grumbled as he dug his keys out. "Jesus, some friends you guys are."

"We're a pretty shitty crew," I agreed.

"I want shotgun," Rebecca said.

Oh great.

Ten minutes north of Dallas, The Dynamic Duo '87 were passed out in the back seat. Stan snored terribly, and I didn't dare turn the car stereo up loudly enough to drown him out. Rebecca sat on the passenger side, staring out ahead into the night, at the black countryside flying away to either side, some dark territory we were passing through. I ignored her as best I could, but it was a three-hour drive, and I was dog tired, and the last thing I needed to do was nod off and drift into a semi.

So after a while, I asked her, "Is there any way you could just leave us alone?"

She looked over at me, her eyes wide and alarmed, her face deathly pale in the light from the dashboard. "I don't know what you're talking about."

"Uh-huh."

We said nothing for five, ten minutes. The highway flew by beneath us. Denton appeared, bright lights and gas stations and cheap motels and fast food, and then it was behind us. We had Q-102 out of Dallas, Springsteen advising us about the tunnel of love. Oh yeah, that's a dark tunnel all right, Boss. Sometimes it doesn't have an end either, sometimes it just swallows you up in darkness.

Someone at the station was feeling dark that night: the next song up was The Smithereens' "Blood and Roses" and wasn't that just all too appropriate. I glanced over at Rebecca but the irony was lost on her. She stared straight ahead as though in a trance. Blood and roses, oh yeah, death and desire, and they were pretty tightly wound together, weren't they? At least they were for us. At that moment I was of two minds, both opposed to each other. I wanted freedom from Rebecca, I hated her for what she had done to us, violations so deep they could not all be articulated. I did not want her attentions, which were a sort of cheap enchantment.

But some part of me still wanted her. It was a vestigial desire, but it was there.

"Do you really have to mess with us all this way?"

She did not answer me.

"C'mon, Rebecca, I'm trying to talk to you here."

No response.

"Goddamn it! Say something!"

"All right," she said, calmly, quietly. "You brought me here, you drew me in, now you're having second thoughts. Why? Am I not good enough for you? Was I not good for you? You didn't put up a fight."

"I was battered out of my mind."

"Oh, I see. Well, they still want me. They still love me. They still *need* me. Both of them."

"Love? That's what you call it?"

She snorted. "Yeah, Eric, you're an expert on the subject, I forgot. They still need me, and I think you do, too."

She slouched down in the seat and drew her knees up to her chest. "I really don't know what you're complaining about. I'll be anything you've ever wanted."

"So long as I don't mind sharing?"

"So ownership is want you want?"

"No. Just the truth."

"I've given you that."

As if.

We flew through Gainesville, crossed the Texas-Oklahoma border. My legs were starting to ache, but we had enough gas to get at least to Ardmore, and I wanted to stop as little as possible. I wanted to be out of this car as soon I could. I felt like I was caught in a pool with something sleek and dangerous and hungry cruising under the surface. The sooner I could get out the better.

We rode for a time with the radio filling the silence.

"Eric," she began, and she let a hand rest on my thigh.

"Don't," I said.

"Okay." But she did not move her hand. I had to slide it off myself.

She said nothing to that.

We came out of the hills and I nosed the Datsun up to seventy-five. Ardmore was not far up ahead; we could stop for gas at a truck stop there, and I could get some coffee, much needed. We still had two hours of driving left.

Soon enough, we hit Ardmore, and even at that late hour the main drag was still lit and somewhat active. I pulled off the interstate and followed the access road until I hit the Love's. There was one car in the lot; otherwise the mercury vapor lights shone down on asphalt desolation. I saw the cashier through the window, and no one else in the store. It looked isolated to me: Ardmore, Oklahoma but at the same time millions of miles away. Maybe it was just my frame of mind. My mood was not improving. I wanted to be home.

I parked by a pump and went in to relieve myself and get a cup of joe. An icy blast of air hit me halfway there; Christ, another cold front. I was not ready for winter yet. Not this year. Like the calendar would wait for me. It was only a week before Thanksgiving, five before Christmas.

I wondered what I would get Sam for Christmas. I'd never gotten her a gift before. I thought about this as I absently nodded to the clerk, a short, pale, thin guy who looked like he had been hitting the No-Doz pretty hard.

The clerk raised a hand and twitched it in reply, mumbled something that might have been "Welcome to Love's" or "Don't cum on the gloves." It was hard to tell.

The men's room stank to high heaven of piss and tobacco. I thought that at least the night creature at the front counter might take a minute to clean the damn bathroom. Jesus, what a skank pit.

But I had to piss and I had to do it now and no way was I going to make it to Norman, which was the next possible stopping point. So I held my breath while I drained the main vein. Much of the stink came from the stall next to the urinal, and I was grateful that I did not have the runs. I could only imagine was the inside of that stall was like.

"So it's still none of your business, huh?"

I jerked and sprayed all over the wall, cursing with every profanity I knew and inventing a couple.

"You think you could ever show up maybe not in a bathroom? You think a little privacy is too much to ask?"

It did not look like Randy was listening to me. In fact, it almost seemed like he was not there at all, it seemed as though he was some vast distance away and I was seeing a projection, a mirage. Maybe that had been true all along.

He was scared shitless. I was an expert in that, I recognized it with no trouble at all. His blue eyes bulged wide and tremors sped through him. He chewed on his bottom lip.

"You got two friends out in the car," he said, "with their brains so stir-fried that if Rebecca says jump, they rip off her panties; you're a walking nervous wreck 'cause you're trying to deny the whole thing and you can't, even *you* know you just can't. And now she's—it's—stronger than ever 'cause it just set the hook good and deep. But it's not your problem. You know whose problem it really is? I think you ought to check on Mick real soon."

I froze, my finger pointing in his face, and said, "What?"

Randy glanced at the door. He ran a hand through his hair and sighed. "Listen. Listen, listen. I can't be here long. It used to be so easy, I was dead, hell, the dead are their own hooks, that's why they make it back so much, that's why we do. But she got strong enough to cut mine. And I think there's only one way she could have done that. I think you better check on Mick."

He stepped toward me and I retreated an equal distance, mybutt bumping into the urinal. Randy looked mad, feverish, about to strain and snap the leash.

"He's going to fucking die, do you get that? Does that *register*? She stuck her pussy in Doug's face, in Stan's face, in your face, and you all got a little of that smell, and then what? You all followed her around like a bunch of toms in heat, and then you're conveniently removed from the scene of the crime. It's how that thing works, and hoo boy! You all fell for it just . . . like . . . that!"

He snapped his fingers in front of my face to punctuate the point. It didn't stir the air, not a bit. I had a feeling I could pass my hand right through him.

"You know why she got rid of him? Because she's got no power over him, and she doesn't need him. She didn't need him. So that's it. He's gone. It wasn't your problem. You couldn't be bothered."

"Mick?" I whispered. None of this made sense to me. Surely Randy couldn't be telling me Mick was dead.

Randy nodded, gripped my shoulders as if to shake me, and it felt like the barest of breezes had rippled my shirt sleeves. An old man's cough, no more. "Now he wakes up. Too late. Because now he's gone and I'm gone and you're all on your lonesome. Hope you like it. Hope you enjoy yourself. Hope she always needs you."

So what, Rebecca was going to kill Mick? She was going to maybe order a mob hit on him or something? Shit, she didn't like him, so what?

"Man, you're crazy. I don't know you've told me one straight thing all along. I don't know that you're not some kind of dementia I'm having. Maybe I've got a brain tumor. But you are nuts enough for any two men. And I am tired of being told one craziness after another. She ain't no friggin' succubus and Mick ain't goin' to die and we didn't ever kill any kid, so just piss off and leave me alone. Okay?"

He opened his mouth to reply to that, and I thought, for a second, that I saw a deeper blackness inside him than I should have. I thought I saw stars. Cold rushed over me towards Randy, and he doubled as if gut punched, as if he were being folded over. He shot a hand out to me, but before I could even blink, he was sucked through some hole that I could not see. In less than half a second, he was gone. There had been no sound. The men's room held silence, stench, and me, no more than that.

I scurried out of the bathroom before another psychotic episode could unleash itself upon me. Enough was most certainly enough.

Rebecca was inside the store now, a Coke in her hand, and she turned a sober expression on me as I rushed out and toward the drink fountains.

She joined me as I plucked a huge Styrofoam coffee cup from a tall leaning stack.

"You look like you've seen a ghost," she said.

"Hah-hah, fuck you." I lifted the coffee pot. The contents did not slosh so much as they oozed, but it was caffeine or die, so the hell with it. My hands shook enough as I poured it that I missed the cup first try and splattered hot coffee all over my shoes. Rebecca watched patiently the whole while.

I took the coffee to the counter and set it down, then snapped a travel lid on it. The clerk, who, judging from the odor that hazed around him, should perhaps have worn a name tag labeling him Dopey, struggled up into some form of somnambulism.

"Be it for ya?"

"Naw, the Coke, too." I yanked the bottle from Rebecca's grasp and slammed it on the counter with a thunk. "And six bucks unleaded on pump two."

"Pump four?"

"Pump two."

"Uh, pump two?"

Jesus Christ on a crutch. "Pump-fucking-two, yes."

"Chill, man, god." He reached over with a lack of speed that I thought tree sloths had to struggle to attain and punched a button on a control console. He spoke into the microphone, even though there was no sign of life outside. "Pump two is now on."

Better even than a chunk of the True Cross.

"Ya'll go to Floyd tonight?" The clerk had a Green Goblin grin on his face and his glassy eyes did not move from Rebecca. Marijuana lust. Rebecca smiled at him, and for a second, just a shaved instant really, I felt the same flickering jealousy that had overcome me at the Sonic a few weeks before. There arose in me a thrusting rage, a compulsion to leap over the counter and smash the idiot's face into his cash register until nothing remained but a soggy, dripping ruin. I actually saw myself doing this; the image was so vivid that it rocked me on my heels. Then it died away, gone, leaving an icy cavity behind.

"No," I said, clearing my throat. "We are returning from a pilgrimage to Mecca."

"Oh."

"Finding Allah and all o' that." This guy had no more idea of who Allah was than a fly knew of Shakespeare. Maybe the fly could learn, though. I glanced at Rebecca. Her head was cocked in a quizzical fashion.

No, I thought, *not for you, not ever again, it's a test I don't want to take, bitch.*

I handed my money over to the stoner and did my best to be patient while he counted it, rang it up, and counted out the change, which only took forever, and Rebecca next to me the whole time. I did not want to be there with her, with my body responding to hers on a level below cellular. I wanted to be back in Oklahoma City with everyone home and no more to think about.

Finally, Old Smokie got me my change, and I grabbed my coffee and got out of there, Rebecca behind me.

"Late night at the shit-n-git," I muttered.

Rebecca said, "Class specimen, huh?"

I reached the car without saying anything. My lucky streak was holding: the attendant had actually managed to turn on the correct pump. The gods did grin. I undid the gas cap and fueled the car while Rebecca stared at my back. I didn't dare turn around. I would have asked her about Mick, and I didn't want to do that. It was all bullshit from my diseased mind anyway. My damaged ego could not handle the fact that Rebecca was sleeping around with all of us and was trying to twist everything around. There was no ghost named Randy.

Which is what I was telling myself, and every time some hidden nook in my brain tried to insist that Mick had seen it too, I clamped down hard on it. Mick didn't know what he was talking about. Mick was crazy. I was crazy. Whatever.

So I glanced back anyway. Rebecca leaned on the rear of the car, on the other side of the hose. Like that was some kind of barrier between us, like it was police tape sealing the scene of a crime. Her arms were folded, showcasing that most ensnaring bosom, and damned if it didn't get my blood going a little bit. Biology is unaware of morality. I resented the hell out of it, cursing my hormones, but that didn't mean a thing, it never does.

She appraised me with those crystal sharp eyes.

"What?" I asked.

Rebecca shook her head, offered me a bemused smile.

I forced my eyes away from her, made myself watch the numbers on the whirring gas pump dials. Six dollars came and went in a blur. I peered over the pump and saw that Dopey the clerk was propped on a stool reading some magazine, Circus no doubt. I shook my head, piss on it. I topped off Doug's tank, something like ten bucks' worth, and the pinhead inside never glanced up. I hooked up the nozzle, grabbed my coffee, and started around for the driver's side. Rebecca did not move. She still watched me.

"Okay," I sighed. "What is it?"

"Nothing," she said. "I was just noticing that you've lost a lot of weight."

I let that hang in the wee morning hour quiet. The only sounds were the buzzing of the fluorescent lights above us, the occasional tired breathing of the northern breeze, and a time or two the passing of a semi on I-35.

"Yeah," I said at last, digging out Doug's keys. "I've gone from whale-like to merely porky."

"Huh-uh. You look good."

Her voice left no doubt where she was going with this.

"Thanks," I said. "I appreciate the compliment. But don't start that, okay?"

Rebecca merely nodded, and got in on her side.

I groaned to myself. It was going to be a long ride back the rest of the way. The Tokin' Twins were still conked out in the back seat, and they remained that way. The Second Coming, in all likelihood, would not have roused the two of them. Certainly my driving did not do it. I kept the speedometer pegged at seventy-five, even when we hit a patch of dense fog about ninety miles south of Norman. Fuck, we'd either crash or we wouldn't, but I wanted to get home.

"You think I don't love you," Rebecca said after a while.

"No, see, I don't care, that's totally different," I said, trying to be helpful.

"You think I'm some kind of manipulative slut trying to keep you all on a line."

"Does it matter what I think?"

She leaned forward and smashed her fist into the padded dashboard. I tightened my hands on the steering wheel.

"Yes," she hissed at me, eyes drawn to slits. "It *does* matter. It's *everything*. What do you think love is, Eric?"

"I know it ain't what you've got in mind."

She sighed. "Love is need like no other. Love is not being able to live without someone. I can't *live* without you."

"Meaning all three of us."

"Do you think it's something that can be sliced up and doled out? Do you think something so powerful and basic can be diminished by being shared? I don't."

I gulped a hot mouthful of coffee. "Okay, princess," I said, feeling awake and nasty, "let me ask the daily double here: What happens if we decide we don't want you anymore?" I glanced over at her.

She glared at me. "You won't," she said.

"What if I already have?"

Her eyes were wide. "You don't mean that."

Yeah, but I did. I am slow but I am solid, and once I get to a place, I generally know where I am.

"You make all this bullshit sound real good, Becca, but you can't hide the fact that it's bullshit. Sprinkle all the sugar on it you want, it don't hide the stink."

That seemed to deflate her. She sank back in the chair and didn't say anything for a long time. The miles rolled on. After a time we came out of the fog, and the brilliant starry night burst out in its full glory.

Stan started snoring heavily again. It sounded like a huge chunk of concrete being shoved across a parking lot a little at a time.

Rebecca said, "I want to live, Eric."

"Don't let me stop you."

"I *will* live."

There was a nasty, combative tone to her words. I thought of my hallucination earlier. Maybe I was still so paranoid, still so screwed up in my head, that I was imagining tensions that were not there.

"I am saying," she went on, "that I need you and I'll have you."

I nodded. "Yeah? Who wants ownership now?

"You'd do the same, to live."

Maybe she was right, if you bought into the absurd notion that she was some sort of non-human entity that needed the attention, no, the *worship* of three schmucks to keep her watch wound. I mean, if I were some kind of sex-hungry thing that needed regular shots of spunk to keep myself up to par, I might stoop to some awful levels. Boy, all of my paranoid delusions from earlier sure sounded tinny and thin now. I was no better than those guys that swear with dark-rimmed eyes that the CIA is bugging their toilets. Maybe I was worse. At least those nuts could prove there *was* a CIA, right?

Okay.

Granted.

But.

I felt like a man dancing around the rim of some bottomless crater, knowing he's got to go in sometime but not sure of the depth or what lies at the bottom.

I spoke without knowing what was jumping out of my big mouth: "What did you do to Mick?"

Time froze.

Imagine hitting a brick wall on a bicycle, imagine that eternal moment of stunned nothing before bright pain streams through the dike and floods over you in a torrent. That sense of being slapped by a giant numbing hand, and everything tumbles and rolls and falls out of its appointed place, its natural time. Sixty to zero and everything flying to pieces.

Like that. My breath was driven away, punched out of me, and nothing moved for a slow instant. Everything outside the car held as it was, dark and two swaths of light that met on the road ahead. Silence fell upon me; no sound, no sensation at all other than pressure and stillness, pressure and stillness.

And the sense of a cold gust blowing across, through, my brain. The shadow of a wind on the mind.

Summer, behind the Texaco, out of breath, chest heaving with exertion and pain and fear, trying to claw my way through the cinder block wall at my back, blood on my shirt, on my shoes, on my skin, and sudden strong smell of roses, roses, and then—

And then the sense of a wind across my brain.

Time flowed again, glacier to river; we were moving through the alien universe. We drove on through the landscape of total eclipse, dark ambiguous shapes flying by with killing speed, the car tearing down the miles as we drew closer to home.

The moon vanished, light was absent from all the world. Someone, Rebecca or myself, had turned the stereo off. It was quiet, save for the sleep noises of my friends in the back seat and the bone thrumming hum of highway rushing beneath. Stan and Doug were piled upon each other like tired vagrants.

Rebecca slid close to me, put an arm around me, gave her warmth as we rocketed through the dark morning. She kissed my neck, my ear, my cheek. Troubled images rose in the lightless waters of my mind and sank again without a ripple. The touch of a feather, the kiss of an angel.

"You're worried about so much," she whispered. Her tongue flicked at my ear. Electricity found hidden paths in my body.

"I know," I sighed. It was true; worry was the acid eating at my sanity. Now perspective asserted itself. How could this beauty be anything but what she was, a love I'd waited my life to meet? How could I not believe that?

Her fingers drifted through my hair. "I think you've been having a lot of nightmares, haven't you? I think someone's been telling you a lot of untruths."

"Randy."

"Mm. But he's not real, you know that, don't you?"

But the blood, everywhere, all over me . . .

The whisper of a feather. The kiss of a spider against my mind. Breath of a baby.

"No," I said. "I was just losing it. . . ."

Rebecca ran a hand over my chest. "We all do."

Sam didn't. I saw her face, for a second, and then it was as if my brain forgot how to remember her. Nothing. Only her name. Rebecca's hand paused.

I forgot about Sam, and then Rebecca proceeded with her caresses.

She said, "All your friends are safe."

"Mick . . ."

She lightly bit my neck, and I moaned. This was unbearable. "Who is Mick, love?"

I didn't know. What had I been babbling about? I was more tired than I thought, and I drained the last of my coffee. Rebecca took the empty cup from my hand and dropped it to the floorboard.

"All of your friends are right here, they are perfectly safe. I would never let anything happen to you."

"I know."

"Eric, look at me."

I took my eyes from the road, for a moment, for an eon. Rebecca brought her face close to mine. "I love you more than anyone else ever could. Don't ever forget that."

Her hand slid to my lap. Her deft fingers worked the buttons on my jeans. I found breathing to be a chore. I forced myself to look back at the road.

"You're always mine," she said, and her hand undid the final button.

Sam.

I shoved Rebecca's hand away and awkwardly used my free hand to button myself back up. She slid against the passenger door, crossed her arms, and glared at me. Now I saw true hurt.

Good.

"I'm not sniffing after you any more, Rebecca. I'm done with that. You might as well get used to it."

"We'll see," she said.

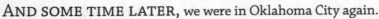

AND SOME TIME LATER, we were in Oklahoma City again.

It seemed that I woke up at the light at 36th and MacArthur. I blinked. Lights swam through my bleary vision. I swept my hand over my eyes to clear them. The dashboard clock read five minutes before four. Jesus, had I driven the rest of the way asleep? I glanced in the back seat, and saw that Stan was gone.

"We already dropped him off," Rebecca said. Not happy, not her usual charming self.

I looked at her, stared at her while I waited for the light to turn green. "Stay out of my head," I told her.

She smiled at me, inscrutable.

I was too tired to pursue it. Better to wait until later, when my head was clear.

Doug sat up. In the rearview, he looked like Thomas Dolby, his hair sticking out at wild angles. He cracked an enormous yawn and vigorously rubbed his face.

"What time is it?"

"Four," I told him. "We already dropped Stan off. I'll take Rebecca home, and you can drop me off at Tate's."

He nodded. "Thanks for driving, man. I guess I got into the weed a little bit."

"A tad."

He leaned forward to Rebecca and kissed her.

Yeah. Sure thing. I looked away from them and proceeded through the light. None of us said another word until we got to Rebecca's apartment. She smiled at both of us after she got out, and walked without a word to her front door. Doug then hauled me up to Tate's, where the Bomb sat unmolested. Like anyone would want it. I got out of Doug's car on legs that seemed made of rubber and wood, wobbly and stiff at the same time. I stretched out and listened to my spine do Rice Krispies. Christ, what a long night. I looked at my watch. Four in the a.m. Hey, in only four hours, it would be time for school. I cursed myself for having been talked into this. I would be even more worthless than usual for the next couple of days.

Doug came around and got behind the wheel. He got in, shut the door, and rolled the window down.

"Eric."

I stumbled to face him. "Huh?"

"Thanks for goin'. It was cool, huh?"

He didn't know the half of it. "Yeah."

He seemed to find the floorboard fascinating for a moment, and then looked back at me. "Are you okay? You looked kind of upset with me and Rebecca. You're cool with it, right?"

"I'm cool with whatever you are, Doug."

Doug grinned. "Great. She's good for us, isn't she?"

In the plural. I glanced down at the new slim version of myself. "I guess so, yeah."

Doug looked off through the windshield at the stars. "Man. How did we live without her? Everything was so gray before."

I couldn't argue with that.

"Have to go," Doug said. I nodded and turned away, content with the evening after all. Doug started the Datsun, and as he was about to pull away, a little bubble burst in my mind. I whirled around.

"Hey, Doug!"

He poked his head out of the window and looked back at me. "What?"

"What about Mick?"

Puzzlement spread over his face. "Who?"

I shook my head. "I don't know. Never mind. I don't know what I was thinking about."

And I didn't. Whatever weird thought had been about to occur to me vanished as quickly as it had risen. I shook my head. I didn't know anybody named Mick. I was just tired. I waved at Doug as he drove off. *Mañana*, man.

Time to get home. Time to sleep. To dream.

No haunted images of pools of water, no swing of rope.

I shook my head to clear it, got in the Bomb, and drove back to the house.

7

I ROUNDED THE CORNER on to my street and my heart slammed against my molars, whirled about, and suicide dived into my feet. I slowed the Bomb down to a crawl, blinked hard, sucked in breath. My brain, roused from the warm and lovely fog surrounding it, scrambled to put together a plan, an excuse, a defense, something, anything.

You see, the lights were on at my house.

Which meant that somehow, defying all rules governing their behavior, my parents were up. And brother, if they were up, you can bet the farm they were waiting for my happy ass to arrive back at the old homestead.

"Oh shit," I whispered, yeah, like they were in the front seat and might hear me. "Oh shit, oh shit, oh shit!"

This couldn't be. I mean, my parents slept like dead rocks. They never, and I do mean absolutely without exception, never, woke up in the middle of the night. *I* was the light sleeper of the family.

Yet here we were.

Okay.

My initial impulse was to flee. But this would only make the water hotter, and besides, would require an effort that I did not have in me just then. Well, what the hell. The worst was they'd yell and threaten and make a big ruckus, mostly serving to keep me awake when I wanted so desperately to sleep. Oh, and they'd ground my ass forever, but what about that? It was five weeks to Christmas, and no grounding would hold through that. I could always play the "Gee, it's my last Christmas at home" card against them. Big deal.

What the hell.

I pulled the Bomb to a stop in front of the house, killed the engine, and sat there. I was too tired to be upset for long at this turn of events, but that did not mean that I was in a great skipping hurry to face it either. Jesus, the worst thing was that the stupid concert hadn't even been worth it, a wash, a dud, a surprising burst of flatulence, flying beds and all. And the ride home had been no great shakes either.

I got out and walked the long mile up to the front door. Somewhere down the street a dog barked with great enthusiasm. I despised the beast.

Okay.

Deep breath.

I opened the door and stepped in.

My mother sat on the couch, in her tattered red robe, worrying at a loose thread. Her eyes were puffy and fatigued. Her mouth hung down in a weighted frown, and maybe that spiked me with a little concern; she didn't look just angry, although that was there. There was something of sadness in her expression in the half second it took her to glance up at me.

My father was in his recliner, looking smaller than usual in his white T-shirt and pajama bottoms. He rose as I entered, and let me tell you, there was *no* mistaking the anger in his face. His cheeks were red and the bags beneath his eyes darkened more as he glared at me.

"Where," he asked, "have you been?"

"Uh, um . . ."

Well, why not the truth? It wouldn't get me any less dead, really.

"Dallas," I said.

My father blinked, as if I'd just blurted a phrase in Mandarin Chinese. "Dallas?"

"Me and . . . some friends, we went to see a concert in Dallas. Pink Floyd."

My father's lips clamped together like a threatened clam, and he lowered his head, closed his eyes, and generally gave me the impression that it was all he could do not to rip my head off.

"We have been worried *sick* about you," he said to the floor.

I gave my mother a look of regret, and I meant it. If I had thought they would be up half the night worrying about me while I sat through "The Dogs of War" I might not have gone. Making other people have a rough time is not my idea of fun. How was I to know they'd wake up, for Christ's sake?

"I'm sorry," I said. "I didn't mean to make you worry."

"We received a phone call," my mother said.

"Jen, that's not the issue here. That can wait."

"A phone call?" Who the hell would have called?

"Yes," said my father, and I could see that some of his anger was reluctantly fading. He wanted to be righteously pissed at me, and I couldn't really blame him. Although, if there had been even a prayer of them agreeing to let me go, I would have asked. I'm sure Doug's parents knew he was going. If I had gone around my parents, it was only because it was always an automatic dead end.

"The phone rang at two-thirty. It rang for almost ten minutes before I answered."

This, I understood, had my father as put out as anything. Having to actually answer the phone at two in the a.m. Having failed to ignore it.

I shivered. At two-thirty, I had been at the gas station in Ardmore. Had something happened there?

My father was saying something, but for a moment I tuned him out, because I could not remember if something had happened in Ardmore, and it seemed awfully damned important. It was our only stop after the show. We'd gotten gas, and coffee, and . . . I'd have taken a leak. That seemed right, but I couldn't remember using the restroom. Everything else was clear as a bell, but I could not remember using the restroom.

"—so I'm sure you'll know more about that later."

"Huh?" I hadn't caught a word of it.

My father sighed, too tired to even continue being angry. "The funeral arrangements. I'm sure you'll find all that out later. Despite tonight's episode, we'll see to it that you can go. Just let us know what's happening, will you son? Talk to your parents, as you should."

Hold it. "Funeral arrangements?"

A flash of the restroom in the gas station, the urinal, whipped through my mind, and I could not grab it.

"For your friend. Mick. Wasn't that the name? I think—"

Mick? Who the hell was Mick?

Someone screaming at me in the restroom, I held that much. But who? Why couldn't I remember?

Now my father and mother were staring at me with raw concern.

"Mick?" I asked.

"Your friend said it was cancer. You didn't know about this?"

"No." Jesus, the name was familiar, but it didn't mean anything to me. Cancer? I didn't know anyone with cancer.

"Who called?" I asked.

My father glanced at my mother. "Someone named Randy."

It all came back so hard, so suddenly, that it was like being punched in the chest. White fire filled my head. Oh god, Mick, Randy, the Swing, the blood, all of it.

Rebecca.

"Oh no," I whispered. Randy, screaming at me in the men's room, at two-thirty in the morning. Randy, who had told me to check on Mick. Oh, Christ, he'd been right, hadn't he?

I staggered backwards. Mick was dead. Randy was right. Randy was gone. Rebecca had done this. And she'd been able to make me forget everything, just like she'd done to us all before. The power to cloud men's minds. Who knows what evil? The Shadow, oh baby, oh Mick, the shadows know. And somehow, somehow, maybe the last thing he'd ever done, Randy had seen to it that I was not allowed to slip gently into that euphoric fog.

Mick was dead. Randy was gone. And whose fault was it?

All mine.

Because I wouldn't listen. Because I couldn't be bothered. Because I had no courage. Randy had shown me what she was, and Mick had sensed it, and both had wanted me to help them fight it. Well, it was too late for that now.

My father was saying something, spouting some nonsense about being in trouble, and though the words were meaningless bubbles to my ears, I could tell that he was pulled between anger and sympathy. And I understood that. And I lifted my face up, to speak to him, to tell him that it was okay, ground me, beat me, hell, throw me out, I understood. But my mouth opened and all that issued forth was a wordless, agonized howl. Tears blinded me. There was nothing to do for it. I turned and ran back out the front door, stumbling, unthinking.

DRIVING, ALMOST BLIND WITH tears and rage, useless seething hatred. It was still dark, almost five in the morning. I found myself in front of Mick's house. His car was not in its customary spot. I laughed. What car? There was no Mick's car anymore; any sign of him would surely have been wiped away, as had happened with Randy. Not a single shred of confirming evidence would be left behind. My god, was her power that absolute?

Yeah, maybe it was. Would my parents even remember the phone call in the morning? I thought not.

I sat in front of Mick's house. It was subtly different in some way, but I could not figure it out. It was right before me, but fatigue and grief blinded me. I shook my head and slumped against the wheel.

The grass.

I jolted up and scrambled out of the car. I ran up into the front yard of the Cornwell house and looked all over the ground. I couldn't truly believe it, any more than I could believe any of it, but I couldn't deny it either. I fell to my knees and ran my hands over the lawn.

The yard was green and lush, recently mowed. I looked at the house, and it was sided, neat, in good repair. The screen door had no dents or holes, the front door was not weathered and fading. The house was well kept. As if a divorced drunkard did not live there with his only son. It looked like the kind of place a bachelor of modest means might keep.

I ran from the truth.

Ran straight to Rebecca's apartment. Or to where it was supposed to be. At first I thought I was lost. I drove over the whole complex, but each time memory confirmed that I was right initially.

Just a few weeks before, I'd spent a very surreal couple of hours in her apartment. Just a few hours before, Doug and I had dropped her off and watched her walk in the front door.

Now there was no apartment. Now there was nothing but a concrete slab illuminated by my headlights, a foundation mostly obscured by the grass and weeds that had grown up all around it. I got out and walked around it. Even in the bad light from the car, I could see the black stains on the concrete. This was one of the buildings that had burned down in the great fire that had gutted so much of this huge complex. This particular one had not been rebuilt.

But goddamn it, I had been *inside* it. I had seen her apartment. The posters, the bed, all of it.

I shuffled around in the dark, lost, confused. Nothing made sense to me; I had the terrible feeling that nothing would ever again. A ferocious desperation took hold of my heart.

I screamed her name, once, twice.

Only silence in return.

And that was no real answer, so I left.

SHE SPOKE TO ME once while I drove. She said, "It's love, Eric. That's all there is. Believe me. Abyss to abyss, and in between, all you have is love. I need your love."

Maybe she was there, maybe not, but when I tried to respond, she was definitely gone.

"Go to hell," I said. Fuck her if she wasn't there.

Black of heart, I raced toward Stan's house, running lights, looping corners, and I don't know how I wasn't picked up. The drive was a blur, a journey without time or place, some kind of blind transference from point A to point B. Time only existed for me again when I slammed into the curb in front of Stan's house, my head smacking the steering wheel. I felt nothing. When I got out of the car, I slipped in dirt and fell down on the lawn. I cursed, got up, staggered for the front door. Fatigue did me in, turned me into an unguided marionette. But Stan had to know. He had been Mick's friend, too. He had to be told. Maybe we could all do it, maybe we could all get together and get rid of Rebecca, although I hadn't the faintest idea how. I remembered where his window was, stumbled around to it, pounded on the glass. I stood in the predawn and waited for him to respond. Nothing. I pounded the window again, and this time I cracked it. Too bad. Poor fucking window. This time, though, I was rewarded with Stan's puffy, bleary face trying to figure out who I was. Then it hit him, and he pointed to the front of the house.

Eventually he came out. His T-shirt was on backwards, and he'd missed a button on his jeans. He moved like a Claymation figure.

"What do you want?" His voice was thick with interrupted sleep.

"Mick's dead," I said.

He looked blank.

"Mick!"

Stan shook his head. "Who?"

I stared at him, exasperated. "Mick Cornwell, you asshole!"

Stan cocked his head at an angle that suggested he thought gears had slipped in my skull.

"Rebecca killed him," I yelled.

A slow grin spread across his face, one of those *oh, I get it now* expressions. He shook his head again. "Man," he said, "it's too early for this shit. And too cold!"

I gaped at him. He thought it was a joke. That set a fire off in me. Mick was dead and doofus here thought I was joking. So I popped him right across the jaw, and it snapped his head around in a very mean fashion, and he went down.

"Mick is *dead*, you asshole!"

He glared up at me from the ground, rubbing his jaw. "I don't know who the *hell* you're talking about!"

He didn't. He had no clue, and I could stand there all night long and try to pound it into him, and he'd never have a clue. He didn't *want* a clue.

I stood and trembled, and then felt ashamed. My anger wasn't with him. I just didn't know how to get to *her*. I spun away from Stan, fell, got back up, cursing. Fury blossomed in my heart like a nova. I scrambled back to the Bomb and roared away from Stan's house.

I drove like a screaming banshee, not knowing what to do or where to go.

Then the decision was removed from my hands altogether. I yanked my car around a corner much too hard and fast, and of course, slid out of all possible control. My stomach took a sickening lurch and the car crossed the intersection sideways. There was no time for thought before it smashed into a curb with a head snapping jolt. I sat for a moment, glanced out the passenger window, and realized I was staring at a light pole maybe six inches from the car. The engine was stalled. My heart raced, and I had trouble catching my breath. Tears formed in my eyes, and this pissed me off. I couldn't even go off on a mad tear without fucking it all up.

When I decided I had control of myself, I pulled off of the curb. I winced as the right rear tire hit the street with a hard thump.

It occurred to me that no one had seen my little stunt, and that I maybe ought to be grateful for that.

Well, now that I was calmed down, I realized there was one place I could go.

BEFORE I GOT THERE, she spoke again.

"Let me take care of you, Eric."

I looked over at Rebecca, and sneered. "Yeah? You can make everything good again, huh? You got that power, that magic power? Tell you what, I'll give you undying devotion, I'll fuck you so much you won't know the time of day, I'll pour my goddamn lifeblood down your throat, if you do one thing, one tiny little thing, one small bitty favor."

Her eyes were like those of a doll, huge and fixed. Maybe she forgot to breathe, maybe she never had to. But she was still and as unmoving as a tombstone. I'm not sure if she'd ever heard such venom from me; I was surprising myself with my capacity to hate. And, oh God, how I hated her.

"Bring Mick back."

"Eric, I can't."

"What? I thought you're this all powerful bogeywoman, able to read minds and leap tall buildings. You can kill and you can erase all traces of it, but you can't reverse it, huh? You can fuck and you can kill but you can't *create*?"

I turned off Broadway onto 3rd, we were in Edmond now.

"No," whispered Rebecca. I glanced at her and she was crying.

"Ah," I said, with a loud false air of congeniality.

No answer. I checked to see that she was still there. She was, and the tears were gone; only a cold hard determination shaped her features. Even in anger she was lovely. But it was artifice.

"Well, listen, bitch. What you've got ain't love, and I don't want it. Get out of my car, get out of my life, just go."

"Eric, you don't want to do this."

"JUST GO!" I screamed.

"You will regret this. We'll both regret this."

"Uh huh."

And then she was gone, and then I was at the gate of Sam's apartment complex. The guard, who by now must have thought I'd moved in, waved me on. I staggered up the steps, reached her door, and knocked. Well, banged my hand on it in low idiot rhythm. I felt myself sliding out of the world.

"You will regret this." A declaration of war? Probably. Who knew? Who cared? I pounded and pounded and then the door opened and there was Sam, oh Jesus, angel, angel, and I was falling, drifting down, and that was it for a long while.

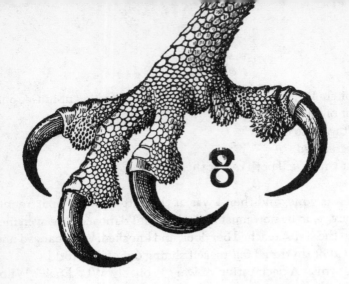

MY WAKING GROAN WAS louder in my head than all the bells of Notre Dame.

"That you, sport?"

I had no idea if I was me or not. The subject was a matter of pure speculation. I was not informed enough to contribute. On the other hand, I wasn't hungover. That was an ideal, genuine plus.

"Uh," I said.

I opened my eyes. Supernova sunlight reduced the inside of my skull to ash. But I got used to it.

Sam's face popped into view over me. Her obvious bemused concern was touching and comforting. She had dark bags under her eyes, and I realized I had probably put the perfect capper on an all-night study session or something like that.

"Want some coffee?"

"Uh," I said.

"Right, coming up. And phew, morning breath."

I closed my eyes.

Mick was dead.

Mick was *dead*.

It was a fact. It was real. And there was no one I could turn to. Who but me had any idea he'd ever existed? I had an idea that even my parents would have forgotten by now. If they'd ever really known who he was. That was the worst of it. No one would remember him, his whole human existence was gone, buried.

Sam came back. "Here."

I sat up, all my innards diving from my head to my ass, leaving me dizzy, weak. I took the mug of coffee from her with hands that trembled.

"Thanks, Sam." My voice sounded like dirty linen.

She sat on the footrest across from me, sipping from a mug of her own. Her hair was pulled back and clipped, and she had her heavy robe on. One of the monogrammed letters hung by a few threads.

"So what was it this time?"

I closed my eyes. Her tone was a little patronizing, a little exasperated, a little worried. I did a countdown before I responded. What good would it do to get pissed off at her? I was just tired and aching and scared. Mick was dead.

"Mick died," I told her.

Her expression did not change. "Who?"

I could not find words for a moment. She'd met him maybe a dozen times, nothing major, just in passing. Maybe it was possible that she wouldn't remember him very well. But this was Sam, who didn't miss much, and I didn't find that very likely.

"A good friend of mine."

She took my hand. "I'm sorry."

"Yeah. Me too."

And my composure collapsed like cold ashes. I fell against her, sobbing like a pitiful child. She held me and nothing more. No false soothing, no powerless platitudes. Just holding and wordless support. I don't know how long I cried, but it was a while, and Sam was there for every second, riding it out, holding me without complaint or demand.

But eventually the tears washed out, and I found, to my amazement, that something was different. It was as though my weeping, like a deluge from dark clouds, had scoured away the landscape of my fear and confusion, my doubt and dread, and exposed a bedrock of anger. Here, at last, was firm ground. Mick was dead, Rebecca was responsible, and goddamn it, I was *angry*.

"Thanks," I said into Sam's robe. "I feel better."

Well, different at least. Stronger.

She brought me to arm's length, holding my eyes with her own.

"You'd do the same for me."

"Yeah. I would."

"Then it's an even trade."

"Sam, it could never be even. You'll always be on the short end of *that* stick."

"Stop it. Want some toast?"

Food. Bleah. "Sure."

"We need to put some meat on your ribs." She rose and headed for the kitchen.

"I see you're still starving yourself."

"I'm—" *not*, I started to say, but I glanced down at myself, and tried to think when I'd last weighed myself. Or when I'd last had a really big meal. My shirt hung on me. I was not just not fat anymore. I was *skinny*.

"I'm just trying to get in some kind of shape," I told her. But was that true? I wasn't doing anything. I thought of Mick, and of cancer.

Why was she doing this?

Rebecca giveth and Rebecca taketh away?

Well, she sure took Mick away.

Sam set a couple of plates of toast on the table, a small tub of margarine and a little jar of Smuckers strawberry jam in the middle.

"What time is it, anyway?" I asked her

She smirked at me. "Two o'clock."

"Excuse me?"

"Two in the p.m., Mr. Lynch. You got a good night's sleep today. You snore, too."

"Um," I said, trying to reconcile three in the afternoon with Sam in a robe. "Don't you have classes today?"

"Midterm at five-thirty. I was up all night studying when you barged in."

"I'm sorry about that."

"Why?"

"Well, I mean, it was kinda late, or early, or—"

"Well, I am kind of put out."

I sat there in silence.

"You didn't call me right off. Instead you go wandering god knows where and show up at my door looking like a drowned puppy. Showing up on my doorstep at the wee hours, I could care less about that, but you could have spared yourself possible pneumonia."

"I thought you said pneumonia was bacterial?"

"Don't argue with the resident geek. Yeah, it's bacterial. It was a figure of speech." She took a bite of her toast and watched me to see if it was sinking in. Then she said, "On the other hand, you weren't drunk."

"It crossed my mind."

"Nonetheless."

"I didn't mean to—"

"I know. It's cool." She reached across the table for my hand.

"Hey, Sam, can I tell you something?"

"Shoot."

"Would it bother you if I maybe fell in love with you?"

Her grip tightened on mine. I thought her smile was the most beautiful thing I had ever seen, and a weird, pale shame came over me: Mick was dead— it repeated in my thoughts like a mantra that my subconscious whispered, and I had no right to joy or love or pleasure. I had survived him. Already that was too much.

"Nope. All I need from you, Eric, is for you to think of highly of you as I do. Okay?"

"Okay."

"I need to get ready to go take that test."

"What class?" I asked.

"Ugh. American history. My last one. Thank God."

"Cool."

"Listen. I've killed myself for this one. History slides right off my Teflon brain. I get done, I'm gonna need a stress buster. Why don't you call your folks while I get cleaned up, let 'em know where you're at—"

"Oh," I said, "joy."

"Hey, they're probably worried about you."

"Sure. I only snuck off to Dallas without telling them. I'm sure they're real happy with me."

"Well, tell 'em you've got a date tonight."

"Okay."

"Maybe we can go grab dinner, rent a movie, see where it goes from there." Her grin following this was very, decidedly, certainly, impure.

"Uh, okay."

"Now I gots to shower."

"I'll clean up," I said, and I stood to put our plates in the sink. I walked past her as she rose from her chair.

"Eric."

"Huh?" I turned to her. "What?"

"Put those down for a second."

"Sure," I said, "Wh—"

She put her arms around my neck and kissed me. For what seemed maybe an eternity. After I got over the initial shock, I put my arms around her, and just surrendered to it. She was warm in my arms, I melted into hers, and it felt like the most natural, comfortable haven I'd ever had. When we finally came up for air, my heart was racing, pounding, and I desperately hoped she hadn't felt my sudden erection. Hell, it was thick robe, maybe she hadn't.

I was made again.

"Just to convince you," she said, grinning. "Hm. And you know, it wasn't half-bad either. You been practicing?"

I watched her walk down the hall. Wondering, did she just do what I thought she did? Oh man. I felt a little less subhuman. I was wholly alive, in a way I wasn't sure I ever had been.

She was right about calling my parents, though. I heard the shower water start as I got up to go to the phone. I tapped out my home number, and listened to a half a ring before my mom picked up.

"Um, hi, Mom," I said, and the silence that greeted this was so tense it hummed. "I just wanted you to know that I'm okay, and I'm sorry for running out last night."

She sighed, either in relief or exasperation, I was not sure which. "Where are you? We've been praying for you all night."

"Well, I drove around all night, trying, you know, to get it out of my system. I wound up sleeping on Samantha Driscoll's couch."

There was a pause on her end. I could tell she really believed *that* one.

"He was a good friend of yours?"

"Yeah, mom, he really was."

"I don't think we ever met him."

But they had. At least a dozen times. He used to come by the garage all the time. Mick loved cars. My father had worked on his Camaro a couple of times.

"No, I guess you hadn't. I, uh, I really can't believe he's gone." Shit, I was *not* gonna cry again.

"I know. You never do when someone leaves you."

We both fell silent for a moment.

"Mom?"

"Yes?"

"I'm really sorry that I didn't ask you and dad about going to Dallas. It was a stupid thing to do. I didn't think you'd let me go, but it was still a rotten thing to do."

"It was. But I think, all things considered, it's bad enough for you. Just promise me you won't lie to us like that again."

I guess it happens to everybody, that strange, twilight moment when your parents begin treating you as an adult, as an individual with rights and problems outside of their sphere, when you blink, and suddenly you're really not their baby anymore. It's part freedom and part regret, and it's liberating almost beyond belief.

"I won't." And I wouldn't. Not ever again. "Um, there's one other thing."

"What's that?"

"I'd like to buy Sam dinner for putting up with me snoring on her couch last night. Would that be okay?"

She spent some time thinking that one over. I thought she was going to say no, that I had done quite enough carousing for the week, that I needed to get myself home that very second. And I think maybe before, she would have. But that Rubicon had been crossed. Things were different now, for good or bad.

"On one condition," she said, finally.

"What's that?"

"You ask her if she'd like to have Thanksgiving dinner with us."

"Mo-om—"

"That's the deal. I don't think you want to be arguing too much with it either. The Bible says—"

"Okay, okay!" After all it wasn't like they'd never met Sam before. And dear god, no Bible verses this early in the, uh, afternoon.

"What time will you be home?"

That was a new one: asking, instead of telling.

"By nine-thirty, latest. Probably earlier."

"I'll tell your father. And I'm sorry about your friend."

"Thanks, Mom."

I hung up and put a tape in Sam's stereo, some new band she'd gotten into named Concrete Blonde. It kicked ass. I cleaned up the table, occasionally glancing over at the stereo and nodding my appreciation.

I was thinking that I'd clean the apartment, vacuum, dust maybe, while Sam was off taking her test. You know, perform an uncharacteristic act of kindness. Earn points. I heard Sam drop the soap in the shower, and I smiled. My lips still tingled from her kiss. My God. The difference between Rebecca and Sam was the difference between a sparkler and the sun. I rinsed off the two plates and the two coffee mugs and put them in the dishwasher, noting that it was mostly full, and I decided to run it as soon as Sam was out of the shower. I filled it with soap, and wiped off the table. I was thinking I would shower myself after the dishwasher was run, scour away the stink of too much time spent in a car. The stench of myself was almost too much even for me. I wondered how Sam could have gotten close enough to kiss me without passing out. The reek could have killed a skunk.

She had laid out blankets on the couch, and I pulled them off and placed them to the side. I took the pillow out of the pillowcase, thinking what the hell, I could go wash the sheets, too. I would be Domestic Boy for the afternoon. It felt good.

It occurred to me that the shower was still going. Christ, I understood cleanliness and godliness and all of that, but this was ridiculous. I glanced at the clock, and saw that it was after three-thirty. Hadn't she said her test was at five-ish? And she still had to get to campus. I thought maybe she'd lost track of the time and so I went down the hall to knock on the bathroom door, to remind her to get a move on. I rapped my knuckle on the door, and it swung in.

Sam was sprawled half out of the bathtub, her left hand clutching the shower curtain and tugging it down from the rod. Her blue eyes were wide open and rolling frantically. They swept over me and it was clear that she did not see me. She spasmed and her free hand beat on the tile floor. Blood poured from her nose in a crimson river.

I screamed, everything in my body turning to ice, and rushed to get her up. I screamed her name over and over, as if by doing so I could freeze the world in its tracks, suspend time, heal wounds. I tried to get her sitting up but she was wet and jerking and slippery. Her mouth flopped open and a choked, wordless moan escaped. Incredibly, the flow of blood increased, and I saw with a slash of terror that her ears were bleeding as well. She was hemorrhaging to death before my eyes; there was so much blood, too much. I tried again to get her up and out of the shower, but I slipped on the bloody tile and we both went down. Her face lay close to mine, dark blood running from her mouth, and then her gaze seemed to clear for a second, she saw me, and she started to try to say my name. I'm sure she did. But then one of her eyes filled with blood, and my name became a weak, gargling rattle. An air bubble formed on her nostrils, ceased expanding, froze. She was still.

I lay under her, unable to move, to think, to be. I called her name once, twice, and still she did not move. The idiot shower ran on. Steam billowed through the bathroom.

"I told you, Eric, you're mine."

Oh Jesus.

Rebecca stood in the doorway. She wore an expression of grief that was as false as a preacher's promise. Black shirt, black jeans, dark angel of loss.

"I told you," she said.

"She's dead?" I whispered, and speaking it made it real, and something inside me ruptured, loosing dark toxins.

Rebecca stepped back, away, and was gone. I wailed, and cradled my dead love, and I really don't remember much for a long time after that.

PART FOUR: PAINTED BLACK

SAM WAS BURIED ON Saturday, November 21st, 1987, four days before Thanksgiving.

THE MINISTER, A TALL, gentle man named Stern, delivered his sermon in a kind cadence. He had known Sam since she was a child, had presided over her confirmation, had no doubt looked forward to officiating her wedding. It was clearly evident that this was deeply painful for him. The eulogy was shot through with pauses and false starts, laced with agonized sincerity. It made me feel no better.

I was in the front row, in a black suit my father had purchased for the occasion. The Driscolls had asked me to serve as a pallbearer. It was the cruelest thing ever requested of me. I didn't hesitate in doing it.

Doug sat on my right, and beyond him were his parents and one surviving grandmother. They all wore the same face. I wore it too, I suppose, because it was the easiest thing for my numbed brain to project. Unlike them, I was not stunned. I was not shocked. I was cast into stone by hatred.

Stan had managed to get a bottle of Everclear the previous night. I don't know how. His brother, I guess. I did not ask. I'd polished most of it off before dressing for the funeral. I had hoped it would help. It didn't.

The Reverend Stern proceeded with his farewell to Sam, and I stared at the white casket, surrounded with numerous floral sprays. The colors, though supposedly muted and respectful, struck me as garish. I could smell them, from where I sat, and the fragrance left me sick.

I did not cry.

I had not shed a tear since the moment the ER physician had delivered the sentence. I had none in me. The inferno consumed them.

Intracavernous aneurysm with epistaxis, the doctor had said. Catastrophic was his word for it. Almost unheard of.

And that would be right. An autopsy would have shown it. There was no doubt in my mind that the doctor was right; the instrument of her death was a burst blood vessel, a sudden, massive cranial hemorrhage.

But it was Rebecca who had killed her.

And the bitch, the savage black bitch, who could have erased Sam, her memory, her existence, erased it all—didn't, wouldn't. That would destroy the lesson, obscure the point.

Pain was the point. Fear was the method.

There would be no love but hers.

Fuck fear. Fuck Rebecca.

The choir sang, an incongruous thing at a funeral if you ask me, but no one did. It was some sort of inspirational thing that was, I guess, supposed to reassure us that Sam had departed for a better place, some sanitized, sanctified afterlife where cherubs and a benevolent deity took care of her. Her pain, we were supposed to believe, was no more. I thought it was all a load of horse shit.

My parents would have bought it. They'd raised me to buy it as well. And I guess I could accept that all manner of strange shit was out there in the world—didn't I have Rebecca and Randy to prove that? But I had no sense that there was anything loving looking out for us in the big black cosmos. What God in any Heaven would allow creatures of Rebecca's sort? And if that God couldn't protect us from the likes of here, then what good was He or She? I saw no Maker to ease our burden, Rebecca would not be taken out by any Savior, no angel would descend from upon high to let this poison cup pass away. I wanted to believe it, all of my upbringing primed me to believe it. But I could not.

Nor would she be taken out by us. Our jones was too strong. Even mine. How long would it be before I succumbed to her condolences, her ministrations? How long would it be before I took her embrace and allowed her erasing wind into my mind so that I would not have to feel Sam's absence anymore? Right now, never. I told myself that I owed Sam my pain, if nothing else. But in a week, a month, six months? Might I not grow tired of it? And would I ever be free after that? It was only through dumb luck and the last effort from Randy that I had regained myself this time. And what about my loved ones, would they ever really be safe from her jealous possessiveness? Jesus, what if someone, some girl somewhere, sometime—coworker, classmate, friend of a friend—developed a crush on me, on any one of us? What then? Heart attack? Convenient car wreck? Would Rebecca respond with the same ruthlessness? How could she not?

Doug nudged me as the organ music rose into some pompous dirge, something Sam would have hated. He nodded toward my end of the pew. It was time to get to the vestibule. I rose, Doug following, and we joined the others already there. There were four other pallbearers, none of whom I'd ever met before the funeral. One of them was a thick, short guy in his early thirties (I guessed) who kept glancing at me as if he had something important to tell me, but always glanced away. There was a cousin of some sort and a classmate. A guy from the church. Strangers, linked by her, bonded now by an empty, icy space.

We lined up as we'd rehearsed and awaited the processional. I could see Doug's parents from where I stood, and my heart wrenched. They looked feeble, little people made of pale dust. Herb Driscoll's eyes were red and leaking. His expression suggested that he was being lacerated over and over. Mrs. Driscoll could have been a statue, a mummy. She looked dazed, and her stare frequently wandered to the stained glass windows. Scenes from the Bible, rendered in jagged jigsaw pieces of technicolor, fairy tales for adults.

There was a pause, and the processional started. We marched out like good dull ants to Sam's casket. The wooden handles were fat and cold. We lifted her as one, and I was shocked that she was so light.

As one, we carried the casket—Sam—down the aisle and out to the waiting hearse, a vehicle almost the same shade of ivory as the casket. It had rained again the night before, plastering the pavement with dead leaves and drowned earthworms. Spatters of red mud caked the running boards of the hearse. Christ, they could have washed it. They could have done that.

It was a crisp, clear November afternoon. No clouds in sight, just the bright blue dome of sky. It was a good day for football, a great day for it. I'd never gone to a game with Sam, I couldn't even remember if she liked it, and my thoughts recoiled. Jesus, anything to keep from thinking of Sam.

I wrenched my gaze away from the hearse and the sky and looked instead at the uglier, more mundane gray and brown buildings of downtown Oklahoma City. First Lutheran was an old, old church, and much of downtown had grown around it. Across the street was an ancient plumbing supply warehouse, as empty and washed by time as a forgotten temple. I glanced at it, and my heart froze.

Rebecca sat on the front steps of the long unused entrance. She was dressed in a long black dress, some somber affair that veered as close to slinky as it could get and not be disrespectful. I could not read her expression.

I closed my eyes as we reached the hearse and slid the coffin into place. The funeral home attendants took over from there, and we all stepped away, none of us looking at each other very much. This was too real, too raw, for all of us.

I looked again at the warehouse, but Rebecca was gone. I closed my eyes again and pulsing lights and strange melting shapes tumbled. I shook my head, unsure just how firm my grip was on reality.

I was supposed to ride out to the cemetery with the Driscolls, and so I followed Doug to the family Cadillac. Halfway there, he turned and faced me. He opened his mouth to say something, but only an anguished croak came out. He blinked rapidly, as if that would dissipate the tears.

"Ah, shit, man," I rasped, and we embraced each other, somehow drawing enough strength to not disintegrate into our constituent atoms, to draw a breath, and after that, another. We held each other, for a minute, two, and then it passed for a time, as much as it could. Doug stepped away from me and dried his eyes. We continued to the car.

The four of us—Doug, myself, his parents—made the trip to the graveyard in shell-shocked silence, smothered in despair so heavy none of us could lift it.

The cemetery was called Restful Oaks, and that really should tell you all you need to know. It was one of the new breed of boneyards that resemble golf courses more than the place where we drop the remains of our loved ones. I will not have my bones put to rest in one of these places; I'd rather be cremated and dumped into Lake Hefner if it comes down to it. The grass was well manicured, the three trees that I saw were healthy and lush, everything was neat and in order, and it had all the soul of a K-Mart.

At the graveside we dutifully gathered around the coffin, which sat on the canvas bands, ready to be lowered into the worm-ridden earth. I sat with the Driscolls. In this time of pain, I was family, it seemed. My own parents were farther back, standing, both dressed in their best, most somber black. I scarcely recognized my father, who wore suits to church that could graciously be considered tacky. Today, he looked appropriate. But my heart wailed at all the black and dourness. This was not what Sam would have wanted. She'd have insisted on a loud slobbering feisty Irish wake, full of energy and a zest to live on, to attack each day in her memory. If anything, to be angry, goddamn it, angry that she was gone from us, to fight back against the impartial and uncaring universe to show that we cared. All these tears, however much we all needed to shed them, were selfish and did her infinite disservice.

And of my grief? It was there, but it was more and more consumed by that furnace of rage, fuel for the hatred that I so wanted to unleash at Rebecca.

I would somehow, someway, use that firestorm of anger in me to destroy Rebecca.

So many destroyed by that creature. All I could do for them now, I knew, was to see that it never happened again.

I don't remember much of the graveside service. My thoughts were churning elsewhere, and I paid no attention to the proceedings. They were dropping Sam into a hole; fine, she was already gone. Rebecca had already taken her.

I blinked, surfaced back to attention. Something had caught me, snagged my sight. I looked across the grave, over the heads of the assembled mourners, and saw Rebecca again. She stood beneath one of the oaks, and the question on her face was clear.

Had I learned my lesson?

Well, maybe it was time for a change to the course.

I waited for the service to drag itself out, to wind down. It took forever. And then afterward, the condolences, the meaningless platitudes meant to give us some measure of comfort but were, of course, only fucking useless mumblings, nonsense syllables. People meant well, but I wanted to choke the living daylights out of each of them. Jesus. What words could ever be said that would fill the gaps, the chasms left by Sam's absence?

Soon it was over, Sam's mother weeping and being led away by Doug and his father, and from their expressions, the tears were catching. I broke away from the other family members and friends drifting away from grave, dodged my parents, and headed for Rebecca.

She was still there.

"I'm sorry, Eric. I know you don't believe that, but I am."

"Bet you are. Bet it just breaks you all up inside. I guess you've been just all weepy. Oh boy. Tell me another one. Maybe you didn't notice, that was a funeral. I could use a few laughs."

She took a step toward me, hesitant, wary. "Put yourself in my shoes. You'd have done it, too. You'd have done it to live. And it doesn't change anything. I still need you."

"I think plenty's changed."

Rebecca shook her head. A rueful smile touched her face. She tenderly touched my face.

I snatched her arm and squeezed as hard as I could. If it pained her at all, it did not reach her face.

"Don't fucking touch me. Don't ever touch me," I hissed.

"You never complained before."

"That's not a complaint. It's a warning."

She walked a few paces away from me. Her arms wrapped themselves around her like a pair of strong black snakes, boas, in a sad mockery of self-consolation.

"You won't hurt me, Eric, it's not in you. None of you would harm me, even if you could. I'm everything you ever wanted. You got distracted, but that's over. You think you're angry, but I think you're really relieved. No choices now."

"What did we ever do to deserve this, huh? Tell me that one, you bitch. What the hell did we ever do to deserve this? We were just a bunch of kids."

"You make it sound so terrible."

And then she laughed.

"I'll never leave you. I'll never grow old. I'll never die on you. Yours for all your days. What more could you want? I'll *always* be here, Eric."

She pointed to Sam's grave. "And I can erase your pain. I can make it like she never existed."

Like Randy. Like Mick.

She stepped up to me. "Eric . . ."

Feather touch.

In my head.

Sam: "I'll always be here for you. When no one else is, I will be."

I think the last thing Rebecca expected was for me to wrap my hands around her throat, but that was just what I did. I meant to throttle the life out of her. I was not joking. No fooling around. I squeezed with all my might. For a second her eyes bulged, her tongue popped out between her lips, and the expression of shock on her face was almost comical. Almost.

I want to say that there was a heat shimmer then, some kind of ripple that warped the air between us. No matter how hard I try to remember this, there are aspects of it that completely elude me. I think there was something about it that my mind, that no human mind, could process, accept. She still felt solid; that is, I could feel her flesh beneath my hands. But what I saw shifted and blurred with incredible speed. And the smell, something ferociously rotten, crotch rot of the dead, evil, foul. I gagged and scrambled away from her, and got a glimpse of something pale and spotted with yellowish growths, and teeth, Jesus Christ, so many teeth, blunted grinding things that would not leave the quick painless shock damage of a piranha but would instead mash you into a pulped but living shred of agony.

I couldn't even scream in the face of so alien a monstrosity.

Then it was just Rebecca again, stunned and gasping, and in a flash she was gone. Not a trace of her remained.

I fell to my knees and sobbed.

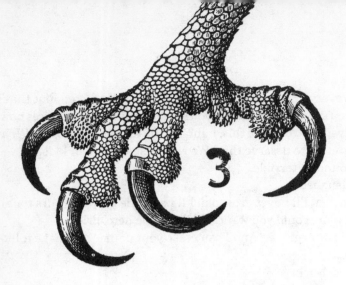

3

THE DAY AFTER THE funeral, I went to see Stan.

I rang the bell and waited for the door to answer. I knew Stan was home, his car was there. Also his mom's Ford.

It was Wednesday, a school day, but I wasn't playing hooky. The school counselor, a nebbish man named Cunningham, had suggested to my parents that I be kept out a few days, to mourn, I suppose. Probably the man did not want my darkness to infect the cheery halls of Wood Wilson. My parents would have done it anyway, I think. They hadn't said much to me at all since Sam's death. Both of them probably misunderstood my dark silence to be an urge to be left alone, to come to grips with my loss, but they were dead wrong; I feared that if I opened my mouth more than necessary, all the rage and hatred I was storing would pour out, and I would be left empty and weaponless. I had stopped drinking after the funeral for this very reason. I was a wreck, shaky, hungover and abominable in appearance, but I was still whole.

Stan hadn't been to school either, from what I'd been told by one of my coworkers when I'd gone into Tate's to give my notice. Apparently, he'd missed a couple of shifts as well, and Craw was *this* close to canning him. I was not surprised. Stan had Rebecca. What else was there?

I rang the bell again. Come on, Livingston.

When the door opened a minute or so later, Stan was a mess. He looked as though he hadn't slept a wink since the Floyd show. His hair was greasy and uncombed, and fell down over the bruise I'd given him the other night. The bruise was faded to a washed iodine orange, and in a day or two would be gone altogether. Why hadn't she taken care of that the way she'd healed my hand after I'd cut it with the wine glass at Sam's?

Maybe the goodies stopped once she had you. Maybe she didn't need to dispense them anymore. Or maybe she wasn't as powerful as she thought. Maybe all this work was wearing her out.

"Hey," Stan said. His worn, red eyes peered at me from dark-ringed holes.

I saw that he was thinking I looked like shit, too. Well. Another little thing we had in common.

"I needed some company," I said. "Just to talk a little."

"Oh," said Stan.

I waited for this to process.

"Well, can I come in?"

"Oh," said Stan. "Uh, sure."

He unlocked the storm door and let me in, rubbing his face to maybe see if it was still there. We paraded through the living room, which smelled strongly of rose incense. Stan's shirt stuck out in the back, and he had no socks on. Like he had to get out of bed to get dressed.

Just missed her, I thought.

At first I thought no one else was home, that maybe Stan's dad had found some day work somewhere, but then I heard a fan running in his parent's room, and knew that his mom was home. She ran the fan during the day to mask out the bumbling racket of day creatures like us. I hardly ever saw Stan's mom. She might have been mythical, except that someone was paying the rent and it sure as shit wasn't Mr. Russell.

Stan went to the kitchen, trailing me, and he got a couple of Buds from the refrigerator.

"Early, ain't it?"

"Shit," said Stan.

I took one from him, so who was I to talk?

"Some shit about Doug's sister, huh?" He leaned against the counter and took a swig.

"Yeah," I said, my voice breaking. "Some shit."

My tone caught his attention and he stared at me. "You okay?"

I smiled. Stan blanched at it.

The kitchen was a mess, a disaster area of dirty dishes and stale food, maybe three, four days' worth of it all piled in the sinks and on the counters. Half empty glasses and crumpled beer cans stood guard over it all. A Pizza Hut box covered much of the dining area table. Maybe half a pizza was still in there. A fat joint, half smoked, drowned in a puddle of beer, lay next to it. I looked for the answering machine, saw it on the floor next to a cabinet, the red LED display flashing ten. Ten messages, Jesus.

"Yeah," Stan said. "I guess I ought to clean house."

I wondered about the fan. And the incense.

"Your dad find work?"

Stan flinched. Only a little, tiny bit. But he did flinch. "Yeah. Manpower got him something."

I finished off my Bud. My stomach was starting to hurt. "You know I was seeing Sam?"

Stan looked at me with genuine surprise. "But . . ."

He didn't finish his sentence, but the rest of it was pretty goddamn clear: Why, when there was Rebecca?

"It's true."

He shook his head. "Jesus, man, I'm sorry."

"I was there when she died."

Now Stan flinched again.

"So was Rebecca."

He laughed nervously. "Oh, come on, Eric. I was with her Friday. We were out gettin' a burger."

Stan's eyes did not meet mine.

"Well, you know she didn't like it." Circling around the matter like warring mongrels judging if the battle would be worth it.

"No," Stan said. "She wouldn't."

The silence stood between us for a minute. I wasn't going to keep at it. What was the point?

Finally, I said, "You been gettin' sleep? You look awful."

Stan shook his head. "I'm fine."

He chugged down the rest of his beer and opened the fridge to get another. He had to search for it, bending over and rooting through all kinds of stuff, and when he did, I looked past him and saw that the door to his father's rec room was slightly ajar.

Maybe that's when it occurred to me. I'm really not sure.

"Learned any new tunes?" I asked him this because I had to say something to prevent my mind from heading down the path it wanted to.

Stan produced two more beers, Coors, and gave me a bright expression. "Well, yeah, actually I have. I've been writing stuff now, pretty good stuff."

I doubted that, but nodded and accepted a Coors.

"Here," he said, "I'll play some for you." He whipped past me and darted off to his room. I glanced at the den, at the open door, and followed him.

He already had his guitar slung on and was jacking into the amp. His room was an even more horrid wreck than usual. A faint, stale smell clung to everything, and there was a lot to cling to: the ubiquitous dirty laundry flung everywhere, tapes and records scattered about, an ashtray crowded with cigarette butts (and since when did Stan smoke?), a half-eaten slice of pizza on the floor next to the bed with funky fuzz growing on it. Only the bed was clear of debris, and it seemed to have been used recently, the sheets in a tangle.

Stan sat on the bed and looked down at the frets, idly noodling, running some scales, scooting through snatches of songs, a wisp of Rush's "Closer to the Heart." Then he paused, looked at me, said, "Check this out."

His fingers moved like mercury, fluid and grace. All expression washed out of face and he closed his tired eyes. He played blindly.

And what he played: an amazing mix of blues and jazz, dark muscle and clever fancy, flowing into a sleek seamless stream, smooth and sure. The piece moved and slunk with the night grace of a jungle cat. Stan played with mastery, with a skill I'd never personally witnessed. I could not breathe while he played; to do so would have shattered the beauty of the song, and that I could not do.

When he was done, the last note faded from the amp, he blinked rapidly, as if clearing his head, and said, "Well?"

"It's incredible."

"Thanks."

"Has it got a name?"

"Not yet. Rebecca—" He stopped short, as if he'd just blurted a state secret. "Yeah?"

Stan grinned sheepishly. "Rebecca's writing some words for it. We're, uh, forming a group. I mean, with her."

Was this supposed to wound me somehow? That Stan had not only shut me out of his "band" but that Rebecca was now in? The idea that I'd ever wanted to play in a band felt like some distant childhood memory now, foolish and insignificant.

Still, I had to ask, "What's Doug think of that?"

Stan said, "Who cares?"

I shrugged.

Stan rested the guitar on his lap and stared at me. "You pissed at her or what?"

I almost lost myself. Pissed at her? Jesus, the sun's heat was nothing compared to that of my rage. *Pissed* at her?

But what could I say to Stan that would mean a damn thing? He was hooked on the worst smack there was. I couldn't change that. Doug was undoubtedly in the same shape. Words would not suffice; they would never be persuaded to walk away from her. Never.

They would never make her leave. They would not spit the hook out.

Then the line had to be cut.

And I knew how to do it. And I wondered if that was the whole reason, the only reason, I'd come over. I felt a thread of shame and fear start working through me as I realized what I had to do, but then remembered the color of Sam's eyes and that stomped those feelings flat. We deserved everything we would get, for no other reason than that Sam and all the others had not.

The idea spun in my head like a gemstone, and its facets became clear to me. It could be done. It would be terrible, but I could do it. And it had to be done soon. While she might still be weak enough for it to work. Like tonight.

"Hey," I said, "I gotta piss, you mind?"

Stan smiled at me, a ghost of his old self. "Long as you don't do it here."

He looked down at the guitar, fiddling again. I got up and closed the door behind me, and briskly walked past the bathroom, through the kitchen, into the rec room.

It was the gun mecca I remembered. I looked around at the rifles. Too big. There were two swords mounted on the far wall, where the garage door had once been. Too slow, and what if they were ceremonial and dull as shit? No good. A pistol would be best. I went to the tall gun cabinet, saw spaces in the hunting rifles. My guess was that Stan's dad was dipping into his collection for smoke money. Oh well. I looked at the three drawers, hoping like shit they weren't locked, because if they were I had no idea where I'd get a gun. Shit, I couldn't buy one. I knew of nobody who would do it for me. My father didn't own any, and I knew for damn sure that Doug's didn't, probably had never even fired one.

I tried the top drawer, and to my everlasting relief, it slid smoothly open. Four pistols lay inside. I quickly tried to decide which I wanted. Christ, what if Stan came out to get a beer or something and heard me? What if his mom got up? But I knew squat about guns. There was what looked like a .45 automatic (at least it looked like the guns you always saw officers carry in World War II movies), there was something that looked like a Luger, and two revolvers. One of those was a monster of a gun, with a barrel that looked like it was ten feet long. Jesus, you could stop a tank with that.

I didn't see myself as the Dirty Harry type, and selected the smaller gun, which was, I was informed by the engraving on the body, a Smith and Wesson .38 caliber. The barrel was very short. I fumbled the cylinder open and saw that the gun was empty. Great. I opened the next drawer and saw a multitude of ammunition boxes, including bullets for the .38. I jammed the pistol down the back of my jeans and opened the box of bullets. I plucked a dozen or so out of the Styrofoam holder and shoved them in my pockets, put the box back, closed the drawer. Everything looked fine. I just hoped Mr. Russell wouldn't be checking in on his collection anytime soon. The bulge of bullets in my pocket was not terribly noticeable. Fine.

I scrambled out of there, feeling that lump of steel pressing against the small of my back like an old accusation. I stopped at the fridge and found each of us a beer, the last ones as far as I could tell.

I paused before Stan's door, cursed myself, and stepped back to the bathroom and flushed the toilet. Verisimilitude.

Coming out, my anxiety lower now, I caught that smell of incense again, but fainter now, and something more unsavory beneath it now. I looked toward his parents' room and stepped that way. No question. It was coming from there. Beers clinking together in my left hand, I nudged the door open. Never mind what I would say if Stan's mother was getting up from her sleep. I would be an embarrassed and sorry shit if I was wrong and she was awake, of course I would be . . . but, damn, that smell.

The door eased open quietly. The room was dark, the heavy drapes barring all sunlight. My eyes had to adjust to the dim. Once they did, I saw the dresser, a fat recliner in one corner, a huge painting up on one wall, the box fan, and the bed.

And in the bed, the Russells. Asleep, maybe, if you didn't look too hard or breathe through your nose. The room smelled of shit and decay.

It didn't take a genius. Maybe they didn't approve of Rebecca, or maybe there was going be a divorce with Stan being taken off somewhere. Maybe. Maybe they wanted to send Stan off to some school farther away than OU, maybe. Like Vermont.

Whatever. Maybe it just came down to Stan having to make a choice, Rebecca or family, and choosing poorly.

Jealousy was a bitch where Rebecca was concerned.

I backed out of the room, closing the door.

Tonight. Tonight for goddamn sure.

I handed Stan the beers when I went back to his room, letting a mask slip down over me. I cleared a space on the floor and sat.

"Here," I said. "I got us some more brewskis."

"Hey, great."

Jesus, what was I supposed to say to him? He sat in here fucking around on his guitar like it was no big deal, like he didn't know his own parents lay dead just down the hall. Probably he didn't. Rebecca's magic touch again.

"What are you going to call the band?"

Stan shrugged. "I dunno. Rebecca'll think of a name."

She would too, and it would be a good one. In fact, I was completely certain that not only would she come up with a killer moniker for their little group, but the group itself would be hot, good enough to get a deal, maybe good enough to make a shitload of money at it. A shitload. And one day, Stan would wake up, old and astonished, and if Rebecca still needed him to stick around, if she had not found some other need strong enough to anchor her to the world of light, Stan would discover that if the lure of lust was no longer sufficient to keep him lashed to this ghoul, then the eternally shining bauble of fame would be.

And for Doug? Some sort of meteoric rise through research and academia, a vaulting over his own limitations, recognition for the clarity and originality of ideas he could not truly claim? Why not? Everyone has a price and everyone has a drug and for the most pitiable of us, it is the same thing.

Stan said, "You could be in the band."

Oh, Jesus wept.

"I mean, we've got a bass player, and he'll do, but you'd be a whole lot better."

"I haven't played my bass in almost two months."

He shrugged.

Was this my drug? I could see it, you know. I would hook up with them, all forgiven, and we would come up with some monster songs. Tour the clubs for a while, build up a live following to make it legit, sign a major deal, have a smash album. Live the high life. Have no other gods before Rebecca. It could happen.

Except my drug, the only one I could ever want again, was in a grave out in Restful Oaks.

I shook my head. "No, that's okay. I appreciate the offer."

There was something like pity in Stan's bloodshot eyes.

The hammer of the revolver dug into the small of my back, and it was starting to hurt. And the image of Stan's parents kept trying to nudge into my thoughts. I had to get out of there.

I looked at Stan. "Listen, there's something I want to do tonight."

Stan cocked his head.

"Something I gotta show you."

"What?"

I shook my head. "I'll show you tonight."

Stan flinched again, that subtle wincing. "Why? It's supposed to be colder'n hell tonight. I ain't goin' out."

"Well, beer is involved. I want to get completely shitfaced. And you'll really want to see this. I mean it, you can't miss it."

"Well . . ."

"I'll bring the beer. And Rebecca will be there."

Stan brightened. "Well, then. Sure, man."

I couldn't help it. "Will it be a problem with your folks?"

He twitched. He looked down at the floor, shuddered again, and I thought then that the whole thing might come apart. I thought that it was such a horrible thing that even Rebecca's tinkering could not keep it suppressed. For a second, it looked like Stan was going to fall apart at the seams and come out of it. But then, like a true junkie, he looked back at me with a shaky, but sincere, smile.

"No," he said. "It won't be any problem at all."

I told him I'd come get him around ten, and left.

Outside of the Russell house, I got in the Bomb but hesitated before sticking the key in the ignition. I looked at the sky for a moment, and then threw my head against the steering wheel and wept for a long time. I have no idea who I cried for. There were so many of us. There always are.

REBECCA CALLED MY HOUSE.

"What are you doing, Eric?"

"I'm about to go help clean my father's shop."

"That's not what I mean. You're up to something. I can feel it."

"Yeah?"

Was that a sob on the other end of the line? Jesus, what baloney. "I'm not your enemy, Eric, I wish you'd see that."

"Guess I'm just too blind there, Becca."

But what I *did* see was this: I wasn't the blind one. The instincts of this monster were good, it's power to warp reality strong, but it wasn't a god. It didn't know all, or see all. And it could read neither my heart nor my mind.

It wasn't lying about one thing: it really did need us. It needed us in the worst way. I was counting on that to be the one stone truth left to me.

"Tell you what, I'm planning to get together tomorrow," I lied. "Maybe we can work this out."

"Eric . . ."

"See you then," I said, and hung up.

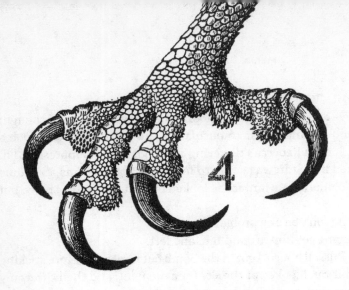

4

I HELPED MY FATHER finish up the jobs he could before shutting down for Thanksgiving. When I got there he was up under a big black Olds 88, checking out the brakes. His hands were busy so he just nodded at me as I came in. I went and got a broom. There was no thought behind this. I just wanted to do something for a while, something that did not involve thought or planning or involvement. Sweeping the floor fit the bill. So I swept: enjoyed the fluid motion of muscles moving past muscles, the rhythmic and soothing repetition of the work, the near absence of being. I could understand why some monastic orders stress hard manual labor. It has a focusing, calming effect. After a couple of hours I was settled in what I had to do.

The whole time, my father did not speak. Never an eloquent man, he was doubly uncomfortable with my feelings regarding Sam and her death. I would see him once in a while pause from his work, idly rearranging grease on his hands with a filthy rag, and regard me. Actually, I felt for him. My father was one of those men ill-suited for fatherhood who nonetheless do the best they can at it. As deeply spiritual as he was, he had trouble molding advice from scripture around real world problems. And, I don't think he ever understood me enough to get close to me. Yet I think he saw the pain I was in, and it reawakened some sense of devotion and empathy in him. He just didn't know what to do with it.

Around six-thirty, daylight gone, we closed down the shop, all neat and packed away for the two-day break.

I watched him lock up the bay door and then check the office lock. It was ritual for him, as his whole life was ritual. I understood that, although I also understood that no rituals would protect me. Rebecca taught me that much. Primal forces always overrode them.

My father slid his keys into his overalls and turned away from the shop into which so much of his life was invested. He smiled at me, a sad and tentative gesture.

"You haven't said much tonight."

I shrugged. I hadn't said anything. I had only swept as though to burn up tears. "I know."

"She meant a lot to you, didn't she?

It was the first time either of my parents had said much about it.

"Yeah. She did."

My father nodded.

I tried to speak, but the lump in my throat would not let me. My father—my dad—opened his arms, and we embraced as we had not done in maybe ten years. He was a big man, as I've said before, but now his very size was a comfort.

"God has a reason," he said.

I doubted that.

He let me go and stood back. "But those reasons aren't always clear to a man, and they hurt all the same. So you let those tears out. A man weeps when he has to, and God don't begrudge it to us. So you cry if you need to."

Through tears, I watched him get into the truck and start it up.

"I'll see you at the house," he said.

He pulled out of the drive as I got in the Bomb. I watched his taillights recede down 36th street until I could no longer pick them out, then got out of my car and used my spare key to get in the shop. I flicked on the big overhead fluorescent lights and scanned the shelves. It took me a minute, but I found what I needed.

People who work with tools a great deal often develop a collector's mentality about them and that's a mentality I can certainly understand. They go to garage sales and flea markets and little hole-in-the-wall hardware stores in tiny little towns and look for odd assortments of tools, most of which they'll never use, some of which they can't even name. My father was no different. And among the odds and ends he'd picked up was an enormous portable lantern, older than dirt, that ran off a fat twelve-volt battery. The lens on the thing was the size of a small dinner plate. Knowing my father, I thought the battery would be charged, and it was. I turned off the overhead lights, locked up again, and stuck the lantern in the trunk.

MOM HAD DINNER SET, some kind of nameless casserole that principally featured ground beef and cheese. It smelled great. I had no appetite, but that was normal now. We ate and offered small talk to each other. I told my parents that I had given Tate's two weeks' notice. I told them I needed new surroundings. They agreed. It was a good dinner. A good last supper. We watched TV, *Magnum, PI*, a show they usually did not care for. At eight-thirty, they wished me a good night, and the last I saw of them was their disappearance down the dark hall.

Once I heard the snoring start, I got a piece of notebook paper and an envelope out of my mom's Bible-study desk. I wrote the following:

> Mom and Dad,
> By the time you read this, you'll know what happened. Please understand that I had no choice in this. Please understand that what I have done I have done out of love for you, for my friends, for Sam. I can't explain all of it & there isn't time and you wouldn't believe me.
> But believe this: we didn't mean for any of it to happen. I don't know if it helps but it's true.
> Your son,
> Eric Peter Lynch

I sealed it in the envelope, left it on the kitchen table, turned the television off, locked the front door and left for Stan's house. It was nine o'clock.

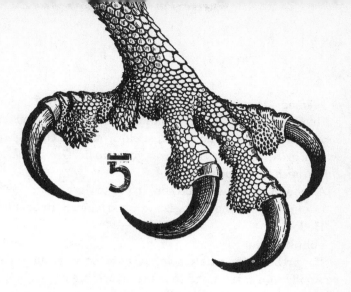

5

THE AIR HAD TURNED savagely cold and the sky was starless. Stan had been right; it was an early taste of winter. This worried me. I had to have both of them willing to go down to the Swing. Well, there was nothing to do but take the chance and damn the consequences.

Before I started the Bomb, I opened the glove box and took the revolver out. I brought out six bullets and loaded the gun. My hand shook as I stuck it in the small of my back. A bump too hard and I'd blow myself a new asshole.

I drove over to Stan's first; it was closer. I was deeply worried that Rebecca would be there. I also half expected that he would have found some chickenshit reason to back out, but I was wrong on both counts. He came out in a heavy jean jacket and gloves.

"Shit," he said. "I think it's gonna snow, man."

"Too early for that."

"Yeah, well."

He rode shotgun with me over to Doug's, the latest Whitesnake on. We talked about that record for a bit, and all the personnel problems of that band as recorded by such respected journals as *Creem*, *Hit Parader*, and *Kerrang!*, and for a while it was like old times. Then he was going on about the band that he and Rebecca were putting together, and how he was getting a lot of ideas for songs, and how maybe they could swing a deal with one of the area clubs to play a few nights a week, and I just tuned him out. Fortunately, it was not a long drive.

We pulled to a stop in front of the Driscoll house and I told Stan to wait for me.

"Hey man, it's gettin' cold out here."

I sighed. "Jesus, I'll leave it running, okay? I won't be long."

There were a couple of cars parked in the Driscoll household that I did not recognize. Relatives, no doubt, sticking around through the holiday. Jesus, what a great Thanksgiving it was going to be. *Gee, thanks, God, for taking our child from us in her prime.*

Although in fairness God couldn't take the rap for this one.

I rang the bell, and my heart stopped when Sam opened the door.

"Hello?"

I blinked. Not Sam.

The girl before me was too old, the nose too long, but Christ, the resemblance was goddamn scary. I had to make myself breathe, talk.

"Yeah, uh, is Doug around?"

She nodded and let me in. "I'm Lucinda, his cousin. You're Eric, right? She told me about you."

I could only offer a feeble, stricken smile.

"Hang on, I'll go get him. We were all having coffee in the dining room."

"Okay."

I closed my eyes and tried to get a bearing on myself. I still had on the T-shirt I'd worn earlier, and hadn't thought to grab a jacket despite the cold. I was sure that the gun was noticeable a mile away.

Doug came out, trailing Lucinda, who hesitated a second and then disappeared back to the dining room. Doug's eyes narrowed when he saw me. He nudged his glasses back up his face and asked me what the fuck I wanted.

I stood there in shock, my mouth working like a fish flopping on a beach. This was what not what I had expected, and I could not pull any words out of my brain that would make the slightest bit of sense.

Doug took two steps toward me. "Hey, I know what you're all about now, Eric. I know what you do."

"Good," I said, trying to keep it light, "'cause I sure don't."

"Outside," he said.

I stepped out the door, turned around, and he grabbed me by my shirt and pulled me to his face. I grabbed his hands and pulled them off me.

"What the hell's your problem?"

"Why," he cried, grooves of anguish carving his face into a kind of fright mask. "Why did you do it? Why?"

I backed away from him. "Do what?"

"You fucked her. You *fucked* her!"

Which "her" were we talking about here? Sam or Rebecca?

"Maybe," I said.

Doug glared at me. His breathing was rapid. He looked like a bull fixing to charge. It was very clear to me that he hated my guts.

"She said you did."

"Rebecca?"

"Rebecca said you were sleeping with my sister!"

Said? Shit, probably ran it through his head in a non-stop porn loop.

I laughed bitterly. "Yeah? Well, I wasn't. I sure *wanted* to, and let me give you a big newsflash here, Driscoll: she wanted it, too. Maybe you never noticed, Sam was a big girl. She could take care of herself without any help at all. Unlike you."

He launched himself at me. It was a clumsy, awkward attack, but I am a clumsy, awkward person, and he plowed right into me and knocked me flat on my back. The pistol drove into the small of my back like a hammer blow. His punches hurt a lot more than I would have thought. He got three of them in on my face while I tried to push him off me. Jesus, where was Stan? Napping in the car, no doubt, or trying to figure out the fingerings on "Still of the Night" maybe. Doug, meanwhile, howled like wounded animal, and did a credible job of beating the shit out of me. He drove my nose out through the back of my brain and sent new constellations to spinning in my skull. I went ballistic at this and in all my flailing and thrashing got a knee into his groin, just like the hero always does in a crappy action film. Doug clutched his jewels and collapsed on top of me.

I grabbed my nose, which proved to be an agonizing mistake. It was broken all to hell. Blood poured through my fingers. My head felt like it was made out of throbbing concrete.

Even so, I shoved Doug off of me, pinned him to the ground, and got face to face with him.

"Don't you ever, ever, talk to me about Sam again. You got no right."

"She was my sister," he rasped.

"She was my love, so fuck you."

"Rebecca—"

"That name does not mean a *goddamn* thing to me."

We panted and regarded each other suspiciously. I'm afraid I bled on Doug a great deal. He was trying make some sense out of my words. I doubted he could. His mind would not be able to assess the information properly. Rebecca had been there. The landscape of Doug's reality was altered. So was Stan's. Mine? Maybe so.

But I thought of Mick and Sam and did not consider doubt.

"Besides," I said, "I *did* fuck Rebecca. It wasn't all that, you know?"

Doug closed his eyes and winced. He moaned. It was hard to tell in the dark, but I think I saw tears. It was funny; Stan assumed I was still getting it on with Rebecca, hell, he was willing to share, but Doug, possessive Doug, had never completely let himself accept the real raw order of things.

I got up, blood pouring all down me, my nose pounding with pain. "We're going to see her now. You might get an answer from her."

Doug made it to his knees, and looked back at the house.

"We won't be long," I lied. "They won't miss you even a little bit."

Doug's look made it clear that he did not trust me at all, but he followed me to the Bomb.

"Son of a bitch, what happened to you two?"

"Nothing, Livingston," I said. "We fell off the swing. See if there's an old shirt back there. I'm bleeding everywhere."

He found it and handed it to me. Some tour shirt. I gingerly held it to my crushed nose and hoped to staunch the flow. Yeah right. I waited until at least it slowed to a syrupy tackiness, until I felt I could drive. The other two just watched me, Doug fuming in anger, Stan, I suppose, in wordless stupefaction.

We pulled away from the Driscoll house.

"I guess you're wondering why I gathered you all here," I said, but neither of them found it funny.

"Might snow," said Stan.

Doug said, "So what are you up to now, Eric?"

"You'll see."

Stan asked, "Where are we going?"

"You'll see."

As far as I could remember, the last time I'd been to the Swing had been in June of '85. I could have been wrong about that, but it had been at least two years. I wasn't even sure that it was still there. Maybe it had been plowed under for apartments or something. I knew the Texaco was still there, I drove past it all the time, but the Swing, who knew? I hoped the place was timeless, I hoped whatever dark magic we had drawn there would have protected it at least this long.

Stan and Doug both knew something was up when we pulled into the lot of the apartments adjacent to the water hole.

"Hey," said Doug. "What's this?"

Stan groaned.

"This is the Mick Cornwell/Samantha Driscoll Memorial Center," I said, killing the engine.

"That isn't funny," said Doug.

"No," I agreed, "it sure isn't."

"Who's Mick Cornwell?" asked Stan. "And where's the beer?"

I got out, touching my back to make sure the .38 was still there, and got out the lantern. Stan and Doug were still inside the car. I shrugged. I couldn't make them get out. But I knew that if I went down without them, curiosity would compel both of them to follow me.

I went around to the back of the Texaco and switched on the lantern. The arc of light it gave off was wide and strong. Shifting shadows made it difficult for a moment to find the path, but once I did I wondered how I'd missed it. The shallow groove was worn in the earth, and as I followed it down, it made me think of a path left by some enormous serpent.

What I most wanted to do was turn around, get back in the car, apologize for the poor joke, and take everybody home. What I wanted to do was run, as far as I could, as fast as I could, leave Rebecca and all this sorrow behind. I did not think I could do that. I did not believe that she would allow that.

The light beam reached the clearing before I did, and I swept it around, making sure no one else had decided to hang out here tonight, maybe smoke some reefer, maybe scrutinize a battered copy of *Hustler*. But Stan was right. It was cold as a murderer's heart tonight. I played the light over the clubhouse to be sure. It had changed little over the years, grown a new board or two, lost a bit of luster. Otherwise it was the same treehouse that we had all sat in those years ago, on that ferociously hot summer day, and drawn a monster into our lives. I had never seen it at night before.

It was a perfect trap.

I started down the bank, working over toward the storm tunnel. Halfway there, I heard cursing and stumbling along the path I'd come down, and I smiled a bit. I waited for them to catch up.

"This better be good," Stan said, teeth chattering. He had on a jean jacket and gloves. I only had on the T-shirt, but I felt the cold only in the most remote sense. It was as though I was already gone.

"We'll see," I said.

They followed me down into the tunnel, into that dark, endless mouth. Three Jonahs in the belly of a concrete whale. I stopped on a dry spot, set the lantern down, and took a good long look around. It was the same boxy tunnel, with the ant farm offshoots every so often. It was cold and dry.

"Well," said Doug, "what was it you had to show us? My parents will be wondering where I'm at."

I looked at Stan, an unearthly apparition in the light given off by the lantern. He huddled in his jacket and blew a frosty plume of breath.

"Doesn't this bring back memories?"

Stan glanced at Doug. "No."

"None at all?"

Doug said, "Jesus, what did you bring us down here for?"

And Rebecca said, "He brought you down here to kill me. Isn't that right, Eric?"

We all looked down the tunnel. Rebecca strode forward, trademark black jeans and black shirt, unaffected by the cold, looking as good as ever, looking better than that.

A voice that lived in my secret-self asked if I really wanted to give this up, Jesus, was she really *that* bad?

Sam.

Yeah, she really was that bad.

"Yeah," I said. "I thought we might have a little shindig. Call it a meeting of minds."

Stan moved to embrace Rebecca, and Doug's face crumpled. It would have been funny if it hadn't instead been so goddamned pathetic.

Rebecca stopped Stan with a look. "Not now, love."

Stan's hands hung at his side. He started to say something, then shut his mouth.

Doug said, "Becca?"

She looked at him. "Love is irreducible. Don't you know that? What I give to Stan, I give to you as well. Love is not energy or matter, it is not finite."

Doug's mouth hung open, and he nudged his glasses up. His look was dreamy. "Yeah . . ."

Now she looked at me. "Eric, why do you hate me so? I am all you ever wanted. Is that not true?"

And that light, light caress on my mind.

And I wanted to want her so badly, oh, man, it hurt. Why fight it? So what if I had to share, big deal. There was enough to go around, right? I could be happy, fuck all this pain, all this work, all this *hurt*. If it meant moving through life as if drugged, what of that? It sure beat this wear and tear of mere existence, didn't it?

Feather touch.

Smell of roses.

Sam, sprawling out of the tub, blood trickling out of her nose, her eyes already far, far away.

I said, "Aren't you just perfect?"

I said, "You want to make me happy? You want me to *need* you, you want my *desire* to keep you here with us?"

She almost nodded.

I said, "Bring Sam and Mick back, and I'll do it."

She opened her mouth. "Eric . . ."

"No? Then how about this?"

I reached around and brought out the pistol, pointed at her belly.

"How about I send you back where you came from?"

But the first shock . . .

THE FIRST SHOCK IS that she is there.

The second, and more important one, is that she is stark naked. And what rapturous nakedness it is. We stare at her as one, four kids on the cusp who have suddenly hit what appears to be the ultimate jackpot.

"Oh man, what is this?" asks Randy.

And I say, "We should go call somebody. Maybe she's lost or something."

But Randy is holding up his sketchpad and looking from it to her more with disbelief than surprise. Doug's eyes are wide like headlights on a Mack truck. I am looking my friends over for their reactions because a part of me is afraid to look back at this girl, this fantasy come to life. Because no matter how much of a male fantasy this is, this is all wrong. This isn't how the world is, or how it should be. This is completely different from furtively trying to unscramble the cable box to see boobs on late-night Cinemax, from sneaking a *Playboy* out from the stash of your dad or brother, from bullshitting with all your friends at school how you've "done it." This girl standing here is some deeply weird shit. Even at twelve I know that.

"Let's get out of here," I say in a husky, strained voice. Doug looks at me in annoyance. Clearly, he would rather stay. Stan is more puzzled. He seems to feel something is wrong as well. He actually takes a step toward the end of the tunnel, towards sunlight.

Doug says, "It's okay."

But it's not, and I grab his arm and pull him toward the outside. The beauty does not interfere. There is something in her eyes—loss? Regret?

Doug fights it, but only half-heartedly. Somewhere inside, he knows that something's off. When we get outside, Stan has gathered his tapes and the boom box, and Randy is climbing up the bank, away from the tunnel. Already, I am wondering if the whole thing was not just some kind of hallucination. Some sort of shared hysteria.

Sure. There is no dream girl. Never happened.
And a loud, short clap of thunder explodes around us.

SMOKE TRAILED UP FROM the barrel of the gun. My ears rang. Rebecca's
eyes were wide, so were Stan and Doug's. She had almost had me, for a second.
She'd almost sold me a past I'd have loved to buy into. I cocked the pistol.
There was no time to play around. Next time, she might scramble my brains.
She might blow apart a blood vessel in my skull as she had with Sam.

She said, "That won't hurt me, you know. I'm beyond that."

"Eric," Doug cried, "what are you doing? Put that down, come on, someone's
gonna get hurt?"

"Hey," said Stan, "is that one of my dad's guns, man?"

"Your dad's dead, Stan. He won't mind me using it."

"You're lying. My parents are fine, just fine." But he looked away when he
said it.

"What are you trying to do, Eric?" asked Doug.

They both looked like they wanted to rush me, but the gun stalled that.

"I'm ending this. No one else pays for our shit."

"And you think you can shoot me, get rid of me?" Rebecca laughed. She
shook her head at my sad presumption. I posed no more threat to her, she
supposed, than a mosquito does to a rhinoceros. The very notion apparently
amused her so much she could not stop smiling.

She was still smiling at me when I spun and shot Doug in the head.

She froze. Stan screamed. Doug's head snapped back and his glasses shot
off into the night and a large black-red flower bloomed on the concrete wall
behind him. He flew back and slammed into the wall, slid down, and slumped
in a sitting position, twitching, the back of his head gone.

"I can't hurt you. I can't pull the hook. But I can cut the line, you bitch."

I turned on Stan.

Stan fled. He made it to the mouth of the tunnel before I could sight and
squeeze the trigger. I hit him in the lower back and drove him out into the
pool. He screamed loudly, wailing.

Rebecca did not use a feather touch. She used a sledgehammer. A white
flash went off in my skull, and a thunderclap of pain followed a moment later.
Fresh blood ran out of my nose. Probably she had just caused some sort of
stroke. Maybe I was lucky she was not stronger. The left half of my body went
numb. I stumbled, knocking the lantern over. Now the light pointed out of

the tunnel, and I could see Stan thrashing in the water. I loped toward him, my bad leg dragging on me like an anchor.

Rebecca said, "Stop it, stop it, you don't know what you're doing, *stop it!*"

I glanced back at her. I had to cock my head, because my left eye was seeing everything through a haze. Rebecca seemed less there. I remembered Randy, sucked into that vortex in the gas station in Ardmore. Rebecca seemed to be fading in on herself, I don't know how else to describe it.

"'M cuttin' the line," I said, alarmed at how my voice slurred.

She tried it again, the hammer blow, but there was no strength in it. I coughed and stumbled but pressed on to the mouth of the tunnel.

Stan tried to swim. He flailed, he was freezing and drowning. He kept screaming about his legs, his goddamn legs, and oh fuck I wanted to throw the gun away and just die, just fucking die, but I couldn't let him go like that, I *couldn't*, so I pointed at his head and fired. The bullet hit and sent something dark skipping across the water like a flat rock thrown by a child. Stan sank immediately.

Snowflakes started falling.

I turned away. I faced Rebecca, the fatty, greasy thing that had once been Rebecca. There was not much left of it. It was just a washed out blur now. It kept crying out my name, kept forcing it out of an alien mouth that was more proboscis than anything else, but words were no more than a meaningless whine and buzz.

"Cuttin' the goddamn line," I rasped. She tried one last time.

". . . love you . . . please. . . Eric."

I put the end of the barrel in my mouth. It was hot and seared my lips and tongue. I did not care. I thought, at the end, of Sam, and Christ, I hoped I'd see her soon.

I pulled the trigger.

There was a sledgehammer blow to my head and I fell and I was able to see, for a second, the night sky, snowflakes drifting down in silence, pure white snowflakes, so peaceful, and then painful blackness.

And then I died.

PART FIVE:
WRECKAGE

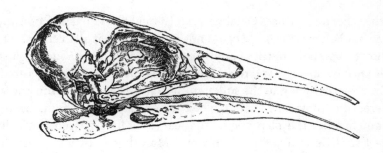

I WAS BRAIN DEAD for maybe ten minutes, they tell me.

The cold helped, they say. I was very lucky, they assured me.

What happened was that I could not even kill myself with any competence. Maybe it was the shock, maybe the stroke that Rebecca hit me with, but I stuck the gun in my mouth at a totally wrong angle, and wound up taking out a lot of neck and enough brain to completely fuck me up, not enough to do the job properly. Typical Lynch competence.

A customer from the Texaco came back to investigate the shots, a braver soul than I would have been. He found two dead young men and a third who was still breathing, but bleeding to death. He raced back up and had the clerk call 911 and that was that. They got there in time and saved my life. Hooray.

The bullet or the stroke, take your pick, did enough damage to make me a quadriplegic. Everything from the neck down, gone. I'm wheelchair-bound as I dictate this into the voice-activated recorder my folks got for me. I must dictate slowly, carefully. The ruin of my mouth causes wreckage with my words.

My parents. Jesus. What this has done to them. They went to bed that night thinking they had a moderately weird, consistently disappointing child, and woke up to a murderer.

Christ, I wish there had been another way. I wish I could have thought of one. I couldn't. I still can't. The line had to be cut.

My mother talks to me about God sometimes. My father seldom visits. I think he can't find the proper words to wrap his emotions around, and it's easier to stay away. I can understand that.

There was a hearing, such as it was, and I was deemed not competent to stand trial, and remanded into treatment until competent. In a lot of ways, that's for the best. If I ever went to prison, they might actually parole me. I'm better off here, where there will never be a reason to release me.

On the other hand, this is Oklahoma, and it might be lethal injection anyway. You may not believe this, but I could not care less how it all eventually turns out. I don't care about much of anything these days. The maddening urge to move is with me always, and my statue body is silent to it. My days are filled with the creep of light and the sullen ministrations of nurses who know why I am here, who know how I came to be this way, and feel I should have gone ahead and finished the job properly. The years have been passed first by books on tape, then CDs, and now books on mp3. Many books, over the years. Doug would be proud of me. I are edumacated at last. After a fashion.

And my nights bring cold sweats and terrors, visions of tunnels and mortality.

I have dreams. In the best of them, I am with Sam, and the dark obsession with Rebecca has never happened, I have not been cursed with her black attention, and Sam and I are at the altar. It is an outdoor wedding, we are being married at the Swing, in the tunnel. There are many flowers, most of them roses exactly the color of blood. In the dream, we exchange vows, rings, we kiss, and as we enter the tunnel toward our happy life, as all of our friends and family shower us with confetti, I reach out and pluck a rose for my bride. A thorn stabs me, and a drop of blood wells from the wound. Sam sees it, and leans over to kiss it, to take the pain away, but once her lips touch the blood, the rose, she looks at me again, but now she is Rebecca. Evermore.

I let the rose fall, and the water rises to take us all into darkness.

I dream this a lot.

In the other dreams, the worst, there is only that smeared thing in the tunnel, buzzing out my name and moving toward me in the darkness. I jerk away from these screaming, with the pointless compulsion to run, and I know in these first waking instants that something still waits for me out in the deeper dark, something that has marked me and will bide its time and will come for me in due course. And I will be more helpless than ever against it.

Maybe someday there will be no dreams.

Maybe, if there is a god. If mercy truly exists.

Maybe.

Acknowledgments

I SHOULD PROBABLY SAY here that this is at once my most autobiographical work of fiction and my least. I should explain, right?

I'm a kid of the 1980s. More to the point, I'm a white male heterosexual kid of the 1980s. Which means I grew up in a culture that taught us all were some hot entitled shit. Entitled to all benefits of every doubt, entitled to a wink and a nod to all manner of shitty behavior, entitled to be first in line for everything, and most dangerously, entitled to have women be our playmates—hell, our property—in whatever we wanted as a matter of course.

Think I'm kidding? Check out any hair metal video from the period. Have a barf bag handy.

Check out the teen sex comedies, even the good ones like *Valley Girl*. Some chuckles, huh?

Read back through your favorite novels from that decade. If you like horror (and I'm assuming you do given what you have in your hands) then go read some of the more popular titles and pay good attention to how women are treated. I'd have a whole case of barf bags if I were you.

That's the autobiography here. I'm not Eric Lynch, but I'm also not going to pretend I was a ton better in terms of how I viewed and treated girls and women. Or LGBTQ, although that wasn't the term we had in Oklahoma in 1987—we had charming terms like "faggot" or "homo" and worse. I didn't know anyone openly gay in Oklahoma until the '90s, because being openly gay in Oklahoma could get you beaten. Or killed.

Things get better. Most of me believes that most of the time. Things are better—the Republican mayor of Oklahoma City this year energetically endorsed and promoted the city's now booming Pride Parade.

The people in this book? Made up, all of 'em. The behavior and attitudes, even the really gross stuff? I'd almost call it reportage.

THIS BOOK HAD A stupid long gestation period, and so there have been a number of people who have helped shape it into what you are holding in your hands.

I couldn't have done this without sharp and early reads by Charles Kerr, Holly Kerr, Christopher Ransom, Rachel Wolf, and my dear and badly missed friend Molly Campbell, whose early feedback was critical to my belief that this thing had a pulse.

I'm also deeply indebted to Paul Michael Anderson, Errick Nunnally, and Sheri Sebastian-Gabriel for their kind words championing *Nightbirds*. When talented writers think you've done okay, you find yourself in tall cotton. Thanks, guys!

A shout out here to my Necon family—life can be lonesome for an introvert scribbler in the middle of nowheresville, but you guys have bettered my life for over a decade now, and the support and love that comes out of this community sustains. It really does. Love you weirdos!

Special and sincere love to Brett Savory and Sandra Kasturi for taking a chance on this, and super particularly to Sandra for the keen editorial eye. Sandra, your patience and precision saved me some embarrassment in more than one place and made this book immensely better. I now know that ship names are italicized! And shout-outs to Leigh Teetzel, who saved me several instances of embarrassment with a keen eye and keener judgement; to Errick Nunnally, again, for wicked great work on the layout and design; to Erik Mohr for the gorgeous and amazing cover; and to Jared Shapiro for his design work (and the logo! I have a logo!). It's humbling to have so many talented people on board, and this book would not be as good or as beautiful without y'all.

Finally, love and gratitude to my wife, Chris, and my daughter, Rachel. It's been a long wait for you guys too, and l can only hope you think it's been worth it.

Oh, hey, and you, reader, have my enduring thanks as well. I hope this took your mind off things for a while and you found the ride worth it. We scribblers write for your eyes, no matter what we say, and a book without readers is just a relic. So, thank you most sincerely.

About the Author

CRAIG WOLF'S FICTION HAS appeared in *Transversions*, *Triangulation: Dark Glass*, *Now I Lay Me Down to Sleep*, and *The Dystopian States of America*, among others. He has published one collection of odd fiction, *Pressure Points*, and a short horror novel, *Trespass*. He is also the co-editor of *War on Christmas*. He is a graduate of the Red Earth MFA, fictioneers in Oklahoma City, and his two favorite words are "bah" and "humbug."